You only know me like the shoreline knows the sea
    – Paul Banks, 'Over My Shoulder'

Salvation

Robert McNair

Matador
Unit E2 Airfield Business Park,
Harrison Road, Market Harborough,
Leicestershire. LE16 7UL
Tel: 0116 2792299
Email: books@troubador.co.uk
Web: www.troubador.co.uk/matador
Twitter: @matadorbooks

ISBN 978 1803136 509

British Library Cataloguing in Publication Data.
A catalogue record for this book is available from the British Library.

Printed and bound in the UK by TJ Books Limited, Padstow, Cornwall
Typeset in 11pt Minion Pro by Troubador Publishing Ltd, Leicester, UK

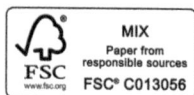

Matador is an imprint of Troubador Publishing Ltd

For Aimie

With thanks to my parents and Yvonne—without whom this book would not be published—and to Lee, Claire and Cath for their feedback and support.

Part One

Arrivals

Chapter 1

Camden woke up early to the sound of the gong. It made sense as the starting point for a day based on routine.

Outside, birdsong welcomed the day. The lama had spoken to him about how, even though each bird sings its own song in its own way for its own purposes, the collective effect sounds harmonious and choreographed. He'd agreed at the time and was reminded of it again. It was as if he could hear twenty different birds as well as their combined symphony. And then came the undignified caw of the grouse that wandered the grounds, always seeming surprised and dismayed that—in contrast to its tuneful cousins—it could only manage the same atonal sound.

Besides that, all he heard was silence.

He sat upright in bed, blinking. His mind was getting used to the discipline he was trying to nurture, his body less so. It always wanted more sleep and he had to drag it along with his wishes. He spent ten seconds looking at the photo on the table at the end of his bed, the only adornment of any kind in the room—the smile that shone from the frame, the loss that lay behind it, the hope still attached to it—then swung himself onto his feet, feeling a couple of reassuring cracks through his lumbar as he did so. He applied his clothes to his body—sweater, joggers, socks—slipped on the sandals, out the door.

Stepping into the yard, he joined the loose, gentle wave of like-minded bodies, all moving in the same direction. Looks and smiles were exchanged, but no words. Up the steps, sandals off and stored on the waiting shelves alongside the others. The door was held open. He lifted the cushion closest to hand and found a space on the floor. Assuming the position, he felt himself find his balance, his centre, waiting for the ritual to begin.

Afterwards, he queued for breakfast in the dining hall. The sky had yet to reveal its plans for the day. The past few weeks had been kind. In this part of the world, a reversal of fortune was soon to be expected. He walked over to a table where several people were already eating and slid onto the end of the bench. Some acknowledged him, others kept eating. Either was fine with him. Both were done silently. One of the rules.

He started to eat. A half-filled bowl of porridge. A single slice of white bread that had been briefly introduced to jam. A cup of water. Each mouthful was chewed fifteen times, slowly, eyes fixed forward. Every chew was deliberate, every swallow savoured. All done mindfully.

Breakfast complete, he rose, taking his bowl, plate, and cup towards the kitchen.

The day was taking shape before him.

Same as the previous day, same as the next.

———•———

Surrounding him was multitudinous timber in various states. The forest was dense and towered above the first few hundred yards of the path, making plain its claim on the land to anyone who walked beneath. Within another twenty strides the rolling hills opened up before him, decorated by a patchwork of felled trunks. Despite the evidence of heavy Forestry Commission machinery having recently been at work, now the only sounds belonged to nature. Rustling leaves betrayed the movements of some of the local wildlife population, too small or quick to be seen by his naked eye.

It was one of his favourite walks. He relished the peace of it.

In total, it would last a little over an hour. He'd follow the downward slope for a mile or so and take some time to himself before doubling back. There was one particularly proud tree stump large enough to accommodate him in the lotus position, its location at the top of a slight rise meaning he would be able to feel the light breeze as he remained perfectly still. He'd taken this walk a dozen or more times, and on every return journey he saw and experienced things differently than he had on his way out.

His practice complete, Camden felt slightly unsteady as he rose. A little unusual, nothing dramatic. Beginning his walk back up the hill, he allowed a thought to drift across his mind about the things he would find altered this time between here and his makeshift home.

———•———

Cresting the rise, he got his answer. Three familiar figures were approaching from a few hundred yards away and broke stride as they caught sight of him. Resolutely, he kept his eyes fixed on them as his mind flitted over potential strategies.

Was it a time for more lies? He could still remember clearly how they all fitted together, but he wasn't sure how many more he could layer on top before the structure would begin to buckle. How much did they know about what he'd told and kept from them? About why he'd done what he'd done?

For the briefest of moments, the question of whether he had sacrificed the right things, made the right choices, flickered into being before being summarily dismissed. He hated that it had even formed.

All important questions. All about to be answered in one way or another.

He hadn't seen them since Santorini. Only seven weeks ago. But in that time, he'd had to bury the life he'd been building. Now, more than two thousand miles away, he was faced with a particular combination of friends and acquaintances who could only know his whereabouts as a result of a sequence of specific events and disclosures, and it gave little cause for optimism.

As he took his final steps towards them, he immersed himself in memories of Crissa and began to form a prayer—

for her to be safe, for her to be free—before stopping himself, recognising its hypocrisy. There was no point pretending things had happened around them. He'd watched the whole thing. He knew what he'd seen.

If she wasn't safe—if something else had happened to her and her world had pulled her under again—then there was no denying that he bore some of the blame.

Chapter 2

"There comes a point where this shifts from being comforting friendship into a level of commitment I'm not ready for."

"Sorry." Tom grimaced and let go of Dean's hand for the first time in half an hour. He'd held it the whole way up, relaxed a bit once the seatbelt signs pinged off, and then grabbed it again when some turbulence arrived to chaperone them over northern Europe.

Dean remembered the last time they'd taken this flight, when he'd feared that Tom may need medical intervention. "Good on you for not letting it limit you. I admire you for that."

"Lucy says the same. Hard to feel worthy of admiration when you're trembling in front of your wife, though."

"If it helps, I'll tell her you were a rock and that you kept me calm."

Tom laughed. "She's too smart to believe that."

The drinks trolley arrived, and Dean bought three

miniature-sized Heineken that cost him most of the money in his pocket. He handed one to Gary, who was uncharacteristically quiet in the adjacent seat, his head buried in a crime novel he'd picked up at the airport.

"Been a quick year," Dean said.

"It'll be good for us all to be back together again," Tom replied. "Almost makes my fear of flying worth overcoming."

"How do you think we'll find things?"

"They'll be a good team. Morton has the cash and the pizzazz; Camden will be the engine and keep them organised. Nothing'll go wrong because of them being underprepared." Tom let the silence hang a few moments. "As for things away from the business, you probably know better than me."

"Camden always plays his cards close to his chest," Dean shrugged, "but when I've spoken to him on the phone he's seemed on good form. Morton hasn't said anything other than that he and Crissa are inseparable."

The seatbelt light came back to life.

"You know," Tom said in a lowered tone, "I was flying Virgin Atlantic once. Really bad turbulence, rocking and rolling all over the place. This stewardess passes and sees me panicking, stops to ask if I'm alright, knowing the answer already but trying to keep my jitters under control. Tells me to think of turbulence the way you think of driving a car along a really bumpy road. You feel it, but it's just part of the journey and nothing to worry about."

"Good way to look at it."

"Yeah," Tom gulped. "Doesn't fucking help, though."

Dean relaxed his hand and let Tom crush it as much as he needed. He checked the time.

Two more hours in the air.

———•———

"Kalimera!" came the greeting.

Morton and Camden were waiting for them at the entrance to the airport, a single storey building with basic facilities. Passport control lasted as long as it had taken the half-asleep border guard to handle their documents, sniff and give them back.

"Looking well," Dean nodded at them both in approval.

"Love suits you," Gary teased Camden, who didn't contest it.

"Right. Who's travelling with who?" Morton asked.

"I'll keep Camden company," Gary volunteered quickly.

Morton guided Tom and Dean to a Toyota 4x4 with more dirt than style.

"Bit low-end for you, Morton." Tom frowned and squinted against the sun.

"No point being otherwise. Good luck finding a car on this island without damage to its paintwork."

"Bad drivers?"

"Wear your seatbelts, put it that way. And be happy you're not booked in with that executive travel company," Morton said, pointing at the matchbox Chevy towards which Camden was coaxing Gary.

"You boys have lucked out," he continued once they were on the move. "We'll be staying at my dad's. Me and

Camden have a place in town and my dad usually rents out his pad, but he's given it to us for the week."

There were approving sounds from around the car.

"All ready for opening night?" Tom asked.

"Yeah, we're ready. We'll grab a few drinks there later on so you can judge for yourself."

"Sounds good. You having any trouble? Been a bit on the news about protests."

"Nah, none of that on the islands. People aren't happy, make no mistake, but it's kept to the mainland."

"How's your partner in crime?" Tom asked.

"Good. Camden's Camden, you know. Impresses everyone but himself. He'll be better once opening night's out of the way. But he's enjoying life. He's under the thumb and over the moon. It's like looking at a different person. That furrowed brow seems like a thing of the past. And Crissa's cool, you know? They seem right together."

They arrived at a T-Junction. As they waited to join the main road, Camden pulled up behind them. A gap appeared in the traffic and as they turned right towards the island's capital, Fira, the heads of all passengers in both cars turned to look out to the left side, where the view of the bay captured their attention.

"That view is awesome," Tom said.

Morton nodded. "Every day I make a point of spending a bit of time just appreciating it. I don't ever want to take it for granted."

A year ago, they'd all spoken about setting up a business together. Each had their reasons for deciding to go for it or opt out. Two had taken the plunge. Sitting in Camden's car, looking out of the window, Gary found himself—not for the first time—wishing he'd committed himself to becoming the third member of the group. Obligation had led him to discount the idea out of hand, yet the thoughts had swirled for a good while after. They felt like a betrayal; of what, he was unsure.

He fished out his phone to see if Jo had replied to his text telling her they'd landed safely. Nothing. Two words into a draft of another message, he thought better of it and returned the phone to his pocket.

There was a sense of relationships fracturing. Strangely, it didn't feel unwelcome.

———•———

Two days later, Morton and Camden kept a distance but proudly watched as Salvation's first sales rang through the bar within minutes of its 6pm opening.

"Yamas," Morton winked and squeezed his business partner's shoulder.

The decor of the bar was monochrome, with marble, metallics and glass featuring heavily. They'd spent a lot of time discussing how they wanted Salvation to look and had visited several interior design showrooms and outfitters on the mainland. There were times when Camden wondered whether they should be paring back what they were spending, but Morton reassured him that the money was there, that you never regretted buying quality, and that it sent the right signs to customers.

They also spoke at length before deciding to have TVs displayed on the walls. Morton was reluctant in case it distracted people from the serious business of having a good time but was won round on the proviso that no sport or music videos were played on them, and that they would be turned off by eleven. By that time, in his eyes, Salvation was failing to do its job if people were more interested in what was on-screen.

By 8pm the place was filling nicely. Gary, Tom and Dean had commandeered a table and seemed to be enjoying both the atmosphere and their friends' success, intentionally keeping things low-key.

Looking back, Morton would recognise that the first indication of anything amiss came soon after that, when a wiry man of around twenty strode bow-legged through the door and straight to a nearby table of six. He spoke in hasty, vexed sentences and showed them the screen of his phone, prompting an exchange of looks. He asked them all a question that they answered by abruptly rising to their feet and following him out of the door. On reflection that was odd and eventually—months later—made itself known to Morton's consciousness. At the time, the relevance of their departure was gone the moment that another group of six replaced them in their seats.

———•———

It was the commotion that brought Morton out from the back storeroom just after 11pm, having transferred some cash to the safe. It sounded like it was coming from all around the town, as though the noise was swelling up from the ground, ready to come crashing back down when it became too heavy for the atmosphere to hold.

He found Santorini's newest nightspot much as he'd left it, yet permanently changed.

Salvation had been a year in the making. The bar took up half of the left-hand wall, ending as the steps began their climb towards where the lights glided across the raised arms of the dancefloor diaspora. Opposite the bar were leather-upholstered booths and some tables and chairs. Beyond the fold-out glass frontage to the right was an uncovered decking area where seating overlooked the bay.

The place was designed to hold three hundred, give or take. The business plan—Morton and Camden's business plan—anticipated a gradual increase in customers throughout May and then a peak that would run through September before tailing off to season's end in early October. If tonight's numbers were anything to go by, their forecasts had been conservative. The place was heaving.

Despite that, nothing sat right in Morton's mind as he took in the images in front of him. His eyes swept the premises and the first thing that struck him was that Camden was nowhere to be seen. Neither were Gary or Tom. He'd only been away for a few minutes.

Morton had spent a lifetime listening to people telling him how calm he was under pressure. The summer would test his mettle. In later recollections he'd swear that before everything started there had been a silence, filled only by the footsteps and menace of eight men wearing black hooded sweaters and scarves covering their faces below the eyeline.

The first man through the door was imposingly tall and every inch the Alpha Male. He reminded Morton of himself in a strange way, but with all tolerance and refinement scraped off. He delivered his words in an angry, bitter howl that Morton wasn't fluent enough to translate. A second man followed, taking two steps inside before swinging one hundred and eighty degrees to his left to shatter the plate glass window with what looked like a truncheon.

Each new entrant put their weaponry to efficient use. Furniture and electrical equipment fragmented in submission. Customers and staff cowered as they scrambled towards the exit onto the agitated streets, punctuating the air with panicked voices.

The staff seemed briefly frozen by indecision before taking their cue from the customers. The DJ sprinted past with impressive speed. It occurred to Morton that he'd turned off the music before leaving his booth, which struck him as oddly considerate. The sounds of destruction that filled the void were deafening.

Morton stood behind the bar, alert and unmoving. He watched the assumed leader coming straight for him and tried to filter through his options. Too late, he saw Dean emerge from behind a piece of wreckage and try to intercept the man, delivering a blow to his jaw which barely seemed to register or interrupt his stride. A black-hooded figure immediately swooped in and struck Dean on the back of the head, sending him into unconsciousness before he hit the floor.

Morton raised his hands in submission but held his ground. The Alpha raced towards him and jammed his hand under his chin, driving him back against the shelves of glasses and sending a half-circle of shards outwards beyond the bar top. Morton was faced with invective and saliva as he struggled for breath and something to hold onto.

Where are they coming from? he thought. There were far more than the original eight now, and the gear and equipment were less uniform. The MO remained consistent, however, as though an instruction manual was being distributed before they entered, showing the quickest way to dismantle the contents of a building with a single blunt instrument.

Morton began feeling more irritation than panic. The grip around his neck had loosened, instead replaced by jerking shoves at his head and a barrage of words too fast to comprehend. The leader showed his increasing displeasure at not being understood by destroying anything within reach during the gaps in his tirade.

Three of the original group pulled down the entrance sign—which had been switched on for the first time only five hours earlier—and slammed it onto the empty dancefloor, taking turns to smash the lights and twist the metal letters spelling the word *Salvation* with an underscore beneath it.

The Alpha left Morton in the care of two deputies and stalked from behind what remained of the bar towards the sign, where he unzipped his fly and began to urinate.

As quickly as they had entered, the group took their leave and without delay sprinted to the right, towards the town square.

Morton already had his phone in his hand as he rushed over to Dean, whose eyes slowly opened, accompanied by a guttural groan, and dialled the police. It rang out. He tried for an ambulance: it rang out.

"What the fuck?" he asked the phone.

The noise from the streets became louder. It had sounded like a disciplined march earlier, but no longer:

people were running now, slowing momentarily to gawp at the damage wreaked on the bar and its residents. There was audible scuffling and aggression but no sounds of other places getting the same treatment as Salvation.

Dean tried to sit himself up.

"Don't move," Morton said, placing a hand on his chest. "I'm trying to call you an ambulance, but I can't get through."

Dean looked at him in baffled despair.

Morton's next comment, after scanning the room to survey the devastation: "Where are the rest of them? Where the fuck is Camden?"

It was 10:30pm on Thursday, 1st May 2014.

Chapter 3

Crissa walked across the town square in the heart of Fira, wondering why her mind was knotting itself up. Maybe the protests. They always carried risk and had been getting more tempestuous recently.

"I wish you didn't have to leave," Camden had told her earlier that afternoon, their foreheads lightly touching.

"I know," she had told him. "But it's important, and it's only for a few days."

It had always been important to her, in ways that few knew. At age twenty-five, Crissa already felt like she had shed more skins than was normal or healthy. Her intermittent trips back to Athens returned her to a world that seemed to look at her with devilish eyes, ready to snatch her back and insist that new skin was the same as old skin.

Pasts can weigh heavy. The move to Santorini had lightened the load. She enjoyed the unquestioning friendship of Irini and Sofia. She appreciated the distance and the relaxed pace of the days. And then Camden had come along, unexpected in ways that invigorated and spooked her.

"Hey, Irini," she said, answering her phone on its first ring.

"Had to hear your voice before you abandon me again. Is Camden there with you?"

"No, I've just left him at the bar. His friends are flying in shortly, so he and Morton are going to pick them up from the airport."

"Are they all set for the next few days?" Irini asked.

"Morton seems to be carrying zero stress and Camden's operating at about ninety-nine per cent, so in some ways they balance each other out."

Irini chuckled. "That's why you're so good for him."

"I'm meeting them for a couple of drinks later. Nothing too much, though. My flight is at 7am."

"Are you going to see your parents when you're over there?" Irini asked.

"I don't think so," Crissa answered. She always felt guilty when she planned a trip back to the mainland without telling her family. "I might see my sister if I get a chance."

"Say hi to her for me."

"I will."

"I'll see you Monday. Look after yourself. I'll miss you."

"You too. See you soon."

As she hung up, Crissa's eyes found their way to the sky, where a plane was serenely heading towards the island, perhaps the one that Camden's friends would be on. She imagined him pacing outside the airport waiting to collect the new arrivals, cursing Morton for being precisely on time with the other car because in Camden's mind that made him late. It was a big week for him, and he'd been doing his best to suppress his anxiety.

"Stop being so British," she had told him.

Camden had given her a smile. It was one of their relationship staples to accentuate each other's national traits.

She walked to a pay phone in the corner of the square, fed it coins and started punching numbers. This call wasn't one that she wanted traced back to her mobile. As it began to ring, she instantly found herself hoping it wouldn't be answered. Julia had been fraying at the edges the last couple of times they'd met.

After the requisite five rings, Crissa replaced the receiver and immediately her instincts kicked in. She swept the dust from her shorts—first from her left side, then from the right—and re-fixed her hair. Doing so had allowed her to take in a panorama of her surroundings in a single second. She saw early-season tourists, unpredictable in their mixture of purpose and indolence. A van driver was attempting to park with such little skill that a casual observer might have thought his vehicle's dimensions were changing by the second. A couple walked hand-in-hand, giving the impression that their bedroom was too far away for either of them to bear.

It was a completely normal scene with nothing out of place, which was exactly why she didn't trust it. Something felt wrong. It was vague but she knew she wasn't imagining it. She'd lived an unconventional life too long and too intensely for it to ever leave her fully.

That evening, after enjoying the first few drinks in Salvation's brief history, they moved on to a restaurant near the town square.

"I hear you're going to miss the opening night?" Tom asked Crissa.

"I'm afraid so." She smiled coyly, first at Camden and then around the table. "I have work to do."

"Work?"

Crissa pointed at the TV screen, where a bespectacled news reporter spoke to the camera in front of municipal buildings. Banners and marching crowds provided a backdrop. "For my country."

"What do you make of it all?" Gary asked. "We only hear snippets back home."

Crissa took a breath and opted for the condensed version. "The country is in financial ruin because the people running it are only interested in money and power. They act as if their friends and business interests are more important than the welfare of the rest of the population. They're not fit to govern, and they need to be reminded that their function is to serve their people instead of expecting us to pay the price."

Nobody said anything around the table, unsure of the role they could play in the conversation. Morton looked like he'd heard this story before. Camden glowed with admiration.

"People have no money, no jobs," she continued. "Everyone's affected. If you're young, the prospects are terrible. If you're working age, you're lucky if you still have a job and even then, it's unlikely to pay you enough to support your family. If you're in your fifties, that pension you've been working towards has disappeared and now you suddenly have to work an extra ten years." She paused for a couple of seconds and smilingly scanned them all. "Sorry you asked?"

The denials she received were unconvincing.

"Some people use that quote about people getting the government they deserve. That's bullshit. Being ruled by unworthy people isn't unique to us, I know. It's the same for you in Britain and people probably feel the same the world over. But we're at the extreme end of things, at least in European terms. A lot of demonstrations will take place tomorrow night. I need to play my part in that. I leave for Athens first thing in the morning, so I won't be here when you drink your final drink of this evening, whenever that may be."

"It won't be too late," cautioned Morton. "Too much to do tomorrow, right bud?"

Camden nodded in reply.

The contents of her Diet Coke occupied Crissa for a few minutes as she stopped finessing the conversation and let it drift onto other matters. She had seen how Camden had looked at her when she spoke, his pride so guilelessly laid bare, as though he understood every truth that lay inside her. There were so many questions she hoped he would never ask.

———•———

A little over twenty-four hours later, Crissa hung limply as the biceps of two men hooked under her armpits and lifted her so that her feet made only the slightest contact with the dust beneath them. They moved her so quickly and smoothly towards the boat that it looked like a feat of wirework.

When she had been deposited into the car that had brought them here, Crissa had almost collapsed across the back seat. She looked sedated, as though struck numb by words, deeds, and fears. Her hysteria had begun to subside. Not that she'd been screaming—and not that she'd come to terms with the chain of events that had set off around her— but a realisation was emerging that resistance wouldn't be in the common interest.

Now, as she was lowered into the back of the boat, she was compliant. Two men stood over her. Her eyes had met the final member of the group for only a second before she allowed herself to be laid flat, and they told him nothing but devastation. He answered with a blink and turned away.

———•———

The police station just outside Fira was abuzz with activity, which would have been highly unusual on any other night.

Standing at its door, Camden permitted himself a moment. A veil of panic had been thrown over him in the preceding hours and gave no signs of being removed any time soon. He let his eyelids gently close as he began to take as many breaths as it would take for him to feel prepared for what would come next. After a dozen, he knew he was getting diminishing returns and that this was as ready as he was ever going to feel for what he would come to recognise as the bridge between his old and new lives.

He strode through the door and addressed the man sitting behind the front desk.

"I'm looking for my girlfriend."

Chapter 4

A year earlier, Camden had stood next to four of his best friends as they traded stories and banter in the way of men on the cusp of their thirties. Santorini's warm air was keeping him company, stroking his face any time he stopped paying it attention. Surrounding him were scores of people dressed to their best and basking in the relaxation of an early summer holiday. Although a couple of hours had passed since they'd watched the only sunset that he'd ever known to receive a round of well-deserved applause, the daytime views of brilliant seas and the stark beauty of the still-active volcano remained etched on Camden's mind. Everything was pin-sharp. At least, that's how it became later.

They'd been in Santorini since the previous night, having arrived under cover of darkness to celebrate Tom's stag weekend. They were staying at Morton's father's canava, one of the island's traditional-style cave houses. None of them—save for Morton—had seen a house built like this, burrowed into a cliff face as though it had patiently out-waited its neighbours before finally manoeuvring itself into prime position for a permanent view of the caldera, as the locals referred to the bay that hosted the volcano. Stepping inside it, they'd been met by a cavernous living room with curved walls and five man-sized oval holes peppered around it. Three generous sofas cradled a large coffee table and faced a vast plasma screen on the wall. Through the hole on the left lay the kitchen, its contents striking the newcomers as high-end as they came to the realisation that the rooms in the canava tumbled into one another, each hole acting like one end of a spoke, corridors of varying lengths leading to new parts of the building that were kept tantalisingly out of sight.

That evening would be their first serious foray into the nightlife.

They started in a bar called Lava, a bullet-shaped cave with three smaller off-shooting rooms, each ringed by wooden seating built into the walls. A lengthy bar lurked at the back of the bullet, a solitary bartender dealing efficiently with the incoming orders of the forty or so drinkers who had found their way there by 10pm. A football match between two teams they didn't recognise was playing on the TV. There was no dancefloor, and when three consecutive groups of young women entered the bar, appraised its merits, and swiftly left, the friends decided not to linger over their drinks.

A hundred yards down the street was a venue called Crystal, where they all instantly fell for a maître d' with endless legs and long hair that started out dark and ended up blonde. She exuded an air of flirtation that they were welcome to appreciate from a distance and led them down steep steps to an open concrete space that was half-filled with people who'd clearly known that Lava wasn't worth the effort. There was a covered area that gave the impression it had been sliced out of the cliffside, bare rock forming a roof, the bar wedged into a crevice at the back and impossibly full of bottles and glasses. There was a roughly-sketched dancefloor that looked set to expand throughout the night, and a balcony that could hold about fifty people and already contained forty-nine.

"Great place," Gary said upon his return from the bar, directing his words towards Morton. "The whole island, I mean."

All nodded agreement.

"Is it tough being you, Morton?" Tom asked with mock jealousy.

"My dad's always loved travelling," Morton replied, sidestepping the question. "When he hit his forties, he decided to pick up a couple of holiday homes in Europe where he could take family breaks or whatever without so much notice or planning. He still does the long hauls and stuff, but he'll come here or to his place in Italy five or six times a year."

"You talk about him 'picking up a couple of holiday homes' like he's grocery shopping!" Tom exclaimed, slapping Morton on the shoulder. "Don't worry, I plan to do exactly the same when I've made my millions. We can be neighbours."

"Imagine the effect that would have on the property prices," Dean observed.

"My dad bought the canava about fifteen years ago.

He'd holidayed here with a friend of his"—the word 'friend' accompanied with a raised eyebrow— "and was back within a month to buy a place. The friend wasn't around long enough to reap the fruits of the purchase."

"Is it your ambition to be like your dad?" Tom asked.

"Not really," was the smiling reply.

"Is it wrong that *I* want to grow up to be like your dad?"

"Pretty wrong, yes."

"I don't think it is." Tom shook his head, undeterred. "I think your dad's secretly disappointed by how rounded a human being you are. I reckon he wants a surrogate son with a bit more edge to him."

"Give me a minute to work out if that's an insult or a compliment."

Camden hadn't spoken or moved. His attentions were occupied by a trio making their way down from the entrance, one of whom had him transfixed. A few words at the top of the staircase had made her friends laugh wholeheartedly while her own face remained a study of calm contentment. Her hair fell to her shoulder blades, incredibly straight and swaying slightly with each descending step.

The navy-blue jumpsuit with cream belt. Cream heels. Matching purse. Caramel skin, the smoothness of which he imagined he could feel from where he stood. Back straight. Eyes forward. Seemingly moving to her own music. Camden took it all in while the others' focus was elsewhere. He caught himself and tried to take a breath, reaching for his bottle. Before bringing it to his lips, he chanced another look as she leaned into her friends, lowered her eyes to the floor and said something to make them laugh again, this time more discreetly. As the laughter faded out, her eyes very deliberately rose to meet his.

He had yet to catch breath.

———|———

From the moment that he saw her descend the stairs at Crystal, something shifted inside Camden, never to resettle in its original place. His eyes sought her out numerous times as she headed briefly to the bar and then the dancefloor, oblivious to anything other than enjoying the company of her friends. She laughed a lot, and moved so fluently that, to his eyes, everything looked like a result of effortless choreography. But she didn't so much as glance his way again. A large part of him saw things for what they surely were: an exchange of looks with a woman he was entranced by while on holiday. A smaller, stronger part of him knew better.

The group moved onto Koo Club around midnight. After a while they followed an outburst of cheering and moved indoors from the sprawling patio to find some of the staff climbing onto the bar top to start dancing.

"Shall we join them?" Tom yelled, trying to make himself heard over a song that none of them recognised.

"Let's act like we've been here before," was Morton's muted response.

"Fuck it, we'll never be here again," Tom argued, looking around for support that wasn't forthcoming. "Who's with me?"

He was faced with a committee of "nopes" and shaking heads.

Tom held his hands by his sides and dropped his head disconsolately, before gradually lifting his right fist and thrusting it into the air with a beaming smile. "Stag Boy goes it alone!" he roared triumphantly before clambering onto the bar to exchange unsteady moves with a few similarly inspired female customers.

"Sometimes you just have to let them grow up in their own time," Gary grinned ruefully.

"My round," Camden stated. "I'll be purchasing from that bar," he pointed as he strode towards the smaller counter at the back of the main room, which remained free of any dancers. "Five Coronas and five Jägermeisters, please," he said to the barman, who nodded and moved off.

Aware of someone standing next to him, Camden glanced left. She was looking straight ahead with a conspiratorial smile on her lips. He looked back towards the bar and realised her eyes were locked directly onto him in the mirror behind the counter. He took in as much of her as he could in those few seconds. There was devilment in her face, as though she couldn't quite believe what she was doing. He noticed how thick her eyebrows were and the scattering of moles to the left of her nose, instantly deciding they were additional reasons to find her tailor-made for him. He also observed the diagonal two-inch scar just above her chin and another etched gently into her right cheek, suppressing his curiosity at what had brought them into being.

She let out a quiet laugh and they turned towards each other.

"Corona or Jägermeister?"

His offer was met with a screwed-up face.

"That's a shame. It's all I'm allowed to order." A playfully despondent shake of the head.

"That is a shame," she lamented, her English assured despite its heavy accent. "We could've done great things if you'd bought me a Sex On The Beach."

"And a Sex On The Beach," he immediately called to the barman, who nodded. She laughed, which was what he'd hoped for.

"I'm Crissa."

"Hi Crissa," offering his hand, which she took with an amused smile. "I'm Christian."

"Crissa and Christian." Her expression remained.

"My friends call me Camden."

"Why?"

It was an obvious question that he nonetheless found unexpected. "It's my last name."

"Ah. Well, hello, Camden. Let's stick with Crissa for now. It's not a good idea to try my last name after drinking alcohol."

Camden was unsure whether it was going well or terribly.

"Not dancing?" she asked.

"Only if you paid me," he smiled.

Crissa immediately produced a twenty euro note and held it out in front of her. "Would that be enough?"

"Erm—" Camden stammered, caught off guard.

"You don't dance?"

"I take some persuading." He knew she was toying with him.

"Are you shy?" she asked.

Camden smiled. His blink reflex had abandoned him, but he couldn't break eye contact. "I'm feeling shy right now," he admitted.

"Thank you for my drink, by the way."

"You're welcome."

"What would you like to talk about?"

"Let's talk about you. Where are you from?"

"I grew up in a place called Piraeus—near Athens—but I live here in Santorini now."

"It's a beautiful place."

"It's been a good move for me."

"What do you do here?"

"I work as a masseuse at a hotel," Crissa's smile returned. "It's renowned for having an excellent spa. You should come. I could give you a massage."

Camden started to try at an answer and gave up.

Crissa laughed.

"You're so beautiful. I'm trying to play it cool here and you're making it difficult."

"You're failing if you're trying to play it cool," Crissa said gently, laying her hand on his.

Camden glanced at their hands, wondering how to react.

"It's up to you," Crissa said, reading his mind. Their fingers entwined. "Why are you here?"

"Stag weekend." The response was almost apologetic.

"Stag?" Her head tilted to the side in confusion.

Camden searched for the right phrase. "My friend is getting married," he said, pointing back at the main bar.

"Ah. Bachelor party." She raised her eyebrow as she took a sip of her drink. "Who's the bachelor? The guy dancing on the bar?"

"Yep."

"And who's his best man—you?"

"No. One of the three who are ready to catch him if he falls."

"You think he'll survive the night?" she asked.

"He's survived worse. And he's got a month until the big day."

"Oh, so the wedding isn't here? We're more used to weddings than bachelor parties. What made you choose Santorini?"

"My friend's dad has a place here. Built into the cliff face, somewhere in town."

"Nice."

"It's very nice."

"And where are you from?"

"A place called Leeds, in the north of England."

"And what do you do in between bachelor parties?"

"I'm a professional table-top dancer."

"Are you really?" she laughed again. "That explains why you didn't want to dance before. You need a break from it."

"Exactly right. My life's one dance routine after another." He swam in her brown eyes for another few seconds. "In between performances, I work for a phone company."

"I prefer the dance story."

"Sorry to let you down. It's only part-time, until the dancing starts paying for itself."

"You're quite successful aren't you, Camden?"

She had a knack for asking odd, wrong-footing questions. "I do OK."

"But not so happy, though."

Camden could only look at her. She seemed otherworldly to him.

"Was meeting me part of the plan for the bachelor party?"

"There wasn't really a plan to speak of."

Crissa held him with her eyes for a few seconds before lifting her hand from his, sliding a card into its place, kissing his mouth tenderly, walking over to her friends and out of the bar, not once looking back.

Camden read the card in his hand: *Crissa Papanikolaou, Emporio Suites and Spa.* It had an address, telephone numbers and email. He stood blinking for a couple of minutes, trying to reconcile what he'd just experienced.

———•———

If the remainder of the night had proven hard to navigate, the following morning was torture. He slept fitfully and tried to get up as silently as he could so as not to disturb Morton.

"What's up?" came a fuzzy voice from the other bed.

"Can't sleep. Don't worry."

"Keys are on the table," Morton replied and was instantly gone from the waking world.

Camden fished a t-shirt and shorts from his case, kicked on his espadrilles and stalked down the corridor through the living room onto the balcony. The town was awakening, the sounds of isolated figures going about their preparations for another day of business, delivered at a leisurely pace. The sun's rays already carried some heft but that didn't concern Camden: he tanned easily under his nearly-black hair and had other things on his mind.

How could he contort the day so that he was free for long enough to visit Emporio Suites and Spa? Would it even be an acceptable option to leave his friends on a stag weekend to pursue a local girl?

He wondered what time she started work and checked his watch. It wouldn't be for a while: it read 7:03am.

———•———

By the time everyone had surfaced, eaten, and got mobile, a firm plan had been made without Camden's consultation: Tom was feeling rough so they were going to spend the day chilling out on the terrace outside the canava. A few hours without motion or thought would aid their collective recovery.

Camden struggled to comply. After fidgeting, playing with his phone and trying to read a book whose words may as well have been Cossack dancing across the page, he decided to take a walk. Kinetic energy often brought about his clearest thinking. Nobody was invited to join him; in truth, most had looked incapable of the required effort.

After climbing the hill, he stopped for some lunch, coffee, and composure. The caldera was a painting of shimmering blues broken only by the flourishes of the languid, dancing white wakes of the boats. The rawness of the sun sent shards of light bouncing off the water's surface.

He ordered a local salad, latte, and water. Feeling a little rushed as his plate was efficiently cleared away, he asked for another coffee and instantly regretted it. Not wanting to arrive looking wired, he left it almost untouched.

The taxi knew where to take him. The destination and price were the only words exchanged between him and the driver, and he got out of the car realising that he'd spent all morning thinking about this moment but none of it planning how to act or what to say.

Unlike almost every other building he'd seen on the island, this one was light terracotta rather than white. It looked well-kept if unremarkable from the outside, but as he approached the steps to the main entrance, his attention was caught by a large sun terrace with a sizeable infinity pool and jaw-dropping views.

A large marble desk waited inside. There was nobody in sight, which was in some ways a relief, in others not. Automatically, his feet drifted towards the hypnotic blue of the water below, and he didn't hear the footsteps behind him.

"Can I help you?" a familiar-sounding voice asked.

Wheeling round, Camden saw that it was only the accent that was familiar. Facing him was a lady in her mid-thirties wearing a mass of curls and a friendly smile.

"Oh, hi. I'm looking for Crissa. I think she works here. Crissa Papanikolaou." He stumbled over her surname and wondered if there had even been a need for the clarification.

"Crissa is not here," came the reply.

"Oh," he nodded as if that should have been obvious. His mouth had become very dry, and his eyes flickered from side to side as he sought the correct next move. "I thought she worked here."

The lady's eyes brightened. "She does work here. Just not today. OK?" Her tone was direct.

"OK," he mouthed.

She hesitated. "Do you know Crissa?"

His nodding gathered a little more conviction. "Yes. We met recently," he said, pausing briefly before the final word, which he had wisely inserted instead of 'last night'.

A white van with the name of the spa emblazoned in blue upon its side had pulled up and two young men in matching white shirts and linen trousers walked in, talking excitedly. The lady—who struck Camden as the manager or owner—immediately spoke to them in a way that suggested she was displeased. They quietened, and one of them turned to Camden and apologised for unspecified reasons.

All three of them were now looking at him expectantly, which Camden quickly came to realise can encourage paranoid behaviour. It flashed suddenly and convincingly into his mind that one of the men must be Crissa's boyfriend. They were both in their mid-twenties, around Crissa's age. The taller of the two seemed the more viable candidate, his hair cropped short with two lines shaved into his eyebrows and an enviable dimple in his chin. It became imperative not to mention Crissa's name again.

"Can I take this, please?" Camden asked, holding up a tourist brochure for the island, as if that was the real reason he had ridden a cab such a distance. He had no exit strategy.

"Sure," said Eyebrows. The manager gave a brief, dismissive flap of her hands as she exited the scene.

"Thanks," Camden said, and tried to adopt a purposeful gait as he left the building.

———•———

"Excuse me!"

Fooled once already, Camden turned around knowing that the voice belonged to a local female, but not necessarily the one he was hoping for. It was nevertheless a pleasant surprise to see the graceful jog of a slender blonde who was a whisker under six feet coming towards him.

"Yes?"

"Are you—" She paused to catch her breath, having just run the two hundred yards from the spa in the blazing sun.

"Can I help you?"

She placed her hand on his right shoulder as her breathing moderated. "Christian, right?"

Her accent was more Americanised than Crissa's.

"Yeah. How—how did you know that?" he stuttered.

"Crissa isn't working today," she replied, as if that explained things.

He nodded tentatively. "So I understand."

"She was supposed to. They called her this morning to change her shift. She's not back in until tomorrow."

"Oh." This seemed like good news to Camden, although he wasn't quite sure why.

"She said you might come here today. She hoped you would."

Despite his best efforts, Camden beamed and looked bashfully over towards the water. "I hoped she would be here."

She smiled at him. "Can you make it to Crystal again tonight?"

"I'm sure I can."

"They don't allow you to dance on the bar in there, you know."

"I'll spread the word," he chuckled.

"We'll be there from ten. Arrive later if you can. Keep her in suspense, just a little."

"I'll try."

"This is your cab," she nodded over his shoulder as a white car pulled up behind them. As he turned back to face her, she held up her phone to show she'd called ahead. "I'm Irini, by the way."

"It was nice to meet you, Irini. I thought I was going mad before you turned up."

———•———

Several times throughout the evening, Camden had to rein himself in from suggesting that they move on. He already felt like he'd been acting strangely. He'd been grilled on his whereabouts when he had returned earlier in the afternoon, but his answer of a long walk to clear his head was accepted both for its potential veracity and the lack of real interest from the group.

At around five they laboured into action, milling between bathrooms, suitcases, and mirrors like a slow-motion production line.

"Did we used to take this long to recover?" Dean asked at one point.

There was agreement that they were getting older but could still take the pace.

"Who was that girl you were cracking onto at the bar last night?" Gary asked.

"I was talking to her, not cracking onto her," Camden corrected genially from the sofa.

"I can vouch for that," Morton confirmed. "I was heading through to help him with the drinks when she walked up to him."

Gary nodded, pursing his lips in a manner that was equal parts mocking and serious. "And where did she go?"

"She left."

And there it ended, as the topic was dropped in favour of laughter as Tom came down the stairs in the tuxedo that he'd been convinced to wear. "Going to be baking in this!" he protested, while seeming to enjoy the look.

There were thirty seconds or so of conversation between them all before Camden drifted back to his thoughts. When he looked up, Morton was grinning at him in a way that said that he alone understood what those thoughts were about.

———•———

Having sat down to eat at almost eight, they lingered over dinner and shared some local wine. Over two hours later, they still hadn't settled the bill and were showing few signs of vacating the table. As the waiter brought across a second complimentary dessert and ouzo, Morton switched with Dean so that he sat beside Camden and leaned sideways towards him.

"Where did you go today, mate?"

Camden's eyes were stuck to his wine glass until he'd delivered his answer. "Just went for a walk."

"Where to?"

He stayed evasive. "Around the cliff streets. Down to the harbour. Around the town. Just wandered really."

Morton nodded. "It's a beautiful island. Relaxing. When I look out at the water, I feel like I'm floating above it. And the views from the hilltops are magnificent. You're looking down on the towns and out into the sea. It looks idyllic, almost unreal."

"Yeah."

A silence hung between them.

"So where are you meeting her?"

Camden's head snapped round. "Huh?"

Morton smiled and raised his glass to his lips. "I asked where you're meeting her." He took a drink. "You know you're going to need some help if we're going to get this lot moving."

Just after eleven, the same maître d' shepherded them down the same stairs. It was far busier than the previous night, making it harder for Camden to spot her. Waitress service was still available but would be some time, so Morton signalled that he would go to the bar and suggested Camden accompany him. They'd barely made it there when soft, warm hands enveloped Camden's and impelled him to follow their lead. He turned in their direction and the hands instantly moved up to hold his face as Crissa brushed her nose and lips against him before delivering a lengthy kiss that caused him to concede a half-step.

The moment that their lips parted she guided him away from Morton, who lifted his chin in encouragement, towards the edge of the dancefloor, which ended with a wall that overlooked the caldera.

Crissa moved with the music and slid Camden's hands onto her hips, back pressed against him as she faced out to the water. After a few moments she lifted his hands from her waist and brought them around her stomach, his arms holding her tightly but naturally. Finally, she turned slightly to him and engaged him again in a kiss, maintaining the movement of her dance. When they released, she was no longer smiling, simply looking deeply into his eyes as if they were the only ones there.

"You need to find a way to stay here with me," she whispered, pulling his head in close to hers.

Chapter 5

Gary had been sitting next to Camden when the pictures from the streets of Athens had taken a sinister turn.

He had thrown an uneasy look towards the others as the television showed police storming crowds, objects being thrown, storefronts demolished, banners waved, fires lit. Images cut with disorienting speed, flitting between a distressed studio presenter, a wired field reporter, and scenes of chaos. As water cannons were shown for the first time, scything the legs from underneath masked protesters and slamming them against the nearest stationary object, Gary's jaw slackened.

He was the first to look away from the screen, sensing that Camden no longer sat where he had been only seconds before. As the others turned their heads to appraise the situation, Gary saw a flash of colour fly out the door.

Within seconds, he found himself following suit, his feet moving quicker than his mind. He paused to get his bearings as he stepped outside. He wasn't that familiar with the town but was in the part of it that he knew best. A hand clasped his shoulder, and he swivelled round to see that Tom had decided to accompany him. As he looked at the long-time friend whom he was no longer sure could be his friend, he decided to focus on the search. All other things would sort themselves out later.

They turned right, the same direction Camden had taken. It was hard to make progress. The crowds on the streets seemed to have competing priorities. The majority were trying to maintain a semblance of discipline as they held makeshift banners, raised their fists and shouted. Neither Tom nor Gary spoke Greek, but they'd seen enough of the news coverage to understand that they were witnessing part of the nationwide unrest against the government.

Another section looked like non-swimmers thrown overboard, their faces marked with alarm and anxiety. Some held children. Some spun full circle as they searched for safety.

The third, most forceful, portion of the crowd was barrelling towards them from a good hundred yards back, some of them making for the steps that led to the harbour. People were being knocked backwards and, occasionally, off their feet as an increasing number made their descent at a speed that seemed unwise given the precipitous nature of the drop.

Gary shouted Camden's name only once, his voice next to inaudible above the crowd. Tom pointed upwards at one of the many staircases that connected the cliffside capital. They were two steps into their climb when there was a sudden increase in the volume and belligerence of the shouting beneath them. The expressions of those around them began to turn to undisguised panic.

They couldn't stand still with the crowd moving so strongly now. They'd barely managed fifty yards from Salvation's front door. Turning round to continue their ascent, they immediately came to a halt again. Between a dozen and twenty figures were quick-stepping down the stairs, sporting helmets, Perspex riot shields and batons.

"Fuck that," Gary said, grabbing at Tom's shirt. "We won't find him in this. Just get back to the bar."

They tried to break into a run but with every step had to either absorb or avoid the contact of a crowd that was moving against them with increasing fervour. They'd covered no more than half the distance to Salvation when the momentum of the throng became too much. Without warning, the tide of bodies reshaped itself as a bow wave, the familiar sight of hooded, scarved youths piercing through and shoving the less dynamic members off-balance into the wake. Tom's face collided jarringly with the head of one of those who had been tossed aside and he dropped instantly to the ground, breath taking leave of his body as his back cracked sharply on the cobbled stones. Gary fought to get across to him. When he was pushed uncompromisingly out of the way he staggered, recovered, and threw his body weight against the closest hood he could see, knocking him down and wiping out two of his cohorts in the process.

Momentary elation was followed by multidirectional pain. A black-clad forearm struck across his jaw, and he felt the push of the crowd as they searched for escape. He was aware of an elbow landing at the top of his spine and kicks briefly hammering into his kidneys as he hunched over, but was surprised when, having lost his footing after a blow from behind, he found himself pinned down with a knee in his back. In his peripheral vision to the right, he caught sight of a transparent plastic convex object. He darted his head to the left where Tom had been trampled by the crowd and was starting to roll himself slowly onto his side, his clothes torn and bedraggled. As Gary's head was forced towards the ground—his mouth filled with dirt and his vision comprised only of close-up paving stones—he realised that on all sides there were motionless bodies, either laying injured or being held in place by crouching figures. Making one final attempt to catch sight of Salvation, Gary heard an assertive shout from his restrainer and yelped as his wrists were brought quickly together behind his back and a thin object snaked around them before being pulled agonisingly taut.

For what seemed like the first time in a couple of minutes he again heard the aggregated sounds of the crowd. Off to the right, it looked like something was burning.

Chapter 6

The boat glided towards the shore, where refuge awaited.

It had been a long few weeks. He needed rest. The engine had been so quiet on the trip that it was almost a surprise to hear its absence as it cut out for the last few yards.

He waited for it to be moored before zipping up his lightweight waterproof as he stood. Slinging his holdall over his shoulder, he nodded to the captain and two crew members and disembarked.

"Mr Andreas, welcome."

They shook hands and embraced. His host extended his other arm behind him, proudly showing off his home. "For as long as you need it."

They patted each other's shoulders and wordlessly swapped positions, his host climbing aboard the skiff after placing the key to the villa into Andreas' hand.

A few years had passed since his previous visit. There were no signs of any renovations, yet the place looked immaculate. He tossed his jacket over one of the stools at the breakfast bar and carried his bag through the living space to the largest of the bedrooms at the rear of the building. He'd used all the rooms here at one time or another, but this was his favourite, and tonight that seemed important. He allowed himself a few moments of contemplation, sitting on the edge of the bed, eyes gently closed. *Breathe in, breathe out.*

He blinked heavily to keep fatigue at bay as he sought out the drinks cabinet at the far end of the room. He poured himself a glass of wine, taking it down the winding stone stairway that led to the infinity pool. As his mind idled, he found himself thinking about playfighting on his grandparents' floor with his brothers, growing up in Athens.

Leaning on the waist-high wall to the left of the pool, he placed his glass on the ledge. The sea looked infinite as he looked out from the southern end of Santorini. Behind him glittered the lights of Fira.

Everything had been business and unpleasantness recently.

He needed space.

He needed this.

Just for a couple of nights. He knew that was all the respite he would be afforded.

———•———

The call came the following night, just before eight.

"Have you seen the news?"

Andreas had not seen the news. The TV had remained off, phone on silent, internet unused. His day had consisted of a dawn rise, thirty minutes of metronomic lengths of the pool, and then mercifully long hours of dozing in the shade, reading a novel and contemplating the panoramas from the infinity pool. He was now halfway through a small bottle of local wine, having taken his time over a plate of high-quality cold meats while his lamb stew warmed in the oven. The villa had been fully stocked with food and drink. He sat at the table, facing south. The lighting was subtle. Classical music was playing. His posture was erect, as always.

"Switch it on," he was told.

Andreas made a sound as he sucked air through his teeth in annoyance. His assistant's theatricality amused him at times, irritated him at others. This occasion was the latter.

"I gave instructions not to be disturbed. Why can't you just tell me what you have to tell me?" he demanded, all the while taking the required steps to turn on the TV with the volume down. A special news bulletin was being aired and the streets of Athens were on-screen, as they had perennially been these past couple of years.

"So?"

"Which channel are you watching?"

"The one that doesn't spend each day saying I'm the devil," Andreas chuckled grimly.

"Turn over."

The demonstrations were also on the next channel, but so too was a red information bar containing white scrolling text at the bottom. It carried four messages in rotation:

The first read: "Demonstrations against government in many cities across country."

The second read: "Reports of more than 250,000 people taking part."

The third read: "Protesters call for resignation of Minister of Finance, Michael Andreas."

The fourth read: "Andreas believed to be staying at luxury villa on Santorini."

"You need to get out of there," his assistant's voice told him.

"I'm running from no-one," he replied. "Keep your line open: I'll call you back in ten minutes."

———•———

"This is what's going to happen," Andreas said down the phone. "I'm going to tell the people of this country why we are doing what we are doing and why there is an agenda against it."

"Think about this, Michael," his assistant warned. "You've said those things before. People aren't won over by a list of facts that they don't understand or recognise. They're angry. They need a scapegoat and you're playing the role."

"I appreciate your concern, Alex, but this is not about being popular. It's about doing what is right for the country."

"For every dramatic bone I have in my body, you have a self-righteous one in yours." Andreas allowed himself a momentary smile at the legitimacy of Alex's sparring. They'd known each other for five years now, since Andreas had first joined the political ranks, and this was the aspect of their relationship in which he found most value. "Grandstanding will achieve nothing here, neither on this call nor beyond."

"People want answers."

"Yes, but they want different answers to the ones you've been giving them, that's the problem. You tell them repeatedly that you are doing what is necessary for the country, what is in their best interests. But where are you right now? In the upmarket villa of a wealthy friend."

"You know," Andreas interjected, "I hate this tendency that has emerged recently to ask a question and then answer it yourself." He enjoyed the sigh that he heard from the other end of the line.

"Hate it or not, you're not disputing it."

"I *am* disputing it. Two years into this job, all I've done is try to clear up other people's shit. Lying was the only thing done competently around here in recent years. Comfortable decisions won't get us out of the mess we're in. You know it."

"Yes, I know that it's true." Andreas could envision Alex massaging his forehead as he spoke, a sure sign he was doing his best to exercise patience under trying circumstances. "But several other things are true, Michael. A politician is a politician in the public's eye: you're all the same. There's nothing about you—your education, your career, your wealth—that they relate to. You are part of a government that can't protect them: they see Germany and the EU pulling the strings and resent what they see as spineless submission from the people they've elected to represent them. This is politics. There are no heroes. Everyone here is compromised, you as much as the next man. Do what you can before the swords turn on you."

"Why do I employ you, Alex?"

Michael heard a sniff down the line as Alex pondered his answer. "To give honest advice that you wouldn't otherwise hear."

"Not just that, but that above all else," Michael agreed. "And what is your advice in this moment?"

"Leave the villa immediately, come back here and get on with unpopular but important work. It's not good for you to be out on a limb like you are there. You know I never liked the idea."

"I know you didn't, but not every decision needs political advice. I needed a break to recharge, on my own. This place achieves that more than any other."

Alex made no sound.

"Thank you for your advice. It is noted. But I am where I am in this world by considering advice and then using or discarding it based on my own viewpoint. I'm a leader in this country at a time when it needs leaders. Leaders don't flee."

"Nor do they grandstand—"

"Use that word once and you're advising me, Alex. Use it twice and you're lecturing me. And I don't like being lectured." He let his words hang in the silence. "I've made up my mind. Shortly, I will record a video message stating my position on our financial predicament and why I have to do what I am doing, for our long-term future. Notify every media outlet you can and be prepared to stream it in fifteen minutes."

There was a pause before Alex responded. "You should speak to the Prime Minister before issuing anything."

"The Prime Minister is not here!" Andreas snapped. "I am. I'm the one who is the focal point here and I'm the one who is under threat. I *will* talk to the Prime Minister directly, but I stress to you that I do not need his approval to speak in public."

Alex's breathing was faint but audible across the connection. "I understand." It sounded like he had forced his mouth shut after his second word. "I'll be waiting for your message. Good luck."

Michael ended the call and started writing outline notes. The call to the Prime Minister went unmade.

———•———

"I speak to you this evening as a leader, public servant, and proud Greek.

"When I chose to enter politics, it was because I believed it to be the most effective way of improving things for my country. I still believe that to be the case. I was not yet in my teens when the military were heaved from power. I have seen the alternative to democracy, and it harmed many more people than it helped. The job of a politician is to improve the lives of the people of the country, present and future. It is a simple principle. What is not so simple is its implementation. That is more complex.

"Our financial system has long been unfit for purpose. It must undergo fundamental change. Previous governments have lost the trust of the countries on which we now depend for help, consistently reporting incorrect figures in order to remain in the European Union. All of this has meant that, when times are hard—as has been the case in this global recession—there is no spare money available. We are bankrupt.

"This angers you. I know it: I hear and see it on the streets and know that there are protests taking place even as I speak. It angers me, too, because I love my country and this was absolutely avoidable. If you save in the good times, you are better prepared for the hard times. Another simple principle. Collect the tax that is owed instead of privately admitting that its avoidance is a 'national sport' that we're willing to accept even though it costs the country twenty billion Euros a year. Make decisions that are right for the country regardless of whether they will be immediately popular or get you re-elected. These are things that should be the foundations on which our economy and politics are based. They have not been in the past. They will be now.

"I will not call on you to return to your homes. You have the right to voice your opinions and concerns. But do not think that these decisions are being made without your best interests at heart."

There was a momentary pause.

"I have here," Andreas looked down to his right and picked up an object which he held in front of the camera, "evidence of why these measures are so unpopular. Austerity has become an ugly word in this country. None of us welcome it, but it should not be an ugly word in our circumstances. Ugliness is tax evasion. Cheating people. The relentless negativity of the media and public figures in relation to austerity is driven by personal vendettas and an underlying fear that important people will be exposed."

Watching from his office, Alex sensed that the earlier poise of Andreas' address had just tilted beyond a point from where it could re-stabilise.

"Contained on this disk are the names of over two thousand of your compatriots—many well-known, all hugely wealthy, several from the very island from which I am sending you this message—who have gone to extraordinary lengths to avoid paying the tax that they owe as citizens of this land. You will recognise scores of names and think:

'*so that is why they have spoken so strongly against these measures*'. They'll no longer have the credibility to appear on your TV screens, newspapers, or radios, decrying the government for the steps we are taking to secure the long-term future of the country."

The pace of Andreas' delivery was quickening.

"There will become a realisation that there has been a game played by untrustworthy people at the expense of the larger population. I respect your right to protest, but I will not sway from the path I have laid out. We must work longer, save harder and live within our means, but we will hand down a country that is fit for our children, and when you see the names contained here," the data stick again appeared on-screen, "you will understand that you have, up to this point, been fed and believed in a lie."

Michael Andreas disconnected the line, ending the broadcast that had been transmitted throughout the country, including on the TV in Salvation. His phone immediately vibrated next to him. The caller showed as Unknown, but he knew it would be Alex—he was the only person who had the number for this phone, which he had purchased on his way to the airport the previous day. He let it go unanswered, instead glancing back at the notes he'd written in preparation for delivering his message with impact but without pomposity, wondering whether he'd regret the fact that he had not stopped talking at the point where his notes had ended, with the words "do not think that these decisions are being made without your best interests at heart."

It was 8:22pm.

Chapter 7

On the final day of Tom's stag weekend, Crissa had looked at Camden with that daring style of hers, in a way that showed she was feeling some of the same things he was but would force him to acknowledge it first.

They sat in a cafe in Emporio as agreed, shielded from the mid-afternoon sun. When he'd arrived, Crissa had walked from inside to welcome him, her entire body carrying such warmth that he almost jumped at her initial touch before settling into full appreciation of the hold. Their kisses were generous, if a little more hesitant than the previous night.

"So," Crissa invited.

"So," Camden replied unsurely. "You live here?"

"Near to here, yes."

He nodded.

"Would you like a drink?"

"Yeah, I'll get them," he flustered.

"Don't worry," she replied and waved a hand towards

the inside of the cafe, which was too dark for him to see into from the sunshine. A man emerged as though he had been waiting for the gesture. He took their order.

"So," she repeated, cocking her head to the side.

"The way I'm feeling is so unfamiliar to me, I'm still trying to get used to it."

"And what way do you feel?"

"In love," he replied without hesitation. "In the space of two days."

"What's the correct time limit?"

"I don't know. I always presumed it would be longer than two days."

"Not at first sight?"

"Actually, I'd always kind of thought it would be at first sight, too, so perhaps none of what I'm saying makes any sense."

Drinks arrived and Camden took a thirsty gulp.

"Did you also expect it to happen in your own country?" Crissa enquired, leaving her drink untouched.

Camden gave that a moment's thought. "Yeah, I guess I probably did."

She smiled at him.

"I don't know what I'm thinking but I do know what I'm feeling. Does that make sense?"

"Perfect sense."

He steadied himself. "You said to me last night that I needed to find a way to stay here with you."

"I did," she replied, and he was relieved to hear that she wasn't now retracting it.

"Well, I've found a way. My friend and I are going to open a bar in the capital."

"Just like that?" She viewed the notion as fanciful.

"My friend has connections that can make things happen quickly."

"This is the friend whose father owns the property you're staying in?"

"Correct. He and I have been friends since university."

They both sampled their drinks, as though that would help with their comprehension.

"So how will this work?"

"We'll be back in three weeks." Camden's brow furrowed slightly as he said it, scanning her face for any type of reaction.

The reaction that he saw was of her hands swiftly cupping together over her mouth, a huge smile leaking out of the side. Her eyes shone. "My life has just changed," she said.

"Mine changed two nights ago," he replied.

———•———

Having completed the most reluctant yet thrilling flight of his life, Camden arrived back at his city centre flat, let go of his bags, drifted across to the French windows at the end of his open-plan living room and looked across the lights of Leeds with utter disinterest.

And yet this made things easier. No doubts existed in his mind. Out came the phone and the words were entered without hesitation: *Just arrived back at my apartment. It doesn't feel like home anymore. Miss you x*

The phone told him it was 1.55am, which made it 3.55am over there. He held the top of the phone under his chin in contemplation, unable to move a muscle until he received a reply. He was released within a minute, flicking the screen in front of him the instant it vibrated to read her words: *Glad you made it safely. I can still taste and feel you when I close my eyes. Speak to you tomorrow xxx*

A goofy smile burst across his face. Images of possible futures drew patterns across his mind like dogs racing across parkland, finally free from the leash.

Suddenly, everything carried purpose.

Having reached a collective decision about their fates the previous night, he and Morton had been consumed by a flurry of ideas and excitement about their newborn joint venture. They shared their intentions with the rest of the group through a sense of compulsion, leaving a brief opening for additional parties to join the fold. Only Gary had given a flash of intrigue, but they had needed to see wholehearted commitment. The moment quickly passed.

Now Camden stood in an apartment that he had already decided to sell and felt like a man renewed. Parts of his person that had previously defined him suddenly began to fall away. Maybe it had been coming. When he had been asked by a group of work colleagues about his New Year's resolution a few months before, instead of taking his usual stance—that he would never commit to such follies—he surprised himself by spontaneously responding: "To be more present in every moment."

"That's a good one," nodded one of his co-workers, visibly impressed.

That memory struck him as noteworthy because it stood apart from one of his character traits that had grown to irk him most: this tendency to drift through days, events, and places without fully engaging with them. His twenty-ninth birthday had fallen on a Wednesday night the previous November and he spent it on his own watching an independent film at the century-old Hyde Park Picture House before walking the two miles back to his Leeds city centre flat in unrelenting rain. Three messages were on his mobile when he switched it back on after exiting the cinema—one from his parents and one each from Dean and Morton, the latter two asking where they should meet for celebratory drinks. A wave of disconsolation hit as he admitted to himself that his dominant emotion was relief at having been able to spend his evening in a form of solitude.

Reality collided with him. *This is not healthy.*

The first few months of that New Year's resolution had been—at best—a qualified success, but Camden recognised the opportunity Morton presented as a sea change. They had never been best friends but shared a mutual appreciation, their stories making each other laugh and their opinions compatible. There was trust in what one another stood for. Though far less commercially minded and experienced than Morton, Camden was no fool, and since discovering Crissa, was possessed by a blissful certitude about his life's new path.

The kettle came to the boil as he finished the first handwritten sentence of his resignation letter. When he handed it to his manager the following morning, she was clearly staggered by the straightforwardness and tone of both the letter and Camden's replies to her inevitable questions.

"Are you sure about this?"

"One hundred percent."

"Don't you want to take a little more time to reflect on it?"

"There's no need."

She eyed him. "I can keep this between us for now. Take a week, think it over."

"That's not necessary, Jane. I've made my decision."

"Is there something wrong?"

"Quite the opposite."

"You know, you have a bright future ahead of you here. I can't believe you're throwing it away like this."

As quickly as that, Camden thought, *we've moved from incomprehension to overt disapproval.* His untaken leave meant he only had to enter the office on a further fifteen occasions.

———•———

Three weeks later, what Camden and Morton would call home was relocated indefinitely.

They sat in the departure lounge restaurant after checking in for their one-way flight. A waitress stood lethargically over them.

"Let's say goodbye properly: large breakfast with a coffee and orange juice, please," Morton said, handing her the menu.

The waitress let her eyeballs fall from Morton to Camden, not writing anything down.

"Same. Tea instead of coffee."

"Sure," she said unconvincingly and sloped off.

"So," Morton said with a smile, "let's have this conversation before we leave home soil."

"What conversation?"

"Why are we here when none of our friends are?"

They were interrupted by the arrival of clumsily plonked cutlery and drinks.

"Neither of us is here for the bar," Morton continued once the waitress had retreated.

Camden's glass of orange juice stopped millimetres from his mouth.

"Am I wrong?"

"Yeah."

"Completely wrong?"

Camden finally took a drink. "No," he conceded.

"I don't have one single, overarching reason," Morton offered, "more a bunch of cumulative ones. I've been getting a bit restless these past few months. Not because I've hit my thirties and feel like I haven't accomplished enough: quite the opposite. Feels like I've done plenty but seem to be enjoying it less. So far, my response has been to put more and more into everything I do in the expectation there'll be a dividend. Then I had a moment of clarity while we were over there a couple of weeks back. You know how something suddenly emerges in the forefront of your mind, fully formed? When it arrives there, you realise it's fully formed because you've thought your way around it in amongst all the distractions of day-to-day life?"

"Yeah."

"In the minibus from the airport to the canava, it just hit me: stop chasing things harder; step back and enjoy life a little more. Give yourself time to appreciate it."

"Slow down."

"Exactly. Slow down. Moving faster doesn't really work. Sometimes it's felt like I've been playing that drinking game when you have to run to a specified point but only after downing a pint and being spun round twenty times before you set off."

"I remember that game."

"And there wasn't much clear thinking done at those events," Morton chuckled. "What about you?"

"Similar in some ways, I guess. I've lived my life by textbook decisions, but they've left me thinking: what's the point? I had no interest in what I was doing. A bit like you, something clicked into place a few weeks back."

"For different reasons," Morton joshed.

"No doubt," Camden replied sincerely. "For the first time, instead of trying to avoid making a wrong move, I'm excited to know I'm making the right one."

Their food arrived; two huge plates with unappetising food taking up less than a third of the surface area.

"This is good to hear from you, mate," Morton said as they began to eat.

"It feels good. As soon as the realisation hit me, everything else—all the things I've made my priorities because there was nothing more worthwhile—just became secondary and faded into the background."

"So, Crissa is the reason you're here."

Camden suppressed a smile as he chewed. "We all need catalysts."

—·—

They collected their luggage as the sun was setting and took a cab to Fira, where their new apartment awaited on the south side of town. They'd seen it online but had left the arrangements to Morton's father, who would be flying in from the mainland to meet them in the morning to show them prospective locations for Salvation.

"Looks good," Morton said approvingly as the cab pulled away. A lithe, fortysomething woman with a runner's body stepped out of the passenger side of a car twenty feet away and greeted them with a smile that looked genuine and well-used. "Mr Morton, Mr Camden." She identified them correctly and shook their hands. She wore a white blouse with black trousers and gave the impression that her wardrobe was well stocked with such unfussy offerings. "Your keys. If you have any questions, my husband and I are five minutes away. Don't hesitate to call." For a country famed for being laid-back, Camden was struck by the efficiency of their welcome.

From the front, the building was an impeccable cream-coloured box, its grey door and window shutters framed in white. It was so symmetrical and uncomplicated that it looked as though it had been designed by a child. A small, paved courtyard ushered them towards the front door. To the left a pathway led to a surprisingly generous patio with an outrageously good view of the caldera.

Camden realised that, up to that point, they hadn't discussed the topic of rent.

Inside was more a case of function over form. It looked as though the previous inhabitants had been modernising one room every couple of years before stopping the project a while back.

They wandered through a self-guided tour. The kitchen was immediately inside the front door and looked as though the exterior of the building had been flipped onto the inside, its counter tops and tiles the same light grey as the door, the cupboards perfectly matching the cream walls. It managed to look both clean and weary in equal measure. A counter separated the kitchen from the living room, which contained a mishmash of furniture. The TV was at least ten years younger than its stand; there was a nest of small tables that complemented nothing else; the coffee table looked as though it weighed so much that it would be standing long after the building fell to the ground. The black leather sofa looked suspiciously new, causing Camden to wonder whether Morton's Dad had shipped it in to replace something less inviting but more in keeping with the period of the other furniture. Sliding glass doors took them onto the patio that they had glimpsed from the front of the house.

Downstairs there was a corridor with three doorways. Straight ahead was the bathroom, with a shower over a tub that looked like it would struggle to host anyone above the age of twelve. Next door was a double room with wardrobes and drawers taking up the entire wall as they entered. It was spacious and square-shaped with a large window that offered unobstructed views of the bay. The other bedroom was longer and narrower with a similar view. They surmised that the bedrooms extended underneath the patio.

"As long as both rooms are soundproof, I don't mind which one I have," Morton said.

He went long and narrow, Camden next to the bathroom.

"Right, I can tell that I'm about to get abandoned because you've got a better offer," Morton grinned, scooping up his keys, "so I'll go grab something to eat and get some provisions. Give you some space to practice your lines."

"Been practising them a lot lately."

"Bet you have. We're meeting my dad and his business guys in the morning. Get Crissa up here tomorrow night, introduce us properly."

Within seconds of being left alone, Camden was dialling her number.

"You're here?" Crissa asked, smile permeating the line.

"I'm here. Can I see you?"

"It's all I've been thinking about. Where are you?"

"Our new apartment."

"How is it?"

"Pretty nice. Amazing views."

"You've got a view of the caldera?"

"We have."

"Can I see it?"

"Sure."

"And then we can come back here."

It was music to Camden's ears to know he'd returned to the shared world that existed only for them.

"What's your address?"

"Erm … come to think of it, I don't know. I didn't think to ask."

"Too busy thinking of other things?"

They were both laughing.

"Tell you what, how about you come to mine instead. I can see your place tomorrow, provided you can find your way back there."

"That sounds like a better plan."

"Get a taxi to Emporio: the town, not the spa. I'll meet you in the main square."

His first unsteady steps away from the cab were replaced by light-headed euphoria as he entered the square and saw Crissa rise to her feet from a large flight of steps in front of an imposing church of traditional colours. She wore a thigh-length lace white summer dress with a brown belt and complimented the outfit with a gold bangle on her lower forearm and a trademark smile that could simultaneously express multiple emotions. She looked exactly how Camden wanted her to look. As she floated towards him, Crissa extended her arms diagonally in front of her, palms facing him, inviting him to take her hands. No sooner had they touched than her arms snaked around his back and up to the nape of his neck, roughing and smoothing his short black hair in rhythmic strokes.

"Hey," he began, but she pulled his head down towards her before he had a chance to say anything else. He hooked his right arm behind her back, and they started a kiss of pure release and relief that what they had tasted so briefly only weeks ago was authentic.

"You look so beautiful," he told her as they paused for air.

"That was the longest three weeks of my life."

They held hands for the five-minute walk to Crissa's compact home, sharing more smiles than words along the way. Everything about her seemed so smooth: her skin, her movements, her awareness of all things happening around her. She lived alone off a quiet street, and from the moment that her key entered the lock and she leaned her back against the door to open it, their embrace remained unbroken as they moved across into the living room, Crissa guiding them through the subtle light so as not to disrupt their flow. Finally, she brought them to a halt and the searching of their tongues and hands eased momentarily.

"This is my place."

"I like it," Camden said, paying attention to little of it other than to recognise that it was an open plan kitchen and living room similar to the one he and Morton had just acquired, although smaller. He caught a glimpse of a bathroom off to the left, behind the kitchen.

"We need to go up there," she said tenderly, pointing at a brown wooden ladder that led up to a bedroom overlooking the rest of the apartment. "That's why I stopped kissing. We can't climb that while we're attached to each other." Her eyes were blinking with remarkable regularity, yet a glistening sheen was there each time her eyelids rebounded into place.

"Then we'd better get up there quickly so we can start again."

Without a word, Crissa turned and ascended the ladder with a grace that left him reeling. They moved together for the rest of the night, exploring and enjoying each other in as many ways as their bodies allowed. At one point, Camden stirred to see her facing him with a look of such complete tranquillity that he couldn't bring himself to wake her. Thankfully, she did so of her own accord, her deep brown eyes immediately consuming him as she leaned into a determined kiss and shifted her body on top of his. When they finally fell asleep for a few hours, the sun had already risen, and he drifted off with the indelible image of her slim, tanned body sliding along his, contrasted against the background of the sheer white walls.

Chapter 8

Slowly pushing his chest forward and shoulders back, Gary felt a crack at the base of his spine. Having waited hours for a seat, he now wished he'd followed Tom's example and remained standing.

By his estimate, they were in a room measuring twenty foot square and he counted fifty-seven inhabitants. When they'd been marched in several hours earlier, he'd clocked a similarly sized neighbouring room, which had been empty at the time but was presumably no longer.

Their transportation from the cobbled streets outside Salvation to this ill-equipped holding facility had been disorienting. Gary's first few words in English—delivered in spluttering protest as he was quickly hauled to his feet— had been met with hostile looks from the other bodies being lifted from the ground in cable ties and he resolved at that moment to remain silent. Either through observation or similar experience, Tom appeared to have decided on the same tactic, so the police made no connection between them. Fortunately, they ended up in the same van but at different ends. Tom was continually dry-heaving. Gary discreetly monitored him. Their eyes briefly met once, and Tom gave a quick nod of affirmation before re-fixing onto the floor—they were both trying to quickly figure out how to survive such an unfamiliar situation.

A photo was taken of every person before they were loaded up. It was the size of a transit van, nothing more, and wasn't fit to hold so many passengers. Neither of them had even seen official police demarcation on its outside, and they would both later recall that they had tried to adopt what they'd seen in films—keeping track of the turns and distances they drove—but coherence was lost within the first four changes of direction.

The journey took fifteen minutes or so, at which point they were stationary for a few minutes before the doors swung open and they were unloaded in two tranches. Gary exited in tranche one without looking back. A few minutes passed before the doors reopened. There was a lot of jostling as they moved from the van into a more orderly line at the front doors, arriving at a reception desk that presumably spent most of its time alone. Another photo was taken, and then the contents of each person's pockets were emptied and placed into a small plastic bag, along with any watches, jewellery, and belts. A third photo of the contents of the bag would match inmate to possessions.

From there, into the room where they had since remained. There was a single metal door with an A4-sized window that mostly remained closed. It didn't look like it would hold up against any determined challenge, yet nobody tried to force their way to freedom. After an hour or so, a senior-looking policeman appeared and delivered an address to the room. Gary had taken it to be an instruction, but it actually transpired to be a question. A dozen or so people raised their hands and two were selected and escorted from the room. They returned within a couple of minutes and the next two were taken: a toilet run, an exercise that was conducted by different police officers another six times, at regular intervals. Gary assumed that each interval constituted an hour, which made sense given the encroaching brightness outside.

Still, they hadn't spoken a word to each other. Gary had shot a warning look as Tom had first entered the room and they tacitly agreed to maintain silence while things calibrated. Tom's was one of the raised hands for the second toilet visit, after which he returned to stand near his friend. Shared space was the most they would venture at this point.

———•———

They had all met at university twelve years earlier, and although they hadn't all been close friends with each other at the same time, they moved in the same social circles and lived out enough stories to make catching up easy to do. A few had stayed in or near Leeds after graduation and would meet up on weekends and evenings in the days before wives, kids and the career ladder started to merit more attention. By that time, the strength of the friendships had grown. As marriage proposals came into play, stag weekends began to add to the library of shared adventures.

Tom's choice of Santorini as his stag destination was unconventional, but they'd done the usual haunts over the previous few years and last time—as they looked disappointedly at the third British stag in two days to be cheered onto the Barcelona beach by friends while wearing a Borat-style mankini—they simultaneously realised that they now belonged to a different demographic.

Next time, they resolved, they would show some signs of maturity while getting blind drunk.

Because the summer season hadn't properly begun, Morton's dad let them have his place for free, save for a minor—but plausible—threat to their health if they caused significant damage.

Tom had found choosing a best man a tough task. There weren't any real candidates from his days growing up as an only child, but he felt proud of the friends he'd made since leaving home and had a few options, if not a single, obvious one. In the end, he chose Gary. They'd been roommates as freshers and shared a house throughout their student days. After university, both had returned home, but they kept in touch, even if their visits had become less frequent in recent times.

They were different animals. Tom was always at the forefront of any mischief-making. Having earned a 2:1 with seemingly little effort, he joined an investment bank on a graduate scheme, working in London but basing himself back at his parents' house in Watford. His generous starting wage was invested in a vigorous social life and a deposit that became a two-bedroom flat in Maida Vale four years later. Girlfriends came and went with alacrity until a weekend trip to Torbay to see Gary. There he encountered Lucy as part of a group who would be spending the night on the town.

"Tom, meet Lucy," Gary told him, clutching her to his side. "My oldest friend."

"Smartest. Best dressed. Loveliest. Most glamorous. So many ways he could introduce me, and yet he always opts for 'oldest,'" Lucy replied. "He's lucky I've known him too long to disown him."

Tom took to her immediately, and the evening preserved itself in his mind as a series of prolonged conversations between them that seemed to cover each and every topic that popped into their heads, until eventually they were passing laughter and prolonged looks across the kitchen table of Gary's flat. When he woke the next morning, Tom knew something felt different even before he glanced over to see Lucy lying on her side, facing away from him, breathing deeply and contentedly. It instantly fascinated him.

Within three months Lucy had relocated to London and they were entwined in all the ways they'd hoped. Eight months in, he proposed on her birthday and the date was swiftly planted into the diary for early the following summer.

Gary's path to marriage and career stability was typically more measured. Although Tom garnered the campus headlines, Gary had relished his early flourishes of freedom every bit as much. The sudden exhilaration of independence became more muted from then on and, although still an active socialiser, his life assumed greater balance. His first teaching job took him back to Devon, where he progressed steadily. In his third year there, a new recruit joined the staff. Gary and Jo Harper tiptoed towards becoming the type of couple who left increasing amounts of belongings at each other's houses while never quite surrendering their independence. The leap was finally taken after seven years, and he moved into Jo's three-bedroom in a nearby village. Six months after performing best man duties for Tom, Gary asked him to return the favour. A date was not yet in the offing.

———•———

Empty plates laid on the table in front of them as Gary sized up his opposite number. The urgency with which Tom had operated when he'd collected him from Maida Vale tube station—ushering him briefly into the flat to unburden him of his luggage before decamping them to a nearby watering hole—had dissipated.

It was the night before they would fly out for the opening of Salvation.

"How are things with the future Mrs Matthewman?"

Gary sighed and twisted his lips as though he had been asked to solve a riddle for which he lacked the curiosity. "We can be hard to figure out."

"Meaning?"

"I think we both expected things to be easier. Getting engaged doesn't seem to have made any difference."

"What did you expect to change?"

Gary shook his head instead of saying he didn't know. A group of new arrivals burst through the doors in escape of a sudden shower. They adjusted to the relief of the indoors in the manner of a recently soaked dog, the brick floor darkening beneath them as they did so. Probably a work night out, Tom decided. They carried that wary tension; the tightrope being walked between their separate worlds and wants.

"Do you think you're making a mistake?" Tom asked.

"Well, we haven't set a date so it's not like the clock's ticking." Gary was allowed to lapse into silence. "That's not the best answer to your question, is it?"

Tom's raised eyebrows were open to interpretation.

"It's not like we've had arguments or anything. It's a build-up of things. I'm a bit serious, she's a bit unaffectionate. Having fun doesn't seem to come so naturally anymore. I see couples in their fifties who've clearly been together a long time and they barely touch or kiss. If they weren't moving in the same space as each other, there'd be no reason to presume they were together. To me, it feels like Jo and I are becoming those people, far faster than I'd ever imagined."

"Have you spoken to her about it?"

"Talking doesn't seem to be one of our strong suits these days." Gary drained his beer. "How about another drink?"

"Hey, your future happiness is only one consideration," Tom told him, trying to provide some levity: "What about me? It would ruin my only chance to be a best man."

Gary forced himself into a wry grin and made for the bar, keeping to himself the fact that his own role as best man had left him privately underwhelmed, reduced to gathering speech anecdotes and standing strategically as directed. The plum job of arranging the stag weekend had mostly eluded him, Morton instead fulfilling the role of booker, buyer, and tour guide.

"What about in the world of functioning relationships?" he asked on his return. "Anything new there?"

"Maybe you can call me a functioning husband in the same way people refer to functioning alcoholics." Tom's phone lit up and he drew shapes across the screen. "Speak of the devil."

"What's going on?"

"She's on her way to meet us." Tom laid his phone on the table.

"That's not what I meant."

"I know. Things change when you get married."

Gary frowned. "In what ways?"

"They become stifling. You don't plan on it happening, but it does. The possibilities that the world has to offer suddenly start to be taken off the table. Spontaneity becomes outdated. Instead, it's all about planning out the future. No sooner were we back from our honeymoon than Lucy was talking me through a list of things we had to do before we start a family."

"You seem to be blaming marriage for issues of your own making."

Tom held up his hand. "Look, I love Lucy. She's the best person I know."

"And she's probably excited about living her life with you," Gary insisted, "doing all the things she's planning out."

"I think she is," replied Tom wistfully, his eyes wandering toward the window and the constant stream of passers-by. "But I don't think it's enough for me."

Gary stared at him. "You need to explain to me exactly what you mean."

"I want to feel the same way towards Lucy that I've always felt—that same energy—but it doesn't feel authentic anymore. I want more living in my life. And I'm finding myself going out looking for more."

He left a pause, which irritated Gary.

"Quit dancing around me and get to the point."

"I have arrangements in place."

"Arrangements?"

"Typically, twice a week. Every Monday, Lucy goes to a gym class with a bunch of her friends and they head out afterwards. Another night I'll invent something that I'll be doing." Each sentence was separated by a few weighty seconds.

"So, you're seeing someone else?"

"Not exactly. Not just one person. They're not relationships."

"Are they people that you know?"

"No, for the most part."

"Is this online?"

"Sometimes. Occasionally through work. Other times I just go to a bar and things progress from there."

"And then?"

"A hotel. Their place. It varies."

"What is it that you're looking for?"

"Nothing more complicated than new sex with new people." Tom's voice was lower now, drawing Gary further across the table as they spoke. "Some of them are beautiful. They arrive all dressed up and looking amazing. Others—especially the unarranged ones—are from all points across the glamour, shape, and size spectrums. Last week was a woman from our offices. I'd seen her around a few times, couple of quick conversations to pass the time in the lift. It was her last day working for us and the team she was part of were all spread throughout the country, so we ended up sharing an impromptu send-off. She was fifty-three."

Tom paused, expecting an interruption, but Gary didn't budge.

"In the end, it's transactional. They're all the same to me and I don't matter to them. If we do meet again, which is rare, we both understand the terms. And then life moves on."

"But it can't last. For a whole host of reasons."

Tom shifted in his seat.

"Why are you telling me this?"

"Who else would I tell?"

"That's not really the point, is it, Tom? I don't know what you expect me to tell you. I grew up on the next street from Lucy. I've known her all my life. Her mum and my mum go for lunch every week. I introduced the two of you, for fuck's sake."

"I remember."

"Yeah? You remember what I told you when you came downstairs after sleeping with her for the first time in my spare room?"

"Not to try my usual shit with her."

"And yet here you are. Within a year of getting married. Proving she deserves better."

"I know she does." Tom was ruffled even as he saw truth in the words.

"Then shut the fuck up and make a change. Talking's not going to achieve anything, and you've just made me complicit."

"You and I are doing the same thing, just in different ways."

"Really? Talk me through that theory." They were both bristling now.

"I know I'm ruining my marriage, otherwise I wouldn't be confiding in you—or trying to. But what are you doing?

When I ask how things are with you and Jo, most of the time it sounds like you're disappointed not to have stumbled across something better, but instead of doing anything about it, you just brood and trudge along."

"Fascinating insight," Gary observed dryly, letting his eyes swim the room.

"Thank you. And I know what's going through your mind as we get ready to visit Morton and Camden: how things would have been better if you'd joined them instead of being trapped back home. Problem is that needed a bold decision and commitment, and although you're happy dispensing advice about those things, they're not really your forte, are they?"

The moment that his phone vibrated, Tom gripped it and jammed it against his ear. "Hi, you nearby? I'll come and find you." He rose vigorously from the table without a backward glance and exited the pub for a few minutes before re-emerging with his wife on his arm. It was with a wide and genuine smile that she threw her arms around Gary in greeting. Although she was instantly aware of an uncommon tension, Lucy was oblivious to the fact that she would not see Gary again.

Chapter 9

"I'm looking for my girlfriend."

The reply Camden received was mumbled and dismissive. He leaned to the side in an attempt to regain eye contact with the man behind the desk.

"I'm looking for my girlfriend." Voice raised slightly this time. It made little difference. The desk sergeant kept moving his papers and looking elsewhere. A third attempt, in beginner's Greek: "I know you understand me. I'm looking for my girlfriend. She lives on the island."

The response came in the form of a shrug, palms held apart at the end of straightened arms as he answered in broken English: "And? Take a look. Crazy here. Everyone from island."

Camden made to move directly towards the overcrowded rooms at the back of the diminutive police station, which was doing its best impression of a clown car.

Suddenly the man leapt into action and blocked his path, palm in his chest and nightstick held as if ready to deliver a tennis serve. Camden breathed deeply and seethed. "I don't want trouble. I want help."

"Relax," a voice suggested from over his shoulder. It was a local accent but far more accessible, and it sounded like it belonged to a much larger person than the one that Camden turned to see. At six foot three, Camden was used to being the taller one in the conversation but in this case, despite having a good four or five inches over the man he faced, they seemed of equal standing.

"Georgios Nikopolidis." The introduction came with a firm handshake, the name offered as though Camden had been told it before.

Nik-oh-poh-lee-dis. Camden turned the name over in his mind, breaking it down into phonetic chunks, as he often did when he struggled to keep pace with multisyllabic Greek names.

Nikopolidis stood with feet shoulder-width apart and gave the impression that this was his default stance, equally ready to move forward or fend off an attack. He wore a chocolate brown suit jacket, white polo shirt and lightweight cream trousers. All items were immaculate and augmented by a full head of dark hair that seemed to raise itself into a curled quiff at the front before making its way lazily backwards. It looked like he could ask for a hundred different styles when he went to the barbers, but within two weeks it would always revert to the one he was sporting now. He said nothing more.

"I'm looking for my girlfriend."

"So I understand," Nikopolidis nodded sincerely. "Forgive my colleague. He struggles with English, and it has been a long night. We've never experienced this before.

As you can see, we do not have the facilities for such an event. But this—," he seemed to search momentarily for the right words, "—civil disturbance and violence cannot be tolerated."

"My girlfriend wasn't involved in any civil disturbance or violence," Camden retorted.

Nikopolidis looked at him steadily. "You say she is from Santorini?"

"Near Athens. But she lives here with me."

"When did you last see her?"

"Two nights ago."

"Where was that?"

"She was with me at the bar that my friend and I own."

"Which bar?"

"Salvation."

Nikopolidis shifted his weight slightly and raised his chin but said nothing.

"Do you know it?"

"I know it. There was trouble there last night."

"Trouble?"

"It was badly damaged. You say you own it with a friend?"

"Yes."

"You should check on your friend."

"I will, I will. But I can't find my girlfriend and I need to find her. I'm worried." Camden tried to empty his mind as dizziness snuck up on him. He knew he was repeating himself.

"You say you last saw her two nights ago. Do you know where she was last night?"

"Back on the mainland."

"She wasn't even on the island?" Nikopolidis let out a short, disbelieving laugh. "What is your name?"

Camden answered.

"OK, Christian Camden. Look around. We have more people here than we have room for. We don't have enough police. There was a lot of trouble last night. A lot. Some of it very serious—and the people in this building were the perpetrators of a lot of it. We may not have experienced this before on Santorini, but that doesn't mean we will not enforce the law."

"I'm not—"

Nikopolidis cut him off. "Nobody has come onto or off the island since last night. I'm sure your girlfriend is still on the mainland. Does she have family here?"

"No, they're on the mainland too," Camden rued the words as they left his mouth.

"Come on," Nikopolidis pleaded, blinking incredulously as he held his mouth open. "Speak to her family."

"I've tried—"

"Keep trying," he replied, and strode towards the rear of the station.

———•———

For the first time in a while, Camden let his thoughts drift onto the other parts of his life he'd left behind. It had all been so clear, so straightforward, like a multiple-choice question in a school exam when all but one of the options are too nonsensical to be considered.

Crissa was the answer to whatever the question was. Everything else simply followed a path of logic and romance and a lack of reluctance to bid the past farewell. He had love for his parents—he saw their remoteness reflected in his habits, the way he would sometimes withdraw into his own head before coming back up for air—but he'd grown up feeling both attached and apart from them, as though a different place and time would have suited them all better.

Camden was an only child, born to his mother the week after her fortieth birthday, his father half a decade older than that. He had no idea why they became parents so late, given their traditionalism. He got the impression that his life choices confounded his parents, like they couldn't relate to any of them but felt it improper to discuss them openly. Lapsed Calvinism at its finest.

Camden did a lot of social things growing up—team sports, swimming, the school band—but never considered himself particularly sociable. He could interact or withdraw with equal ease, and the latter sometimes felt easier. His parents' habits were resolute: Darts & Doms for his father on a Wednesday; twice-a-week racquet sports for his still-spry mother; a few quiet drinks together in the lounge of the local pub on a Saturday night. There was no intersection between their interests and his, no Venn Diagram. They both taught—Maths at the local high school in his father's case; primary school for his mother—and did so dutifully, if not enthusiastically.

When he chose Leeds as his university destination, Camden acknowledged that it was at least partly motivated by its distance from his hometown of Kinross. He visited home between terms his first year before finding holiday work in Leeds from then on. He phoned home occasionally. His parents hadn't visited him in any of his homes since that first university year. When he had told them he was abandoning his career and relocating to Greece to start his own business, the news was greeted with such a subdued reaction that you would have thought it concerned a friend they'd met a couple of times, not their only son. There had been no questions. No discussions about motives. No enquiries about departure dates or location. No send off. It would have surprised Camden if it had been any other way.

Crissa looked at him from the screen of his phone, a photo of them taken a few weeks ago, her smile a symmetrical flash of white across a canvas of browns, his face turned towards her, brushing against her insistently straight hair.

He pocketed the phone, took as deep a breath as he could manage and turned the corner towards Salvation.

As he approached, the sun was rising, its first rays illuminating the tiny fragments of glass that remained embedded between the cobbles on the streets, giving them a marble sheen.

Morton emerged, dustpan and brush in hand, taking two steps outside before stopping when he registered that he had company. He took a long inhalation through his nose, filling his chest with as much air as he could, slowly releasing it through lightly pursed lips. It was an action Camden had only seen a few times and which he knew was exclusively reserved for those rare occasions when extra composure was needed.

Steadily, Morton turned to face his friend outside the remnants of their bar. "Where were you?"

Camden seemed unsure how to answer. "I ran."

Morton frowned at the unsuitable response. "What does that mean?"

Ignoring the question, Camden kept walking until he

got to the doorway of Salvation and saw the full toll of the previous night's incursion. "Jesus Christ! What happened?"

"You'd know if you'd stayed with us."

"Look, I saw how bad the trouble was on the TV and I ran."

"Where?" Morton shot back.

"I had to help Crissa."

"How could you help Crissa?"

"I didn't know what to do. I couldn't think of anything but trying to get to her."

Morton was struggling to comprehend Camden's thought process. "So where did you go?"

"First, I tried to phone her and couldn't get through. Then I tried to phone the friends she was with. That didn't work either." He spoke with increasing rapidity. "So, then I got a taxi to the other side of the island to try to catch a boat."

"A boat? To the mainland?"

"To anywhere!" Camden crouched onto his haunches, hands clutching his head.

Seven hours of pent-up anger that Morton had been waiting to unleash evaporated at the sight of the anguished figure before him. He stayed quiet.

Letting his hands fall to lightly touch the ground, Camden spoke softly, almost sheepishly. "It was pointless. I couldn't get anyone to take me anywhere. Besides, nobody was allowed on or off the island."

"Then what did you do?"

Camden let out a dry chuckle. "I spent a long time trying to convince people to take me. Then I just walked and walked and walked. Getting back up to the capital took forever."

"Have you heard from her yet?"

A shake of the head.

"Things'll settle down."

Camden squinted up at Morton as he asked a question that he realised should have dawned on him as soon as he'd arrived: "Where is everyone?"

"Dean's inside. Took a sore one to the head. Was unconscious for a bit, been throwing up a lot. He spent the first few hours trying to avoid falling asleep. I think he's drifted off now."

"Gary and Tom?"

"Arrested."

"What?"

"Mate, it was crazy here. Obviously, this shit happened," he jerked his thumb over his shoulder, "and things got out of hand on the streets. Before we knew it, riot police descended on the place. It was chaos. Gary and Tom got caught in the maelstrom. I went to the station soon after to try to get them out. Couldn't even get near the place."

"Yeah, I was just there," Camden offered.

"What were you doing there?"

"To see if they would help me find Crissa. They weren't interested."

"Probably not much they can do if she's on the mainland."

"That's what they said. I didn't see Gary and Tom, though."

"I was told they're safe but being held for the time being. Dean's the man for that job. Once he's feeling up to it, he'll head over there."

A pause descended.

"Weird thing is," Morton resumed, "look around. Seems like we were the only place to take the brunt of it."

Camden's mind seemed elsewhere as he asked: "What were Gary and Tom doing out amongst the crowds?"

Morton gave a look that Camden couldn't quite read, like he was suppressing annoyance so as not to burden him further. "They were looking for you, mate."

Camden breathed in and looked out to the water. "Shit." He shook his head.

"Go inside. We could use an extra pair of hands."

Chapter 10

The way Morton looked at things, the money he'd grown up around was an unmistakable asset that had come at a price worth paying. His father, Anthony—never Tony—left school at the first opportunity, high on ambition and self-confidence, fully intent on his joinery apprenticeship being a steppingstone to bigger things. In future years he would wryly observe that he mastered networking before networking existed in Manchester, where he was raised.

Anthony habitually moved quickly. The first of his friends to become self-employed, he'd acquired his second property while most of his peers were still in their childhood homes. By age twenty-three, his growing workforce was providing services to homebuilding companies. Four years on, with trademark exemplary timing he formed a partnership with two fellow businessmen to buy some land on which they would construct the first privately built student accommodation in Manchester. It was the game changer he'd been seeking.

Clare Wallace was still at university when she met Anthony. As he approached the table that she shared with half a dozen friends in a pub on Deansgate, a self-assured flourish of charm and tailored clothes, he instantly separated himself from every other guy she'd met. Taking the hand he offered as he stood before her, all other suitors—and there were plenty—faded into the background. Although barely into his twenties, Anthony carried himself like a man.

Clare had retold that introduction to numerous people over the years, ruefully adding "but not all men grow up". They married in 1983 and a son was with them inside a year. By the time Adele was welcomed into the family two years later, the marriage was listing and never righted itself. The fact that divorce took a further four years to materialise was largely due to Clare's determination that her children grow up under the same roof as both parents. It was also partly a result of Anthony having no need to pursue one, since he had never modified his premarital womanising once he wore a ring on his finger and didn't desire to ever marry again.

Clare moved her children to Didsbury, where they lived throughout secondary school in comfort and surprising amicability between their estranged parents. Financially, Anthony was generous with his support and was there for most of the childhood milestones, but Clare was the glue. Resentment was forbidden to seep into her home. She'd graduated from university as an optician and carved out a career that achieved professional success, financial independence and a work-life balance that enabled her to be the mother she wanted to be. There was only one further relationship after Anthony's departure: with Gareth, a doctor whom she had met at a New Order concert that they had attended as part of a group of friends. They first dated in 1993 but waited until 2004 to marry, once both children had left school.

For his part, Anthony continued to look beyond his immediate horizons. More acquisitions meant that he had conquered as much of Manchester as interested him by the mid-nineties, at which point he turned his attention to the capital. Chiswick, Shoreditch, Dalston: few false moves. Ten years later it was time for his portfolio to get a suntan. He felt that he'd mostly been a good father, given how poorly cast he was for the role.

When talking about her children, Clare would swear they had never had an argument worth remembering. They shared common interests, often going together to concerts, movies, parties, pubs. Friendship was the dominant characteristic. Both shared their father's confidence, balanced by their mother's genuine care for others. Their relationship with their father was functional, and each would confess to occasionally indulging themselves in his displays of generosity when he felt he had an absence to atone for.

Morton's studies at university were a masterclass in economy. The same unconstrained clear-thinking that had characterised Anthony's career were present in his son, allowing Morton to finish at or near the top of his class with none of the deadline rushes that beleaguered his peers. He had his father's dense, light brown hair, contrasted by his mother's piercing blue eyes. A combination of Anthony's height and Clare's swimmer's shoulders gave him a tapered torso. The fawning attention he received mystified him, yet it led to him rarely being alone unless through choice, although he was pathologically determined to be clear about his intentions with any and all prospective partners: there would be no casualties in the wake of his promiscuity, at least not as a result of wilful cruelty on his part.

His skills were a natural fit for the two consultancies that came looking for (in their words) "brains on legs" as he completed his Business Economics degree. He chose to join McKinsey, but that quickly started to feel like handing control of his life to a cause and central office that left him unimpressed. Within a year he moved on, his unruffled approach having crucially won the admiration of several senior managers to such an extent that he had multiple references to accompany him on his way out the door.

Creative projects were what floated his boat, he decided, but he needed to self-fund them to feel fulfilled. His father insisted on one purchase: a house at the far end of Headingley, close to where he and his friends had spent their student years, and which was bound to appreciate in value with the market continuing its relentless ascent. Morton didn't mind—it had always been Anthony's stated intention for both of his children to have their own home without the usual attendant financial burden, and it meant Morton could instead plunge his money into other pursuits.

Two years at a wealth management company saw him pick up a good wage, his incentive package fully unlocked by outstanding performances and acute investment acumen. Importantly, Morton found the work easy and, despite two rapid promotions, managed to keep his priorities firmly where he wanted them. Capitalising on his father's construction contacts, he spent a good deal of his evenings and weekends establishing his first venture: a recording studio on the banks of Leeds-Liverpool Canal. Clare had looked intrigued when told of his plans, his father a little perplexed, unclear on where the income would be generated. Both trusted his judgment. Adele was jubilant. "I can practise and record there!" she enthused upon hearing the news. Drifting towards her final year of Interior Design at Manchester School of Art, Adele was more devoted to her musical collective than her studies. They got their free recording space, which served them well for eighteen months before an implosion of egos and epic chord progressions tore them apart. Other artists benefited, too. In fact, Morton had always planned to run the place at a loss for the first six months and he saw that plan fearlessly through to fruition. Towards the end of that initial period, Anthony took his son out for a meal in San Carlo's in Manchester with the goal of broaching how to move on from his unsuccessful first foray into business onto something with a more reliable revenue stream. Instead, before they'd even placed their drinks order, he was already listening to Morton enthusiastically deliver the vision for his next enterprise, a church on the edge of studentland that he had heard would shortly be up for sale and which he planned to turn into a live venue.

"Think of the acoustics," he extolled. "The place will be unique."

Anthony knew his son well enough to keep his reservations to himself, hard though he found it.

"A friend of mine has a show on BBC Radio Leeds. He does a spotlight session once a week on local bands and he'll do a special feature on us. There are four acts that have material ready to go. We could even produce and release their music."

Despite his best efforts, Anthony's eyebrows rose.

"It's 2007, Dad. You don't need big investment to release and publicise music anymore. The internet does it for you."

Eclectic opened its doors in late summer, just before the universities welcomed their new enrolments, and immediately drew increasingly strong crowds who experienced different types of religious experiences under its ornate ceilings. The recording studio started to more than pay for itself and also adopted the Eclectic moniker, its graduates enjoying both the stage time and radio play that Morton had envisaged. So too emerged a record label, its main aim to help its acts embark on their first tours with a product to sell. There were twelve bands signed and touring when, three years in and at the age of twenty-seven, Morton abruptly decided to step away.

"It's running itself now," he explained matter-of-factly to unbelieving friends. "It doesn't need me. I've put people in position to run each of the places. I'll stay on the board but it's time to let it take its own direction."

He'd always been single-minded. Early in his university days, he'd been part of a group—two parts male to one part female—that had gone to a gay-friendly night at one of the clubs in town. It was on its way to being simply another night out amongst many in those days, up until the point at which Morton moved from having his lips on a girl near the bar to gripping the hair of a guy wearing a slim-fit white polo shirt as they exchanged a lustful kiss on the dancefloor. Upon deciding that the guy wasn't an indispensable part of the evening, Morton returned to the group as if nothing consequential had happened. Those who reacted accordingly remained friends; those who didn't quickly became inessential.

And so it went. "Don't hurt people, live the life you want to live," was his instinctual reply to a young student with a microphone and camera-toting sidekick who approached him as he walked with Tom and Gary through Leeds city centre one day in their final year and asked him to sum up his philosophy of life in ten words.

"Corny bastard," Gary said.

"What is this, a project?" Tom asked.

"Yeah," the girl nodded, adjusting a ladybird hair clip, and smoothing her fringe back across her forehead. "We have to do a vox pop."

"What's a vox pop?" Tom asked between mouthfuls of a Subway.

"Vox populi. It means voice of the people. Latin, I think." Her tone suggested there was no task she could have been asked to perform that would have added less to her life. "We ask ordinary people broad questions and see what they say."

"Hold on—he's not ordinary," Tom nodded in Morton's direction. "He looks like a male model and he's intelligent, rich, and bisexual. Nothing ordinary about that. Ask Gary a question. He's completely ordinary. Bordering on irrelevant."

"OK," said the girl, turning to Gary. "Describe your friend's dress sense in three words or less."

Gary quickly scanned Tom—blue plaid shirt, white t-shirt, khakis, Converse. "Dressed in the dark."

Morton threw out an unbridled laugh.

"That's four words!" Tom shot back.

"We'll accept it," the girl acknowledged, as if the answer was a valuable contribution to medical research.

"That just shows the ordinary man on the street can't count," Tom persisted, trying to press his case as his friends prised him away from the camera.

"Are you going to have 'Don't Hurt People, Live The Life You Want To Live' as a neon sign above the new place?" Tom asked five years later. Morton had just informed them all that he was opening a new bar in Headingley, defining its target demographic as the late-twenties, early-thirties crowd who had stayed in the area after university and still lived for the weekend, but were less inclined to spend the end of their night in a club.

"It says a lot about you that you still remember that from years ago and that you know me so little that you think I'm considering neon," was Morton's riposte.

Add in a sports bar and an independent coffee shop and Morton had accumulated an impressive portfolio of businesses that he nurtured and then outsourced to assorted partners, each of whom seemed to appear from the ether as if they had been acquaintances for decades.

"Been thinking about setting up shop here," was how Morton first mentioned the prospect of Salvation to Camden.

The two of them were sitting on the wall that ringed the patio of the canava, watching the sun flaunt its colourful glory one last time while the others were getting dressed. Upon hearing the words, it struck Camden that it was no coincidence that Morton had dressed in greater haste than normal, leaving them alone for their current conversation.

Morton smiled at him and gave an imperceptible nod. "I'd been wondering about the right approach, the right partners." He looked along his eyes to gauge Camden's reaction. Wordless though it was, there was little doubt in Morton's head. "This trip's given me a few good ideas for the approach." He left a playful pause. "Any thoughts about who the right partner might be?"

He turned to see Camden grinning guilelessly at him.

Chapter 11

Eleven hours had passed without word.

Morton had spent most of the morning trying to get workers to come and help with the repairs to Salvation, but nobody was answering their phone. To begin with, he decided it was the after-effects of the protests—maybe some of his workmen had got involved and found themselves sharing communal space with Gary and Tom—but as the day went on that felt less plausible. Some of his contacts were solid family men, yet none were obtainable. Finally, he phoned one of his joiners from the unlisted landline in the bar and got through.

"Kostas? It's Morton."

"Mr Morton," came the flustered voice.

"I've been trying to phone you and everyone else for help all day."

"I have trouble with my phone."

"It worked fine when I just dialled you from a number that didn't tell you it was me calling."

"No, no, Mr Morton, do not act like that. That is not true. Today has not been a good day."

"No shit. Did you know that our place got smashed up last night?"

"I had not heard that," Kostas replied after a crucial pause.

Morton stayed quiet, trying to work things out.

"Mr Morton?"

"Forget it, Kostas. I'll talk to you later." He ended the connection, looked at the phone and rested his chin on his hands. *Something isn't right.*

The television was on a loop. The national news was showing unrest on the mainland at a different scale to what had taken place on the island the previous night. All transmissions started with footage of the capital's streets filled with banners and people shouting and gesticulating, before segueing to scenes from what was presumably later in proceedings. By this stage, the banners and marchers were replaced by images of missiles and protesters who had become detached from larger groups scuffling vainly with oncoming riot police. The spectacle was replicated amongst numerous cities across the country. When it was the turn of the local news, the scale of the trouble on Santorini looked paltry, but still told a tale.

———•———

"If they're not going to help me," Camden announced, "I'll do it myself. I'm going to the spa. Try a couple of her friends as well." Multiple calls to Crissa's phone had gone unanswered.

"I'll come with you," Dean suggested.

"No, it's fine. There's stuff to be done here."

"I need some fresh air to clear my head."

"Go, mate," Morton averred, looking first at Dean and then Camden. "Nothing more's gonna happen here today."

The spa was eerily quiet. Dimitrios stood behind the reception desk, flicking distractedly through a magazine. He seemed surprised to see them, or anybody.

"Christian, hello. Hello." The second greeting was aimed at Dean, who lifted his chin in reply.

"Hey. Have you heard from Crissa?"

Dimitrios shook his head, frowning. "I thought she left the island for a few days?"

"Yeah, she did."

The frown was complemented by a shrug and a grunt.

"Anyone else in? Irini? Sofia?"

"No. Quiet today. Few visitors so only two people working, George and Zeta."

Camden saw that his line of questioning had already reached its end with Dimitrios. When they'd first met, he'd feared that Dimitrios was Crissa's boyfriend, but he subsequently turned out merely to be an admirer of hers—and most other attractive women he encountered.

"He always that talkative?" Dean asked as they got in the car.

"I'm the wrong sex. Dimitrios can have lots to say, so long as you meet the criteria."

They headed to the east of the island, passing the foot of the hill leading to the monastery. The engine of the Chevy battled gamely to keep pace with Camden's requests as they made their way up a series of gradual, extended slopes and down elongated, meandering S-shapes on the other side. Pulling up outside a thin, long white house with blue doors and windows and an empty five-stride-deep front porch, Camden took a moment of reflection. Dean wondered if he was gathering himself.

Unclicking the seatbelt, opening the door, and exiting the car in a single movement, Camden was marching confidently onto the porch before Dean had even had a chance to budge. The driver's door remained open, and the house looked uninhabited. Three knocks, after which Camden took a couple of steps to his right to look through the window. He gave a wave in response to whatever he saw. Dean didn't recognise the young woman who appeared in front of them. Her light brown hair had a slight kink which she swept around her right ear as she pushed open the door. She had slightly rounded shoulders and, though not tall, gave the impression of feeling lanky. Her facial features were angular: all cheekbones, forehead, and jawline. Dean couldn't take his eyes off her spectacular eyebrows, which darted up and swooped wide, reminiscent of the way he was taught to draw birds in the sky, off in the distance, in the art classes he had pretended not to enjoy at school.

"Hi Sofia," Camden said gently as they exchanged kisses on the cheek. "This is Dean, one of our friends who's visiting from the UK."

"Welcome."

"Nice to meet you."

"Have you heard from Crissa?" asked Camden.

"Crissa?" A gentle, searching head shake. She held her hands in front of her and massaged the thumb webbing of her opposite hands. "I don't think she's on the island anymore."

"Yeah. No, I mean, I know she's on the mainland," Camden clarified, seeming to will himself to remain encouraging. "She went over there a couple of days ago for the protest march, but I've been trying to get hold of her and I can't. I keep getting voicemail."

"Oh." Sofia's eyes dashed between both men and settled back on Camden.

"Have you tried to call her?"

"No," she replied softly.

"Would you mind calling her now? See if you have any luck?"

"Oh, ok," Sofia acquiesced, as though the suggestion only sunk in as a good idea two seconds after Camden had finished his sentence. "Just a moment."

She shambled back into the house. Dean looked at Camden as if questioning Sofia's mental capacity. Camden shook his head in a show of support for her. For someone who moved without urgency, it was a surprise when she suddenly returned to the doorway. They stood in silence for twenty seconds or so before she took the phone away from her ear and held it in front of them. Crissa's name and photo was on the screen and her recorded voice was talking from the mouthpiece.

"Did you get any texts from her yesterday? Before she was due to be in the protests, I mean?"

"No." Again the slow shake of the head. "You know Crissa. She would have been completely focused on the demonstrations."

Sofia shifted and looked around as though she suddenly needed to get the phone out of her hands and put it down somewhere. She settled on the windowsill as the best storage option.

"Will you let me know if you hear from her?"

"Of course. But I'm sure she's fine. Perhaps there's a problem with her phone."

"Maybe."

It was as if Sofia had lapsed back into standby after her last sentence. Camden stepped in to give her a hug, which lasted longer and looked more natural than Dean expected; there had seemed little connection between the two while they'd been talking.

"Everyone's a little edgy today," he observed back in the car.

"Understandable," Camden answered, and pointed the car north.

———·———

Irini was pushing an infant girl on a small swing-set in the back garden. The house was one of half a dozen or so on either side of a quiet street that had taken a few turns from the main road to reach, and which seemed to disappear into nothing as it stretched towards the water. Its colour scheme matched Sofia's, a tall, thin rectangle of two storeys with steps leading upwards from the ground to a white door at the side of the building, hinting at separate apartments on each floor.

Camden pulled into a gravel driveway in front, and Irini stood up straight, shielding her eyes from the low sun as she identified her visitors. Bringing the swing to a stop, she moved round to face the girl as she spoke to her, lifted her out and held her hand. Irini waved stiffly at them and the girl—who was three or four and looked like she was transplanted from a TV commercial with her blue and white dress, blue shoes, and very dark brown pigtails—waved, too, after a friendly prompt.

"Hi, Irini. Hello, beautiful."

The girl looked up at them with delicate, perfectly clear eyes and half-hid behind Irini's legs.

"Are you shy, Maria?" smiled Irini. "You've met Christian before. My niece," she clarified for Dean. "She'll be OK in a minute."

They exchanged kisses.

"Sofia called. She said you'd been to see her."

"Right."

"I haven't heard from her either, Christian. Last time I spoke to her was just after you'd gone to pick up your friends from the airport the other day."

Camden nodded.

"I wouldn't worry. It looked like there were a lot of people at the demonstrations and quite a bit of disturbance. Not that unusual these days. Crissa's smart enough to stay out of it. She's probably getting ready for another demonstration tonight."

"I know. It's just unlike her."

Irini held his eyes unblinkingly. "I'm sorry to hear about your bar, by the way."

Camden eyes seemed frozen in Irini's gaze for a few long seconds before snapping back to the present. "Thanks," he answered distractedly.

Their eyes re-locked without words. Dean felt like a voyeur.

"Perhaps leave it another day," Irini finally suggested.

"Maybe."

Maria started tugging on Irini's arm. "I have to go," she told them. "I'll let you know if I hear anything, and I'll call you tomorrow either way."

They kissed again and held briefly, and Camden blew a kiss to Maria which elicited a coy smile as she was walked back to the front door by her aunt. Irini was holding her in her arms and waving goodbye as they reversed off the drive and down the road.

They reached the junction to the main road before Dean asked a question he'd been holding in for a few minutes.

"How did she know about the bar being damaged?"

"I don't know." They could see the lights of Fira ushering in the transition into night. "I can't piece things together."

—————•—————

Once he and Dean had returned to the canava—after a quick detour to Crissa's eerily empty apartment—Camden couldn't settle, unsatisfied with the information he'd gleaned. He squirmed, paced and channel-hopped, plainly uneasy, prompting Morton to calm things down by discreetly phoning in some food and plating it up around the large wooden dinner table.

"Frustrating, mostly," was Camden's verdict when invited to talk about his day. Dean gave a nod of agreement.

"In what way?"

"In that we got no answers. Nobody at the spa knows anything. We went to see Irini and Sofia," his eyes met Morton's, who knew both women, "and neither of them have heard from her."

"Yeah, what was with those two?" Dean piped up.

"How do you mean?" Morton frowned.

"They both seemed a bit off."

Camden offered his perspective. "I think they were both just worried. Maybe I was freaking them out. I text her every hour and call her, too. Nothing." His eyes flickered around the faces at the table and the room beyond. "Hard to keep a rein on where my mind is going."

"I can imagine," Morton nodded.

Placing his hands on the arm rests, Camden rolled his shoulders in a vain attempt to free them of tension. "One thing's for sure," he said, "I can't stay still waiting for her to turn up."

He got up, lifted the chair off the ground and placed it back under the table, as though he didn't want to make any unnecessary noise.

"What's the plan?" asked Morton.

"Go looking."

"Where?"

"Well, there's no-one else here who can help me, and if Irini and Sofia hear anything they can reach us, right?"

Morton nodded with his eyelids.

"So, I'm going to go to the mainland. I don't know it at all, but I know where her family and a couple of her friends live. I'll find someone who can help me. There's an early flight in the morning."

"Have you met her family before?" Dean asked simply.

Camden released a brief chuckle. "No, crazy as that sounds. Been too busy getting the bar ready and she goes to visit her folks rather than have them fly here."

"Be an inventive way to introduce yourself," Morton

said, offering up a hesitant smile and noticing how Salvation was now being referred to as 'the bar' rather than by the name they'd jointly given it.

Chapter 12

Dean woke with his mind set on making Saturday productive. Moving quickly to silence his 7am alarm, he let out a moan as pain stabbed behind his eyes from several angles. Slowly lowering himself back onto the bed, he pinched the bridge of his nose firmly and held it for a few seconds before blinking his eyes wide and re-rising. He moved more tentatively to reach his full height in stages, imagining the contents of his brain as a spirit level. The concussion he'd been served two nights previous was proving hard to shrug off.

The mental dust that had gathered on top of parts of his law degree was also proving hard to shift as he tried to establish the best methods to extricate Gary and Tom from jail. Despite the piercing pain, he had made it to the police station late on Friday, still feeling like his legs belonged to someone else, but was rebuffed within minutes and impatiently told to come back later. He resolved that a more considered approach was needed if he was to make progress.

The keenest student of the group, Dean had moved from the South of Scotland to study at Leeds University while the others—bar Morton—attended its less accomplished neighbour, which at the time was named Leeds Metropolitan. Possessing a character of little drama, he navigated life efficiently. Having made it clear from his first day of work that he wanted more than an existence of twilight shifts at the office, he achieved a couple of well-paid promotions by virtue of rigorous, quality work and felt like he'd almost progressed to the level to which he was willing to commit.

These days, Dean lived alone in Chapel Allerton in north Leeds. Up until two years ago, he'd shared a city centre apartment with Caroline. They were often cited by friends as an ideal couple, designed for each other, which made it all the more devastating when she informed Dean that she was leaving him to be with her boss at work, who was twenty years her senior, with three teenage daughters and a now-estranged wife.

There had been no histrionics from Dean, but he cut a slightly diminished figure as he made the clean break, selling the apartment and not once speaking to Caroline after she delivered the news. Socially he withdrew, other than to share the company of long-established friends on a reduced basis. Female colleagues made tentative approaches towards him; the more maternal members of the office clearly adored him and felt like he needed a good woman in his life; acquaintances and other halves would be more overt in trying to matchmake. It was all well-intentioned but entirely unwelcome. Unfailingly polite, Dean nonetheless showed no interest in any of it. His male colleagues were bemused at him passing up such opportunities; closer friends knew to let things run their course.

———.———

By the looks of things on TV, trouble was continuing at a lower level on the mainland, but Santorini had lapsed back into peace, albeit a slightly chastened version. It was by no means business as usual; the streets carried little foot traffic.

Morton had taken Camden to the airport and was yet to return. Sitting at the breakfast bar in the canava, Dean sketched a plan. He would try once more to see Gary and Tom and get them released. If the police were still delaying things, he would contact the Foreign Office in London and go from there.

The officer on the front desk gave a look that spoke of recognition and displeasure at his return.

"I'd like to see Thomas Drummond and Gary Matthewman, please." Dean adopted a civil but professional tone. "They're both being detained here."

"You were here yesterday," the officer replied with a voice as tired as his eyes.

"I was," Dean assented with a confident nod, "as were Mr Drummond and Mr Matthewman. I'd like to see them both."

"And who are you?"

"Their friend. And their lawyer."

The eyes held him intently.

"I would like to see them, please," he repeated, maintaining his tone.

"Not possible," the officer snapped and diverted his attention to the paperwork on his desk.

Dean measured him up for a few moments, waiting to see if the head would lift to resume their exchange. When it didn't, he looked left and right. To the left was ostensibly a staff room, holding two police officers smoking cigarettes and drinking coffee. To the right, another man was on the phone while reading papers spread in front of him on a large work desk. Having decided this was the person with the most power in the building, Dean started towards the room.

"Hey!" called the voice behind him as it scrambled up from the desk too late to intercept him.

Dean knocked twice on the door, swung it open and leaned in. "I'd like to speak to Thomas Drummond and Gary Matthewman."

The seated man eyeballed him. The desk officer appeared and pushed in front of him, ready to launch apologies and complaints in his superior's direction before he saw a cautioning palm raised, accompanied by a shake of the head. The man spoke briefly and calmly into the phone and pressed his finger on the receiver. A sideways nudge of his head sent the officer back to his post at the front desk, and an extended hand invited Dean to sit in a chair opposite him.

"You're a different one."

It seemed to Dean an odd start to a conversation. "Excuse me?"

A smile emerged on the man's face before settling back into neutral. In contrast to his colleague, he made a virtue of being exhausted. His white shirt looked like it was on its third day of wear, rolled up to the sleeves. A light brown tie hung loosely around his neck, its knot ready to give up the ghost. A chocolate brown suit jacket hugged the back of the large chair.

"I may have met a friend of yours yesterday. But he wasn't looking for the friends you're looking for. He was looking for a girl."

Camden, Dean realised, and nodded briefly to move the conversation along. "My friend did come here very early yesterday. Friday," he added for clarification. "I came in the afternoon and received no help from your man on the front desk. I would have come earlier but I was knocked unconscious by a group of men who smashed up my friends' bar with truncheons."

The man raised his eyebrows with interest. "What is a truncheon?"

"A stick, like your police officers had the other night. Not exactly the same, but similar. Metal."

The man straightened his back in the chair and resumed his previous aloofness, as though he'd solved the mystery of Salvation's ransacking merely by understanding the definition of the word truncheon. "My name is Georgios Nikopolidis," he stated. "What exactly can I help you with?"

"I would like to see—"

"Your friends, yes, you said. Thomas and … Gary?"

"Yes."

"What makes you think they are here?"

"Because your men arrested them during the riots on Thursday night. They'd gone to find a friend of ours."

Nikopolidis looked contemplative. He made an impression on Dean as a man who was rarely careless with words or actions.

"I think you know the two men I'm talking about."

"If they are here, then like everyone else here they participated in the trouble on Friday night."

Dean considered his next words. "Have you charged them?"

The temperature dropped across the table. "What is your name?"

"Dean."

Nikopolidis looked at him in a manner that told him he had no patience for incomplete or evasive answers.

"Dean Lockwood. Have you informed the British embassy that you've detained two British nationals?"

"Mr Lockwood, are you a lawyer?"

"Yes, I am."

"Do you know the direction you are taking this conversation?"

"I don't feel you've given me any other option."

Nikopolidis raised his chin, his manner inscrutable. "That is unfortunate." He stood up and walked across to the only window in the room. Dean remained silent, letting things play out.

There was a customary pause before Nikopolidis resumed the conversation on his own terms. "First, let me explain things from my perspective, Mr Lockwood. I think I know the men you are talking about. This country is going through challenging times; you will know about this. I understand people's anger. We are all affected. But there are limits to how anger is displayed. In my view— and, more importantly, in the eyes of the law—those limits have been overstepped many times by many people in recent months. Until Thursday night, my wife and I would shake our heads and hope it would stop, but it remained a problem limited to the mainland. We have a small police force here on Santorini. When Thursday night started to take shape, I called colleagues from nearby islands, and they hurried to help. We went into the back of our storage area and retrieved protective equipment that we laughed at when it was delivered to us, years ago. We never thought it would need to be used. Without it, things would have been far worse. And yet look. We still are not ready to deal with this."

He pointed to the wall with his palm, indicating the room next door. "You come in at eight in the morning and see two police officers sitting with coffees and cigarettes. You encounter a man trying to do a job he's never had to do before. Of course, it's not ideal, and maybe you think we're sitting around doing nothing, being unhelpful." He returned to his chair. "I assure you that is not the case. None of those men have seen their families since Thursday. They have slept in shifts, one at a time and barely for a few hours. They're exhausted. We have been promised officers to assist within a couple of days but are under orders not to release people until then. Serious crimes have happened here."

"Yeah, I was caught in the middle of one. My friends' business was destroyed, and we were assaulted," Dean retorted. "Other than that, there was only fighting in the streets."

Nikopolidis looked askance at him. "More than that, Mr Lockwood. Far more than that."

Unsure of what was meant, Dean said nothing.

"The bar you talk of: it is called Salvation, yes?"

Dean nodded.

"Your friends who own it: one of them is called Morton, is that correct?"

"Yes."

"His father is well-known in these parts. He owns some nice properties. Well-connected."

Again, Dean was unclear what was being said or why. "And?"

Nikopolidis waved him off. "You said they were looking for another of your friends?" He nodded in the direction of the adjacent room in his first firm admission that Gary and Tom were housed there. "Was this before or after the attack started on the bar?"

Dean elasticised his patience, not wanting to jeopardise his chances of speaking to Gary and Tom. "Before."

"Why wasn't your friend with you?" The question was joined by a furrowed brow.

"He was trying to find his girlfriend. He was the guy who came here yesterday."

"I thought as much. But I'm confused—your friend told me that his girlfriend wasn't even on the island."

"No, that's right. I think he must have wanted to talk to her on the phone." It felt like he was talking more than he should, even though he had no reason to withhold information.

"With such crowds on the street, it must have been hard to hold a phone conversation," Nikopolidis suggested.

"Perhaps he walked somewhere quieter and that was why Gary and Tom couldn't find him easily."

Nikopolidis nodded and rose. "Let's get your friends for a talk with you, but I must make myself clear: you will see that they are safe and well, but we must hold them here for now, until we get support. You may visit them twice a day if it reassures you, but orders are orders. I cannot stress enough that these are extraordinary times."

———•———

It had been well past dark the previous night when Gary and Tom finally initiated conversation, surmising that their prolonged proximity to each other marked them out as allies.

Their clothes also differentiated them: both wore dress shirts and trousers, with Tom adding the flourish of a blazer. They'd been happy with how smart they'd looked when they stood in front of the mirror prior to going out; both subsequently wished they'd gone more casual. Not only did their expensive garments fail to blend in; they were also now in an irrecoverable state of disrepair.

"What are you going to tell Jo?" Tom asked, shifting as far as he could to create space on the bench.

"I've been thinking that through. Still not found the right answer. The only way to tell her is once this is all over."

"It can't go on that much longer, surely," Tom continued. "People are going to get restless. There's no reason to keep us here."

The slow pace of their exchange was in contrast to the staccato statements and sudden gestures that dotted the room.

"Jo isn't a big one for texts."

"Lucy would expect one," Tom lamented. "She'll start wondering if she doesn't hear anything, especially if she's sent me a message and I don't reply."

Gary had nothing he was inclined to add.

"Do you think the guys know where we are?"

"I'd think so. I'd imagine it was difficult to miss what was going on."

"Then why aren't they here?"

"For all we know, they may be in the next room." Gary allowed himself a rueful chuckle. "Maybe they have been here. They might have been turned away. They'll be doing what they can."

"Maybe they've already told Lucy and Jo."

"I doubt it. They'd know that would freak them out. I did think we'd have been allowed a phone call by now, though."

"Me, too," Tom agreed.

"Who would you phone?"

"Good point. Couldn't call Lucy. 'Having an eventful time but struggling to sleep because of all the angry looking men and immense back pain.' How about you?"

"Probably Morton. Or Dean. Would have to be one of the boys. Nobody else is in a position to do anything other than worry."

The conversation had served its purpose. Having briefly ceded ground, remoteness again entrenched itself between them.

The door swung open and Nikopolidis entered. He addressed the room in three or four economical sentences which invited little discussion but were nevertheless met with dismay, then paced across the floor and stood before Gary and Tom.

"You two come with me." It was a statement of fact. Voices were raised in protest at the perceived preferential treatment, to which a reply was delivered over Nikopolidis' shoulder as he led the two Englishmen through the door and into his office, where Dean stood up stiffly, in a way that struck Gary as comically formal. He hugged them both in turn.

"Sit," Nikopolidis advised them in non-negotiable fashion. "You have ten minutes."

———·———

"How you both doing?" Dean asked as soon as the door clicked closed.

"Fine," Gary replied.

"Just want to get out," Tom added. "We're fish out of water here."

"You being treated OK?" Dean could hear his words sounding more professional than intended.

"Yeah," Tom answered. "Not much legroom, and the facilities could do with an upgrade, but OK. It's the waiting that's the problem. None of us know what's going on."

"Food and water? Toilet breaks?"

"Three yeses. How is everything, Dean? Everyone alright?" Gary had taken control of the conversation.

Dean recognised that, although they ultimately would need his legal expertise, they initially needed him as a friend. "Hard to know where to start." He rocked back in his seat and let momentum bring him up to standing. "Soon after you left to look for Camden, a big group of guys came into the bar wearing ski masks."

"Sounds like the same guys we ran into. Literally," Gary said.

"I thought they might have been part of the protests, but they were carrying these metal sticks and started smashing things up right, left and centre."

"Oh fuck."

"Morton's OK, but Salvation is in about a million pieces. Getting it back in order is going to take a while. Camden turned up the morning after the trouble. He'd been out looking for Crissa, seemed to panic when he saw things getting out of hand on the TV. We went to visit her friends yesterday to see if any of them had heard from her."

"Have they?"

"Not yet, so he's getting more frantic." He didn't elaborate further.

"Morton?"

"Gutted, understandably. There's barely a scratch on any other business and he's struggling to get people to help him."

"After all that planning and build-up," Gary observed. "I feel for them. How about you?"

"I tried to take on the leader of the group that stormed the bar. Landed my best punch on him and woke up on the floor after they'd cleared off."

"No way!"

"Morton assures me it was a pretty good shot. A full swing of the baton. I didn't feel anything at the time. It only started when I came round. If I could've shaken it quicker, I would have been here sooner."

Gary waved away any hint of an apology. "Just glad to see you upright."

"So, what happened with you two?" Dean asked.

Tom gave an outline of proceedings.

"What happens from here, mate?" Gary asked. "The patience is going to run out in that room unless something changes soon."

"I'm trying to catch up as best I can. That guy was pretty honest with me." He nodded in the direction of Nikopolidis' office door. "They're waiting for extra staff to come over from another island to start processing everyone properly. It may take a couple of days."

"A couple of days?" Tom complained.

"Apparently, they've been told not to release people until then. I don't know where that order came from," he continued, anticipating the question. "They're out of their depth here."

The information settled on the room for a moment. "What options do we have?" Gary asked.

"The thing I understand best is your rights. I tried to contact the embassy on Crete yesterday but by the time the room had stopped spinning every time I moved, they'd already closed, and they don't open again until Monday. Next option would be to phone the consulate in London, but I wanted to speak to you first. I came yesterday and didn't even get past the monkey on the desk.

"By rights, I'm fairly sure the police should've contacted the British embassy as soon as they arrested you. When I asked Nikopolidis if he'd done that, he went frosty. I took that as a No."

"They haven't even taken our names," Tom said.

"That would explain why, then. I'll call London as soon as I get back. They'll ask me whether you want them to contact your family." They both gave definitive headshakes.

"No point worrying them," Gary said.

"I thought as much. I think a phone call will be enough to give the police chief headaches he doesn't need. I'm sure this will all run its course soon but that seems our best chance to get you out of here quicker."

"Thanks, mate, appreciate it," said Gary, and Tom added agreement.

"Don't thank me yet. This is all new to me. Just hang in there. He's told me I can visit you twice a day until this is sorted, so I'll be back later today."

A shadow appeared in the window to the side of the door, Nikopolidis readying himself to twist the handle before turning to answer someone behind him. Shooting a glance in that direction, something occurred to Dean. "By the way, he was talking as if something major had gone down. 'Serious crimes have happened here,' he said."

"Things were out of hand," Gary said.

"I got the impression it was more than that." There was no recognition or reaction from the faces looking back at him, so Dean dropped it.

The door swung open and ended the conversation.

———•———

Gary and Tom avoided all eye contact from the heads that turned their way as they re-entered the room and had been seated for five minutes when a man crouched on his haunches in front of them, wearing a black hooded top that was unzipped to reveal a deep necked white t-shirt over khaki cargo shorts. His heavily scuffed trainers looked like they had started off white years ago and his black hair was closely cropped. He said nothing as his eyes measured them both, a smile occasionally threatening to dance across his lips.

"Can I help you?" Gary asked.

"No," came the instant reply and the smile emerged fully now along with emphatic gasps as if he had heard something funny, before rapidly disappearing.

Glancing towards Gary, Tom was surprised to see him holding their new acquaintance with a steady look that bordered on amusement.

"Do you expect us to be scared?" Gary asked finally, voice unwavering.

"No," the reply was again quick-fire and brought with it a flash of teeth and breathy laughter. Tom became very aware of the eyes of the room upon them.

"I have two questions for you," the man informed them after another ten seconds of frantic eye movement.

Neither of them said anything.

"Would you like to hear my questions?"

Neither of them said anything.

"You don't want to hear my questions?" He continued after allowing them a pause that they refused to fill. "It's no problem. Perhaps the questions are better directed towards your friends."

Neither of them said anything.

"That way, I could see their faces when I ask them why so many people waited until their opening night before paying them a visit with their sticks."

Gary leaned forward, hands out in front of him in case they were needed. "It's taken you thirty hours to pluck up the courage to come and speak to us so don't act like you're a tough guy. Now fuck off back over there."

The man continued undeterred: "And I could assess how truthfully they answer my second question. Which would be: 'Can you be trusted?'"

Chapter 13

Camden's hastily formed plan was to visit Crissa's family home in Piraeus and, if necessary, head into the capital to seek out a couple of names that he knew from stories that Crissa had told him.

It was to be a two-day round trip so an extra pair of clothes had been stuffed into the single bag that jostled on the seat beside him as the taxi driver weaved amongst the traffic on his way from the airport. Each change of direction was taken with assured confidence and absolutely no consideration for other road users. All the windows were down but the air outside was heating up. After a little over an hour in the cab, a sudden right turn was succeeded quickly by a left and the volume of traffic thinned. The driver spoke to himself as he slowed outside a building and then pulled away again, having wrongly identified the address which Camden had handed to him. A few hundred yards further along the road he was satisfied.

Camden found himself standing on the pavement looking up at an unassuming apartment block comprising seven floors on its right half and five on its left. Each apartment had a balcony that could be reached via sliding doors. Some had brown sunshades pulled down even though they were westward facing. It was 9.10am.

He checked his piece of paper for the umpteenth time. *Apartment 514.* He stood, nodded uncertainly, and blew out his cheeks. He hadn't expected his first visit here to be made without Crissa. He placed the bag on the ground, lifted it again and decided to go for a mind-settling walk around the neighbourhood.

Fifty minutes later, he circumnavigated back to the same spot, and this time there was no hesitation. "Here goes," he told himself, already pressing the buzzer next to the front gate. A female voice came through the two-way.

"Kalimera. My name is Christian," Camden said slowly and precisely, mixing between the native tongue of the female voice and the English with which he hoped to conduct most of the rest of the conversation. "I'm a good friend of Crissa's."

He smiled inwardly at his wording.

There were a few seconds of silence, then a buzz. Camden pushed open the gate and followed the signs along corridors and up staircases. A wiry man of six foot stood in the doorway when he reached 514. "You know Crissa?" he asked.

"Yes," Camden offered his hand. "My name is Christian." It didn't seem like the right time or place to mention the nature of the relationship.

"You are English?" the man asked, accepting the handshake with a strong grip encased in thick hair and abrasive skin.

"Scottish." There didn't seem to be much else to add.

The man nodded and looked at him, at a loss for what should come next in this unexpected Saturday morning visit.

"Are you Crissa's father?"

"Antonis," he nodded vigorously in confirmation.

"It's a pleasure to meet you, Mr Papanikolau. Would you mind if I come in?"

———•———

Having been led inside, he walked through a hallway past a series of open doors and entered a living room of browns and creams. To the left was a kitchen that looked immaculately overstuffed with equipment and ingredients. Straight ahead was the balcony, with a pleasant view across other similarly sized buildings, the port in the background.

"Hello." Camden spoke formally to two women, one of whom was seated on a sofa, the other in the doorway to the kitchen. They looked like they had been in the depths of conversation before the foreign intrusion. Camden placed the lady in the doorway as Crissa's mother, the straight hair a dead giveaway in a long ponytail down her back. He knew her second-hand as Silvia. He surmised that the younger woman, who looked around twenty, was Crissa's sister.

He introduced himself, eyes sweeping the room as he said it, waiting for name recognition to flash across their faces. Instead, his words were returned undelivered. "Do you speak English?"

"Yes," answered Antonis, perturbed by the question. "We all speak English. Please. Sit."

"Thank you," Camden replied, taking his seat and seeking clear-headedness.

"How can we help you?" Silvia asked in the gentle voice that she had bequeathed to her daughter.

Camden's eyes drifted out of focus as he tried to regroup. After a glance at the floor and a gulp, he lifted his head. "Mrs. Papanikolau, Mr Papanikolau," he addressed them both individually, dry-mouthed, "forgive me for asking, but has Crissa mentioned me to you?"

A haze of unease emerged, the parents exchanging searching looks.

"She has," said the youngest member of the room. "Mama, Crissa has spoken about seeing a man on the islands."

"Oh," came Silvia's reply, neither confirming nor refuting the suggestion.

"She didn't say you were British, though," Crissa's sister continued. "Not specifically. Christian isn't necessarily an British name."

That the point was valid was of only minor consolation. "My friends call me Camden."

The girl shrugged. "She called you Christian."

"You must be Nina."

Nina gave rapid, shallow nods but kept her lips tight as she did so.

Tentatively, he tried to establish a foothold. "Crissa and I have been in a relationship for around a year now. I moved to the islands from the UK eleven months ago to be with her and to set up a business with a friend. I must admit, Crissa was a bigger reason for the move than my business." He smiled and nodded as he spoke. "I'm very much in love with her. Forgive me, I'm a little taken aback. I thought she would have spoken to you about me."

He felt his Adam's apple hoist itself up, catch and dive-bomb in his throat. His decision to come here felt like an excruciating misjudgment.

"She has spoken about you," Nina threw him a lifeline. "Crissa and I speak every week."

Camden nodded. He knew about the weekly phone call to Nina and the less frequent ones to her parents. Although he couldn't understand the conversations, Crissa always seemed happy and relaxed when she talked to them. He'd made the presumption that some of her excitement about their relationship had made its way down the line.

"It seems like you make her very happy," Nina continued. "She probably discusses these things more with me."

She looked in the direction of her parents for their opinions. Silvia nodded and smiled in reluctant agreement; Antonis remained stolid.

"We have given her ... distance ... on the islands," Silvia said by way of faltering explanation. "If we had been able to visit, I'm sure we would have had the chance to meet you before now."

Camden appreciated the words for the comfort they were intended to bring. "When Crissa has visited you in the past year, I've always been too busy working. Another British friend and I have set up our business from nothing."

Antonis gave a nod and an approximation of being impressed.

"We don't see Crissa so much these days," Silvia lamented. "We talk but not always so freely. She lives separate lives, you know?"

Camden nodded without understanding.

"And Nina's right—she has spoken of you. Don't worry about that." She smiled soothingly at him. "I'm glad she makes you happy. She's a wonderful girl."

He beamed agreement.

"Would you like a drink?"

Camden asked for a glass of water, which seemed to be a two-person job, given that both Silvia and Antonis migrated to the kitchen and took several minutes to re-emerge.

Nina smiled sympathetically at Camden's awkward predicament but said nothing for the first few minutes of her parents' absence, instead leaving him to tread amongst his own thoughts. Finally, she spoke quietly and earnestly.

"Try not to look so worried."

"I'll try. This isn't how I imagined meeting you all."

"She'll turn up."

Nina's second sentence seemed so out of place that Camden couldn't help but keep his eyes attached to her until she looked away towards her parents as they re-entered the room.

Two sips into their drinks, Antonis spoke up.

"What is the reason you are here?"

The wording sounded brusque, but Camden recognised it as a combination of Antonis' demeanour and the language barrier.

"Well, I have a few friends visiting from the UK for the week to celebrate the opening of our business. Crissa decided to take a trip for a few days to give us guys a chance to catch up."

His ad lib was solid. Camden felt the tension lifting.

"The thing is, despite having all my old friends around me, I miss Crissa. They're off doing a few tourist trips for a couple of days, so I wanted to try to surprise her. My first thought was that she may be staying with you and," he shrugged sheepishly, "I've wanted to meet you all for some time."

"No, we haven't heard from her," Silvia said, her voice perpetually laced with a wistful air. "We didn't know she was coming."

Camden's hands were back out in front of him again. "Perhaps I misunderstood her. I presumed she may come to see you, but my mind has been very busy lately."

"What is your business?" Antonis enquired.

"It's a bar. In one of the best spots on Santorini. Amazing views."

"Hmmm." He seemed less impressed than before. "Is it successful?"

Camden swallowed. "It will be, yes."

The ensuing silence began to feel terminal, and Camden found himself drinking in gulps. "I should get going."

"When is your flight?" Silvia asked.

"This evening."

"But you have luggage," she observed.

Again, he swallowed. "In case there's a late change of plan. If I'd managed to see Crissa, I would've stayed overnight in a hotel until tomorrow, so I brought a few things."

"You can stay here," Silvia suggested, exchanging looks with Antonis, who seemed unsupportive of the idea.

"That's kind, Mrs Papanikolau, but I couldn't possibly impose myself on you. I'll return to Santorini tonight to spend more time with my friends while we're all together."

Silvia nodded gingerly.

"It's been lovely to meet you." Camden rose, taking Silvia's hand and kissing her politely on the cheek before turning to Antonis and shaking his hand. "Sir," he said deferentially, and nodded at Nina, who remained seated. "Sorry for interrupting your Saturday morning."

"Not at all," Silvia replied. Antonis' steady look acknowledged both the interruption and the apology.

"I hope to see you again soon," Camden said as a parting comment. "Take care now."

His last image was that the room was awash with Crissa's family members exhibiting quizzical looks.

Except one.

———•———

Before he'd driven Camden to the airport that morning, Morton had placed a note on the coffee table in the living room and went for a walk to clear his mind and motivate himself ahead of what he hoped would be a more successful second day of dragging Salvation up from its knees. It felt like he spent most of the morning moving things around rather than making any real inroads, so he resolved to take an early lunch and headed back to the canava to recharge. He walked through the door to find Dean cradling a coffee at the breakfast bar in the kitchen.

"Hey, you ok?"

Dean nodded. "Yeah. Been to see the boys. Holding up fine. About to give the embassy a call."

"Good. Let's hope it makes a difference. Feels like there needs to be a jolt to the system."

"Too right."

"Been up long?"

"Since seven-ish."

"Wet the bed?"

"Heard you guys leaving. Plus, lots to do." Dean wasn't big on convoluted sentence structures until the first coffee had worked through his system. "How's the clean-up going?"

"It's felt like a wasted morning, really."

"What's the plan for the rest of the day?"

"Hopefully not more of the same," Morton replied, flicking the kettle back on. "Time to shake myself out of it and take things by the scruff of the neck. Doesn't seem like the local handyman industry's falling over itself to help and it's gonna take a lot of work to put things back together. Who knows how much of the summer we'll have missed."

"I feel for you, man."

Morton was giving a look of thanks when his phone rang on the tabletop. "Maybe one of those TV shows that renovate your property in the space of a couple of days," he suggested with a smile before answering.

Dean was draining his mug of its contents when he saw Morton's expression change as he stood up straight.

"What do you mean?" he asked the phone. "What allegations?"

Chapter 14

Morton appeared trapped in homeostasis as he stared at his phone for a full five seconds after the talking had stopped. He rebooted himself and started punching numbers an instant before Dean had the chance to redundantly ask if everything was OK.

Anthony answered before the first ring had ended. "Son. I was half-expecting a call from you. Are you alright?"

He knows, thought Morton. "I'm not sure," he replied. "Been trying to make sense of a phone call I've just received."

"I feared as much. There's no truth in those stories." As though he knew all the details of all the stories.

"Always one step ahead, right, Dad?" Morton bristled. "Why didn't you get in touch as soon as you heard?"

"I'm certainly not one step ahead in this case, Anthony." His father was the only person who called him by his full first name. His mother and sister called him Ant; to all others he was Morton. "And I've only just found out about your bar. Are you hurt?"

"No, we're fine. The bar sustained significant injuries."

For the two generations of Morton males to have a testy conversation was hardly unchartered territory, but less common these days. They were similar enough to rub each other up the wrong way but different enough to reconcile their differences. Still, Morton was aware that, by default, Anthony would try to control the narrative of their conversations, so details of Gary and Tom's predicament could wait until the main purpose of the call had been achieved.

"Glad to hear you're OK. Sorry about the bar," Anthony answered.

"I get the feeling you know what my last phone call was about, but I'm going to tell you anyway."

"Go ahead, son."

Morton began, determined to achieve unerring accuracy in both the telling of the story and the reading of his father's every response.

———•———

"May I speak to Anthony Morton, please?"

Morton had stayed quiet, wrong-footed by an unknown female voice addressing him by his full name.

"I am looking for Anthony Morton."

Still Morton said nothing but became aware of Dean's eyes on him and a chill hitting the back of his neck, despite the heat.

"Hmmm," said the voice, as though arriving at a decision after a lengthy two-way conversation, despite the fact she had yet to receive a single word of reply. "My name is Elena Ralli from Antenna. I believe I am speaking to Anthony Morton—either father or son—and I would like to ask what you think about the allegations being made against you and your family."

"What do you mean?" Morton couldn't help but ask. "What allegations?"

"Anthony Junior." Elena Ralli seemed satisfied to have resolved the identity of the person who'd answered her call. "Thank you for speaking to me. Tell me, did you watch the broadcast by the Finance Minister, Michael Andreas, on Thursday evening?"

Her voice was relaxed and conversational, although Morton could tell that the tone and content could instantly change if required. Without waiting for a response, Ralli continued: "Mr Andreas made allegations against many wealthy people in his broadcast, claiming that they were evading tax on an industrial scale and that they are behind the criticism his austerity crackdown is attracting."

It was notable how the phrases 'industrial scale' and 'crackdown' seemed to come out of her mouth unnaturally, as if plucked from a film or TV show and force-fed into her syntax.

"What do you think about that point of view?" she asked.

Morton had expected a more piercing question, but still found himself at a loss for how to answer it. "I didn't see the broadcast," he stated. "I don't really understand what you're asking."

"Are you familiar with the names Manos and Nikos Melas?"

There it was. "Yes." Inexplicably, he felt like he had been caught out.

"How do you know them, Mr Morton?"

"They're friends of my father. Associates." He cursed his clarification.

"These *associates*, Mr Morton, are widely believed to be leading names amongst those to whom Mr Andreas was referring."

Willing his brain to catch up, Morton held back to see where things went next.

"The Melas brothers are magnates. They appear in lifestyle magazines all the time, always in the company of glamour and power. They own an enormous amount of land around Athens and other cities. In recent times they've turned their attention to developing upscale resorts on the holiday islands. For some islands that task is easier than others, especially if they are already well on their way to being commercialised to cater for the tourist industry.

"For other islands, history and integrity are not to be negotiated. There are specific laws in place to make sure that buildings do not rise above a certain height and complement the existing environment. By chasing the tourist dollar, the appeal of such islands would gradually become diluted. To places like this, individual identity is important. Such is the case for Santorini."

There was an unfilled pause.

"Your father's business ventures have made him a wealthy man, Mr Morton. He owns numerous properties throughout this country as well as in several others—Monaco, France, Italy, the US, the UK of course."

Morton only knew portions of this list and had never been inclined to ask.

"Have you ever met the Melas brothers?" she continued.

"Yes, I have."

"What did you think of them?"

"Have you ever met them?" he countered.

"Ah. Has the tone of our conversation turned defensive, Mr Morton?"

"Ms Ralli, put yourself in my shoes. You've called me unexpectedly. I don't even understand the questions you're asking me. And now you're bringing into question my father's integrity."

"You're right," she conceded, "I'm not in your shoes, in any way. I personally am not questioning your father's integrity, but others are. Investigations, cameras, microphones: all are pointing at the people who are believed to have their details on the data disk that Minister Andreas showed on his broadcast on Thursday night. They're calling it the 'Andreas Archive'."

Morton could sense her fingers drawing quotation marks in the air.

"The country is boiling, Mr Morton. There's a deep sense of injustice. If it becomes apparent that influential people have been robbing from the country while it sinks to its knees, that rage will only intensify, and it will be focused squarely on the people on the Andreas Archive."

Nothing occurred in Morton's mind as worth adding to the conversation.

"How did you acquire the property for the business that you recently opened, Mr Morton?"

"My father bought it," Morton answered on impulse.

"Just like that?"

"This conversation is over, Ms Ralli."

"Haven't you been asking yourself, Mr Morton, why amidst all the unrest and trouble that happened that night, only one property was destroyed? And on its first night of business?"

"This conversation is over," he repeated, although what he really meant was that, while he would no longer contribute, he would allow one more rejoinder before terminating the connection.

"None of this is a coincidence."

The conversation was over.

———•———

A drawn-out sigh was the extent of Anthony's response at the end of his son's retelling of the phone call.

"I need more than that, Dad."

"You know as well as I do that business is all about greasing the wheels. I have business contacts in every country where I have or want properties, and a lot more countries besides. It's how things get done. What are you asking me?"

"I don't know," Morton replied, a split-second too late.

Audibly annoyed, Anthony said: "I can't begin to tell you how much your lack of trust disappoints me. You should know me better than that. And these questions are pretty far down the line, don't you think? Shouldn't you have been asking them at the time? All you wanted was the perfect location. You picked it, you pointed it out to me, and I got it for you. You trusted me then. What's changed?"

"A lot's changed in the past forty-eight hours, Dad. The government are more or less accusing two of your business contacts of tax evasion; our business was in smithereens before the end of its first night; Camden's now trying to track down his girlfriend, who's suddenly dropped off the face of the earth; a news reporter has called me to ask what I think about allegations being made against you—" He cut short the list he was reciting.

"What else, son?"

Morton pressed his eyelids tightly closed. He had spent his early teenage years establishing himself on an even footing in conversations with his father and hated giving ground, but he knew he had just tipped him off.

"The only time you end a sentence as abruptly as that is when you realise you're about to tell me something you don't want to. What are you holding back?"

"Dad," Morton tried to keep him at bay.

"I'm coming over there anyway. You're my son and you're in trouble and some of it may be my fault. I'm coming to help you, like it or not. But I can help you more if you tell me everything I need to know before I arrive."

After only a slight vacillation, Morton let him in. "Gary and Tom were arrested." He left a pause in expectation of an expression of dismay or outrage, but his father remained studiously stoic. "There were a lot of arrests made on Thursday night; they got caught up in it while they were looking for Camden. They're still in jail. Dean's been to see them and they're OK, but we're struggling to get them out of there."

"OK. Thank you for telling me. I'll get the first flight out tomorrow. I'll be there early in the afternoon. Let me know if anything else happens, alright?"

Anthony laid out the words calmly, robotically, as though reading the cooking instructions from the back of a sauce packet.

———•———

Morton had first encountered the Melas brothers at his father's canava eleven months earlier.

It was late morning on their first day as residents of the island. Morton and Camden met Anthony at the canava, where he had already spent a few days. He looked as thrilled as them at the prospect of their new enterprise.

"I've lined up a handful of places for you to look at for the business," he enthused as he clasped Morton tightly to him. "And there are a couple of people you should meet."

It was hard to imagine Manos Melas having ever had anything other than the crown of fine but plentiful grey hair that he sported as he shook their hands upon arriving soon after. Dark at the roots and styled into a side parting that gainfully battled the mishmash of waves across his head, it vied with his crooked hook of a nose to be his most defining feature. He stood six-three with a spine that suggested that it could stretch him ten inches taller if fully unravelled. Every movement was languid as he tumbled his limbs towards them and beamed a well-worn smile. "Pleasure to meet you, Anthony Junior," he said.

"Morton. Makes it easier," Morton corrected with a smiling shrug.

Manos went on beaming, head bobbing in appreciation at what he seemed to assume was easy chemistry. "And you must be Christian."

"Camden. People call me Camden."

"It is your last name?" Manos roared as Camden nodded. "All last names with you guys! That would not work for us. Melas and Melas!" he boomed, flicking his index finger between he and his brother.

Casting Manos a look of weary familiarity, Nikos Melas took the steps required to make his introductions. He shook their hands in turn, maintaining eye contact throughout. In contrast to his elder sibling, his words were selected thriftily, but their parents had done a consistent job of doling out limbs that seemed to flail while accomplishing the most basic of tasks. Tousled, unstylish black hair sat atop a vulpine face housing flickering brown eyes and thin lips that constantly alternated between pursing and disappearing completely. He was in his late forties, around five years younger than his brother.

"Manos and Nikos are great people to know here, for many reasons," Anthony said by way of introduction, and they shared a laugh as he did so. "They've been helping me scout out suitable places for you."

Manos nodded eagerly; Nikos kept his eyes set on Anthony, as though rapt with every word.

"We've done business together before, very successfully. They're good people. Trustworthy."

Morton kept quiet but thought his father was laying it on a bit thick.

"You'll like the places we've lined up for you. No pressure for you to rush into taking any of them, mind you—entirely up to you guys to call it—but they'll be a great starting point if nothing else."

Manos' expression suggested he'd be mortally offended if they decreed that none of the locations met their approval; Nikos' almost seemed to challenge them to do exactly that.

As it happened, all three potential venues were far beyond their expectations. Each was built into the cliff-side in the heart of the town and looked like an immaculate blank canvas on which to work. After visiting the first two, they felt sure that they would end the day agonising over which to choose. Instead, something just felt right as they approached the third.

"I like this," Camden murmured as they entered, and Morton was already sold.

No down payment, just a healthy but fair cut of profits. They couldn't believe their luck and asked few questions—including why three prime locations were available at such short notice with the new holiday season having just hit full swing.

———•———

"Mr Morton?"

Morton squinted up in the direction of the voice, any distinguishing features obscured by the bright sunshine framing it.

"Can I help you?"

"My name is Angelos Karatzas, I'm from The Daily." He extended his hand at the start of his sentence and began to withdraw it as it ended, as though used to such an offer being rejected. Morton removed the protective gloves he was wearing and shook it firmly anyway.

"What do you want?" he asked, putting them back on and picking up the detritus of what used to be the plasma TV screen, before carrying it towards the storeroom at the back of the bar.

"I have some questions that I thought you may be able to answer."

Morton walked back towards the doorway, where Karatzas remained. "Oh?" he asked noncommittally.

"The damage to your business is one of the subjects I want to talk about." Karatzas had a lilting voice, delivered like a tune from a music box that needed wound up.

Morton resolutely refused to fill any silences. Most of the conversation that had staggered on from there covered similar ground to Elena Ralli's earlier phone call, but two questions resonated in Morton's mind afterwards.

The first: "What do you think about the plans that your father has been working on with the Melas brothers to build a luxury development just south of Oia, at the top of the island?"

Morton hadn't expected that question: he'd been on Santorini for eleven months, seen his father three times in that period, and heard nothing about any such plans.

———•———

The following morning, Morton awoke to the single buzz of his phone. His father.

About to board. Arrive at 1340. EasyJet 8765. Pick me up if you can.

It was a little before nine and he had only allowed himself to be coaxed to sleep five hours earlier. He hauled himself out of bed and trudged downstairs.

"You look like I feel, mate," Dean remarked from his position at the breakfast counter, facing out to the caldera with a coffee for company.

Morton tried to blink his eyes into life and sunk slowly into a chair.

"Struggling to sleep?"

"Yeah. Been to the jail already?"

"Indeed. Starting to feel like I fit in there."

"They ok?"

"Seem a bit testy with each other, to be honest. Probably just cooped up too long. Said some guy was acting weird with them after I saw them yesterday."

Morton looked querulously at him. "In what way?"

"Didn't say. Think they struggled to understand him, just said he acted odd."

"Any progress on getting them out?"

"The head police guy is squirming more as time passes. The embassy's been in his ear. When I spoke to them yesterday, they seemed confident they could put enough pressure on to get them released today. So that's the plan: call at ten and wait for word. I'll be ready for that call any time it comes." Dean sipped his coffee. "What's with you not sleeping anyway? Never normally an issue for you."

Morton shrugged. "Probably just the past few days catching up on me." Slapping his hand on Dean's knee, Morton rose to his feet. "But the place ain't gonna fix itself, so making progress is one of the things that helps. I'm going to take a shower and head over to Salvation."

"I'll come with you."

"Nah, you've got Gary and Tom to worry about. Speak to the embassy and spring those boys as soon as you can. Just let me know if you hear anything."

———•———

A little over two hours later, as he approached the open door that led from the side alley into the bar after positioning another boxful of debris in the back yard, Morton could sense that people were waiting for him inside.

"Can I help you?" he asked.

There were four of them, all dressed in dark suits of varying styles, three men plus a woman, who was clearly in charge and stepped forward. Her hair was auburn, and her manner was so immaculate that it looked like it had taken years of practice. She held an A4 envelope in her hand.

A buzz went off in his pocket. He deftly silenced the phone call with a press of his thumb.

"Are you Anthony Morton?" he was asked.

"I am."

"I believe that you are the owner of the business that is based here."

"One of the owners, yes."

Again, his phone vibrated. Again, he thumbed it quiet.

"I believe that your father is one of the owners of the building in which your business is situated, yes?"

"That's right."

"Do you know where your father is, Mr Morton?"

He wasn't sure how to answer. For a third time, his phone made its presence felt. Tutting, he pulled it from the pocket of his cargo shorts and saw *Dean* written across the screen. Something felt off.

"I need to take this," he told them.

"Mr Morton, this is very—" she protested, but he cut her off by raising his index finger.

"Everything alright, mate?" he asked his phone.

"I'm at the canava. There are four people here, Morton. Say they're from the government."

The woman was waiting to receive his attention when his eyes shot back towards her. She gave a diminutive nod, as though answering a shared, unspoken question between them. The envelope made its way towards him, and he took it from her.

"Mr Morton," she informed him, "pending an ongoing investigation into the potential illegal evasion of tax, all the assets in this country which are owned by your father and his associates, Manos and Nikos Melas, are being taken under the control of the government."

———•———

In amongst the dizziness that he tried to wade through as he was led away from the besuited figures buzzing around the inside of Salvation—clipboards and tablets in hand—Morton's mind kept latching onto the second unexpected question that Karatzas had asked of him the previous day.

It had been asked in response to Morton's enquiry into why—if he had so many questions about the people whose details were on the Andreas Archive—he didn't approach the Finance Minister directly.

"Mr Morton," Karatzas dropped his voice conspiratorially, "Michael Andreas has been missing since he sent out his broadcast on Thursday evening."

Chapter 15

In an attempt to ease the anxiety that had been building inside him in the forty-five minutes since Michael Andreas had delivered his speech, Marcos tried to savour the warm, refreshing breeze as the boat undulated rhythmically across the black water. A spray of lights came into view from Oia and Fira to the northern end of the island, where unbeknownst to them, demonstrators had just hit the streets. The south—from where they were making headway—offered pure darkness, silhouettes distinguished from it only by the reflection of moon on water.

They were pointed towards an islet hosting a sole property, opposite the main island. It was known locally that the Finance Minister had holidayed there before, so it was worth the calculated gamble. To them, it was incredible that he had the audacity to preach about the need to tighten belts from a luxurious living room that was the same size as the average family's home, a large glass of wine visible at the corner of the camera shot. "He has no idea," Grilla seethed to those assembled on the sofas in Marcos' home.

The boat carried four and they were each decked out in all-black, having stopped at Daniel's for him to change clothes while Grilla kept the car running outside. From there, he drove them to the house that he shared with his cousin, Salvo, who immediately offered the services of both his boat and wiry physique. The cousins re-emerged from their bedrooms so quickly that it caused Marcos to wonder if they'd had the outfit already picked out for such an unforeseeable occasion.

"Take these, and put them on when we get there," Grilla said as he tossed two ski masks to Daniel and Marcos. Although Marcos questioned the motives for storing multiple ski masks in the Aegean climate, he resigned himself to the fact that the time for objections had passed thirty minutes ago.

Grilla's day job was as a baker, but he eagerly assumed the bearing of a military leader issuing instructions to his cohort:

"Salvo takes us in his boat," he dictated, lifting an index finger to show that this was just the first in a series of directives. While Grilla spoke, Salvo repeatedly took himself to different parts of the house and returned with new pieces of equipment, some carrying a clear purpose, others seemingly plucked at random: two metal baseball bats, a tennis racquet, a hammer, bedsheets torn into strips, two slim paintbrushes, a petrol canister, four pairs of ski gloves, a sponge, a carving knife.

"Andreas is staying at the house on the island next to Aspronisi." Grilla spoke as if Salvo's accumulations were perfectly in line with his expectations. Marcos noticed how speculation about the Finance Minister's whereabouts had quickly turned into fact despite the absence of any new, compelling evidence.

"That house is the only one on that island, so he won't be expecting anyone. We get in however we get in and we get our hands on him. Rough him up a bit but not too much. The masks will keep us anonymous. And then we flick on that magic camera of his and have him broadcast a different kind of message. You're good with words, Daniel: have a think and add a couple of flourishes."

"No problem," Daniel agreed with a conviction that caught Marcos by surprise.

Salvo's boat was one of a dozen or so moored near to a jetty, a short walk from his home. Having deposited their gear in the back, he and Grilla rowed the first hundred yards or so before starting the engine. Initially heading south to escape earshot of the few neighbours Salvo had, they then swooped around the southwest finger of the island and made a beeline for the islet. A couple of other boats criss-crossed the caldera to their right—much closer to the island proper—but far enough away that their engines were inaudible. Clear water now: between them and the Minister there was only the sole resident of the volcanic island and the goats he kept for company, and they would pass the volcano on its left, at the opposite end to its inhabitant.

To Grilla, the boat passed over the water too slowly: he wanted to be there immediately, his adrenaline anticipating the moment of confrontation, capturing that glint of fear in the Minister's eyes as he realised he was cornered.

For Marcos, the waves skidded under the hull at a dizzying speed. His twenty-first birthday was less than three weeks away. This next year was supposed to be all about him gathering together enough funds to resume his halted university career. No advisable plan had him sitting where he sat, cursing himself for his consistent inability to say no.

The engine was silenced a few hundred yards from the islet, the Minister's presumed abode well-lit and introduced by its own landing jetty. They idled in with little noise, although the others held their breath when Grilla's haste caused him to sclaff his shoes along the wooden jetty as he stepped ashore, grabbing the baseball bat from the bottom of the boat before making his way round to the back of the building. Looking impatiently over his shoulder, he waved at them to hurry up. Their ski masks were already in place.

They rounded the corner to see him with his back pressed tightly against the wall. Every step to his left would expose him to a glass frontage which encased the remainder of the impressive house, facing out to sea. A door lay ten yards from them, bisecting two floor-to-ceiling windows.

Grilla held his right arm straight out to the side, palm extended, before lowering it slowly to the ground. It was a theatrical gesture that nevertheless conveyed its message to the others: *stay here, I'll go.* There was no discernible activity from within the house. Marcos wondered if they even had the right place. Grilla crouched so low that he looked as if he were about to start a forward roll but instead pumped his legs furiously as he darted to the door and then flattened himself on the ground. Still no movement from inside. He lifted his head and uncurled his back from the floor, cobra-style. Satisfied he hadn't been spotted, he coiled himself up and stood side-on to the doorframe.

After a final sideways glance, he gently pressed down on the handle. It was important to him that the Minister was caught unawares: it would heighten the spectacle. The door edged open without resistance or sound. Even through Grilla's ski mask, Marcos could see his eyes bulge and a smile present itself in recognition of the Minister's arrogant presumption of safety.

Grilla moved swiftly inside, resuming his crouch position. Salvo was close behind, as was Daniel. Marcos hung back as far as he dared. They were in a utility room that opened onto a hallway. Grilla pointed left and Salvo and Daniel headed in that direction, towards what looked like bedrooms. Tapping his chest and then pointing the opposite way, he indicated where he and Marcos would go. Despite himself, Marcos gave a nod to confirm he understood the instruction and followed as Grilla wheeled into the open. To his surprise, as he turned the corner he almost ran straight into the back of their de facto leader, who stood fully erect at the top of a small flight of stairs which led from the kitchen to the living room and out onto a balcony.

The room spoke of money and sophistication with its minimalist, modern refinement and was the same room they had seen in the background of the Minister's broadcast. They were in the right house. Grilla turned to observe Salvo and Daniel coming back into the room with their palms spread to show they'd found nothing.

Two things occurred to all of them: firstly, the stool in front of the laptop lay toppled on the floor and had scraped a black rubber scrawl over a couple of tiles in the process; secondly, one of the two couches that faced each other across a vast coffee table was pushed diagonally out of alignment and the table itself was shunted to an asymmetric angle, a whisky glass smashed on the floor at its far left-hand side.

"Someone's beaten us to it." The frustration was audible in Grilla's tone.

Salvo moved to his cousin's shoulder. "We need to move fast. We can't be here."

Without further words, they both spun around and slunk past Daniel and Marcos towards the door through which they had entered minutes before. Marcos watched them from the light of the living room, peering to make out their dim shadows moving purposefully outside. Salvo bundled something up in his hands and leaned against the door to open it; Grilla was bending over to assume the weight of the petrol canister that revealed itself as he came back into the light. Marcos hadn't noticed Salvo empty the boat of its contents.

The cousins weaved towards the sleeping quarters, Salvo dropping half the bedsheet strips on the floor at the kitchen entrance on his way. There wasn't so much as a glance in the direction of Daniel and Marcos, who had become superfluous. Daniel took a tentative step towards the exit before thinking better of it. Marcos' head strafed the room for security cameras. His untrained eye saw none but he knew they must be somewhere.

The first wisp of burning met their noses as Grilla marched back into the room, leaping down the stairs and across to the long curtains that hung in six pairs around its perimeter. One by one and with striking efficiency, he and

Salvo doused the bedsheets in petrol, lit them and lay them at the floor of each set of curtains. Swiftly drawing a swirl across the sofas, floor, tables, and worktops, Grilla emptied the canister, threw it towards the far end of the room and nodded as he walked past Salvo, whose hurl of a final bunch of sheets was followed by a whoosh and a sudden backdraft.

All of them stalked to the door, Grilla holding it open for them in a curiously gentlemanly way, surveying his work a final time before squeezing the door closed as though not to disturb those inside.

This time they gunned the boat as soon as they were all aboard.

Chapter 16

After gate-crashing Crissa's family's Saturday morning, Camden had taken his time over lunch, mulling over his next move. He tried two addresses without success so decided to book himself into a clean-looking chain hotel, centrally located. Resigned to having to resume his search in the morning, he was snaffling a burger in a diner in a busy part of town when the mood changed appreciably. Instinctively, he aborted the meal and hurriedly overpaid the bill. By the time he'd sped back to his hotel, the demographic on the street had morphed into a broiling concoction of barely constrained energy, mostly young and dressed in black. Once he was inside, the hotel doors were locked behind him, the staff sheltering behind the reception desk, necks craned like meerkats, both inquisitive and fearful of the events unfolding outside.

He tucked himself away in his room and the percussion of shouts, smashes, chants, and bangs faded within twenty minutes, after which a normal Saturday night seemed to occur. When he switched on the TV to see if there was unrest elsewhere, a reporter told the camera of the disappearance of the Finance Minister and a dark knot of worry took hold of Camden's stomach.

The night before flying to the mainland, he had leafed through Crissa's address book and picked out two names: the one of whom she had spoken most often, and the one to whom she had spoken most recently. It was the door of the former that was opened on the Sunday morning.

"Evelina?" Camden enquired of the young woman who stood before him. "I'm Christian Camden. Crissa's boyfriend."

Her expression conceded little, so he used the address book and a photo of them on his phone as evidence of his credentials.

She nodded and blinked at him in recognition, drawing her lips tight and pulling the door to as she stepped into the hallway.

"I'm looking for Crissa," Camden said deliberately. "She came to Athens a few days ago and I haven't heard from her since. With the trouble that's gone on here, I'm worried about her."

He gauged Evelina to be in her mid-twenties and found her quirkily attractive. Enthusiastic waves of hair sprung forth at outrageous angles, proudly presenting a high forehead and somewhat bulbous nose that turned up slightly at the end. She struck him as someone who would have a multitude of expressions at her disposal, but who wouldn't necessarily deploy them at the appropriate times.

Accordingly, her reply was ushered his way with a look of incredulity. "And you think she would be here?" The expression was held in place long after her question was posed.

Small movements mapped across Camden's face as he sought the right response. "I don't know where she is," he said, settling on simplicity. "I visited her family yesterday."

At this, Evelina narrowed her eyes, forcing him to continue.

"They don't know where she is either. I don't know what to do, Evelina. This is the first time I've even been to the mainland. I feel like I'm making this up as I'm going along."

Returning her facial features to neutral, Evelina seemed to make up her mind about something. "Stay here," she instructed, closing the door behind her as she ducked into the apartment. Camden could hear her talking in hushed tones, with no audible response other than the sound of jangling keys as the door eased narrowly open and she re-joined him, a light denim jacket hanging on her slender shoulders.

"Let's go for a walk," she suggested.

———•———

They sat outside a restaurant that had taken twenty minutes to reach, two pizzas laid in front of them that were twice the size indicated in the pictures on the menu. Evelina was making the better headway, with only a quarter remaining uneaten. She gave the impression of pausing rather than quitting as she shifted the plate slightly to one side. Camden's was almost untouched.

"So," she said, speaking for the first time since she'd advised him that conversation would not be initiated until a pepperoni thin crust was served. Camden had been surprised that anywhere could meet her demands at that time in the morning, but she'd known exactly which place to come to. "You can understand that this is an odd situation for me."

Camden agreed. "What would help to make it less odd?"

"If I ask you questions and you give me answers," she stated after a pause.

The cadence of Camden's breathing slowed. "Of course."

"I know the story of you and Crissa. I don't need any details about that."

"OK." He seemed both surprised and disappointed.

"How would you describe her?"

"Intelligent. Kind-hearted. Beautiful."

Evelina's face fascinated him; its constituent parts capable of moving completely independent of each other. At that moment, they were contorted in a manner that could be read as a sneer. "Those are just words said by lovers the world over. Speak about her in a way that tells me how she makes you feel."

Camden almost snapped at her but instead took a moment to ponder his answer: "Like the only worthwhile things in life are the things that Crissa and I experience together. The world can seem shrink-wrapped around us and still feel more substantial than it ever did before."

Evelina nodded, apparently satisfied. She nudged just over five feet tall, and a crease had taken up residence on her spacious forehead. "What about before you knew each other?"

"That she grew up in Piraeus. One younger sister, Nina, who I met for the first time yesterday when I freaked out her parents by turning up unannounced looking for their daughter." Camden gave a sharp, mirthless chuckle that went unacknowledged. He was on surer footing now, so he pressed on. "That she went to the University of Athens to study Political Sciences in 2007, the same time you did, and that she dropped out after her second year."

A passer-by could have been forgiven for thinking that Evelina was studying complex code on a computer screen.

"In the summer of 2011 she moved to Santorini. She'd planned on it only being for a single summer season but found work at a high-end spa there and liked the pace of life. 'The best plan I ever made was to have no plan.' Her own words."

Evelina tilted her head querulously, eyebrows arcing up like an exponential graph.

"We met last year when I was visiting for a bachelor party—"

"I know that part," she cut across him brusquely.

"You're making me feel like I'm sitting a test," Camden retorted.

"You've got more right than wrong so far," Evelina conceded. "Let me colour in some gaps and make some corrections."

Camden reclined and laid his palms flat on the arms of the uncomfortable metal chair. "OK," he said quietly.

"Crissa and I met at university, you're right about that. I started a year earlier. Crissa was always older than her years, though. We started working together at the same cafe, doing the same shifts. We hit it off pretty quickly and would hang out all the time with a few other friends. I'm sure you've heard their names: Julia, Adrianna, Rosa, Yannis, Spyros." She gave the names a second to register. "In my third year of university—Crissa's second—we moved in together. Funny times. Crazy times." Memories passed behind her eyes. "Some great, some not so great."

There followed moments of no sound or movement.

"Do you know why Crissa dropped out of university?" she asked with sudden urgency.

Camden had no answer.

"University was very important to Crissa. She'd done everything she could to make it there and was top of her class. To understand why she abandoned that is to know who Crissa is now."

Seeing there would be no reply of any substance, Evelina changed course. "I've not had what you would call a nice life." She had hesitated before deciding on the right words, then took a large bite from her penultimate slice of pizza and seemed to ruminate on how or whether to continue. "It's why Crissa and I are kindred spirits, in a way."

Camden swallowed with a struggle.

"Around the same time Crissa dropped out, I had some issues and took a year off. We would spend a lot of time walking the streets of the city, talking for hours, letting the days wash over us. We'd go out. Partying. A lot."

A cigarette had magicked itself already-lit into Evelina's right hand and she inhaled purposefully. "You said that Crissa dropped out after two years and you're pretty much right. That was 2009 and she moved to the islands in 2011. Do you know what happened in the time in between?"

Camden couldn't establish whether Evelina was savouring the cigarette or the question. "Tell me."

Three long drags filled the pause before she lifted and dropped her eyebrows and looked away aloofly. "The things that bonded us were the same reasons we would have grown mutually destructive. One of us had to make the break and it was me."

No relevant questions or comments made themselves known in Camden's mind.

"Am I the first of her friends that you've spoken to?" Evelina asked.

"Not quite. I tried friends on Santorini, but none could contact her. I flew here yesterday and tried her family. Then you."

"Why?"

He cocked his head to the side. "What do you mean?"

"I haven't spoken to Crissa in three years."

Frowning, he said: "But she speaks about you a lot. More than any other friend."

"We'll always be close, but from a distance," Evelina nodded, pulling out the remaining chair from under the table. "That's why I invited Julia."

"Of all places, you brought him here?" asked the fragile-featured blonde girl who warily took the seat opposite him.

———·———

Evelina kept her eyes on Camden, ignoring Julia's question. "Sit with us," she finally said. It didn't sound up for debate.

Julia was unmoved, not yet acknowledging Camden with a look.

"Where would you have brought him, Julia? Where would be the right place? What would you have done if he'd knocked on your door?"

Julia let her shoulders drop slightly as she answered. "I wouldn't have brought him here."

"Sit down," Evelina repeated, staring imploringly at the empty seat that was pulled out beside her. "This is Crissa's boyfriend."

Camden stood and introduced himself, offering his hand, which Julia hesitantly shook.

"Hello," she managed.

Evelina pushed her last slice of pizza along the table and Julia immediately sat, as though the offer of leftover food had been the deciding factor of whether she stayed or bolted. She was petite and, despite being a few inches taller than Evelina, looked even more diminutive in every way. Her bedraggled blonde hair fell to shoulder length, her fringe partially obscuring her face so that she had to continually brush it sideways with her hand. Her facial features took up only a tiny part of her face, round eyes straddling a nose so wafer-thin that it looked like it could cut glass, dainty lips constantly pursed as though that was the only way to prevent them quivering. The way she clambered into her seat suggested she was more used to perpetual motion.

"I'm looking for any information that can help us find Crissa," Camden explained. "Where she was staying, who she may have been with. That type of thing."

Julia barely looked capable of comprehending the questions, let alone constructive response. She took a few seconds to steady herself and then made as if to answer. Instead, she scooped up the pizza slice and munched it inelegantly, each new mouthful beginning before the previous one had been swallowed. Evelina looked amused by the scene.

Camden was unsure whether to be irritated or concerned by the detachment of the new arrival. "I tried to get in touch with you yesterday because I know she spoke to you in the days before she left for the mainland."

Julia's chewing abated and her jaw hung loose before springing shut as she swallowed the contents of her mouth with newfound resolve. "I did speak to her," she confirmed. "We speak now and again. I'm still in touch with some of the groups here and we try to coordinate when she comes across for demonstrations."

It had seemed as if this would be the start of a lengthy discourse but instead Julia stopped abruptly, as though those three sentences would erase any uncertainty. It forced Camden to probe further. "Did you coordinate this time?"

When conversing with people for whom English was not their first language, he'd developed a habit of adopting their phrases to bridge any ambiguity between them.

Julia weighed up the question and looked at him cagily. "I wasn't sure if she was coming over this time or not."

"What made you think she wasn't coming over?" Camden asked, eyes narrowing slightly.

"I don't know. She asked for Malachi's new number because he changes phone every few weeks. I gave it to her, but she didn't talk about concrete plans." Julia seemed to drift off into her own thoughts and was given space to do so. "But then again, she was pretty vague. I'd already told her that I wouldn't be joining the demonstrations this time. Things have been getting out of hand recently."

"Do you have a number for Malachi?" Camden asked.

"It doesn't seem to be working. But that's not so unusual after an event," Julia continued, as though she viewed each of her counterpoints as being of great help. "He'll often get rid of his phone and change number. I wouldn't be surprised if he did that, especially this time."

"Do you know where he is?" Camden tried.

"I don't know of anyone who has seen Malachi since Thursday night." Her manner implied that such a disappearance could be either fatal or inconsequential.

Evelina maintained a stillness akin to someone who had wandered into the frame of an incriminating photo.

Camden's eyes searched the surroundings as though suddenly cataracted. Eventually, he managed to locate his next question. "When was the last time you actually saw her?"

Julia wore a look that suggested she was surprised she hadn't already provided these details. "I don't know." The pizza plate apparently held the answer, as five seconds of sharing her thoughts with it produced an extremely specific response. "April 12th. It was a Saturday."

"OK," Camden said with a cautious nod. "Was that one of the protests?"

Julia stiffened slightly. "Yeah, I guess."

His optimism ebbed. "What aren't you telling me?" he muttered quietly, before shifting his weight forward and leaning his elbows on the table. "I've got so many questions," he said with renewed purpose. "I'm going to ask them all, one after the other, OK?"

Julia's eyes were wide and unblinking; Evelina's weight adjusted onto her right elbow as though a formal event had just ended, and this was the beginning of a catch-up with old friends. "Ask your questions," she said with a smirk lurking nearby.

He was glad to have brought Evelina back into the conversation: his judgment was that Julia could give some useful facts, but Evelina held the key to knitting everything together for them, if she were so inclined. "When did you first meet Crissa?"

"Six years ago," Julia's chin slanted briefly to her right as she answered. "2008."

He decided against taking issue with the fact that she'd partially checked her answer with Evelina as she delivered it. "Where did you meet?"

"We had similar circles of friends. We'd often find ourselves chatting to each other at the end of long nights. We'd make each other laugh back then."

Unbidden and without a glance, Evelina offered a cigarette which Julia eagerly grabbed and leaned in to gain a light.

"Go on," Camden encouraged, in case Evelina had made the gesture to disrupt the flow.

"I'd dropped out of university by then. I hadn't lasted long, less than a year." She chuckled at this in a way that could be construed as either pride or embarrassment. "There was nowhere that made sense for me to go. Groups of us would meet up, sometimes to party, sometimes to talk, sometimes not to talk."

"What kind of things would you talk about?"

She shrugged. "All kinds of things. The usual."

He didn't explore this further. "This was 2009?"

"Probably. The years have been hazy recently."

It was the type of puzzling answer that jeopardised Camden's best efforts to navigate the conversation smoothly. "What does that mean?"

"Things haven't gone so well since those days."

"In what ways?"

"Lots of ways. I barely notice the seasons anymore."

Feeling marooned, Camden decided on a different tactic. "What do you do now, Julia?"

Evelina twisted round to fully take in the answer Julia was about to give, seemingly entertained.

"What do you mean?" Julia's confusion seemed genuine.

"Do you work? Did you ever go back to university?"

"University was never a good fit for me."

"Right," he nodded, as though the answer was just the one he was looking for.

"I'm not really sure how I'd describe what I do."

Camden held his palms apart. "Try," he shrugged with an unthreatening smile.

"I don't really think that society works here," she replied. "I guess that's what this is all about."

"What what is all about?"

"What we do. These past few years. By the time I left university and got to know Crissa and Evelina, everything was starting to change. We'd speak about what that meant for us if we did nothing, and what it would mean if we did something. Some people find it strange that I'm a member of several of the different movement groups. They don't like it; they think I should pick one and throw myself into it. Some call me a tourist. I don't think it matters."

He blinked away Julia's answer. "What about you, Evelina? What are you a part of?"

"Who do you think you are?" she answered, nostrils flaring in unexpected anger. "Elbowing your way into our lives with your stupid fucking questions."

"Put yourselves in my shoes—"

"I hate that expression," Evelina retorted, "it's so redundant."

"Let me put it a different way, then," he said, volume rising. "I'm desperate to find Crissa. You're supposed to be good friends of hers and yet when I ask questions that might help me find her, Julia avoids them because she's scared, and you dance around them as if it's some kind of game."

"Julia's not scared, she's just Julia. It amazes me that these are the questions you think will bring you to Crissa. It makes me wonder what you've been talking about these past twelve months. Whether you've really got to know each other at all or whether you've scratched the surface and decided that's enough."

Camden made to speak but was cut off before he had the chance.

"There's a reason you're here, by the way. Specifically, here," Evelina clarified, "in these seats, in this restaurant."

Despite her objections upon arrival, the way Julia was perched on her chair—listening intently to each word—made it hard to tell if she was entirely clear on that reason.

"It's because it's opposite that cafe." Evelina pointed across the road at a building with a brown wooden frontage and writing scrawled across it in cream coloured paint: *Stoicheía*. The chairs outside looked as though they'd been haphazardly mixed up for the start of an elaborate version of the cup and ball game. The furniture inside was no more structured. Had Evelina not specified, he would never have guessed it was a cafe.

"University ended badly for Crissa and if she hasn't told you the details about that then she has her reasons. Neither of us liked the skin we were in, so we did all the standard things that make you feel better about yourself for a short amount of time and then worse about yourself over the long haul. Do you need me to spell it out for you?"

Camden discreetly shook his head.

"By the time things had started to recalibrate for us they were tipping out of control across the rest of the country. When we started university, one out of every five young people couldn't find a job. That had ticked up to one in four within a year. The next year it was thirty percent, then forty percent, fifty percent, sixty percent," she clicked her fingers as she revealed each number, her speech gathering pace. "What was the point of taking on debt with those types of prospects waiting for you?

"Everyone could see what was happening. I can't believe it's taken so long to come to a head but here we are. Young people have always been at the vanguard of that. They saw a future that they knew their parents would never have wished for them, which they had no intention of passing onto their children and—in our land's finest tradition—protest groups sprang up, pockets of discontent amongst those who were worst affected or least willing to take it lying down. There wasn't much in the way of structure at first, but you had to admire the passion and the verve, so long as you could get past the unruly factions that always crop up, whether through stupidity or infiltration.

"You probably don't understand the writing on the sign over there. It means Elements. Crissa named it. You remember that night, Julia?"

Julia nodded enthusiastically, as though being read a bedtime story.

"By that stage, Crissa had become the glue for disparate groups of protesters who previously hadn't been able to fit their egos into the same room. She pulled strings, got them exposure, built alliances. Her more impulsive tendencies were under better control," Evelina said, choosing her words with precision.

Camden sat straight in his chair.

"Crissa didn't want to be front and centre, but she held serious sway. Malachi was enraptured with her, and his quest for her only increased Crissa's influence over the members of the movement.

"We would meet there," she said, again nodding towards the cafe. "Malachi's uncle used to own it. The movement had to shift its meetings elsewhere as its presence grew. The name remains. Would you like to know how it was christened?"

He may have nodded.

"In the initial stages, when Crissa had brought the group together, we decided we needed a name. There was a lot of talk, some terrible suggestions. Julia came up with an idea that resonated for us." Evelina looked at Julia invitingly.

"I said I thought we should be like the wind, able to rise up or disappear at any time," she beamed.

"Crissa let everyone get comfortable with Julia's concept, then added her own. 'We should be all the elements,' she said, and it stuck."

The image he carried of Crissa living out an episode from her past—regardless of whether he could relate to its context—was enough to bring to Camden a smile and a wave of warmth.

"And here again," Evelina continued, piercing the moment, "she's become elemental."

Chapter 17

For each of the friends—for differing reasons—that Sunday was a chaotic, churning, pivotal day.

Dean waited in a cafe off the town square. He was one of a handful of customers. On the table in front of him a third coffee sat half-empty and cold, partnered by a large still water that had been bought in the hope it would bring him calm.

"How you holding up?" he asked Morton, who arrived looking like he needed a drink that would deliver more concrete results.

Morton's eyebrows twitched in reply, and he held up Dean's bottle to the advancing waitress by way of placing his order.

Within seconds she arrived at Morton's side with a glass full of ice, a bottle of water and an approving gaze. He thanked her without meeting her eyes and she lingered a little longer than necessary before retreating inside.

Morton gulped his water. It was his first drink in over an hour and came under the midday sun. His clothes were streaked with dust and grime from his earlier exertions at Salvation, when it was still in his possession. "I can't get in touch with my old man."

"He'll be in the air now, right?"

"Yeah. Due in at twenty to two."

"I'll come with you to pick him up."

Morton swept his head away from the square towards the milling tourists. "Any joy with the embassy?"

"Spoke to the same woman that pissed me off the last two days. You'd think I was trying to order a new bin or something. No fucking urgency. Might have raised my voice a little. It got her attention anyway: that and a call to Rosey."

"You called Rosey?"

"Seemed like he could get our voice heard."

Morton smiled. "How's he doing?"

"Good," Dean nodded. "He's an editor these days and there's been some coverage of the riots over here. He fancied the 'Brits trapped abroad' angle. I told him it was Gary and Tom, and he was more interested in them being OK than running a story."

"You hear from him much?"

"Not as much as I'd like to. I spoke to him first thing this morning—felt like things needed a fresh approach. Sounded like he'd had a late night, but once I gave him the details, he was wide awake. He called me soon after to say he'd phoned the embassy asking for a response to a troubling emerging story he'd been made aware. Suggested it would be a good time to give them a call."

Morton nodded approvingly.

"She says they're 'pulling out all the stops.'" Dean permitted himself a small grin.

"Good. Keep that phone handy for when the call comes in. Let's go," Morton said, finishing the water in his glass and taking the rest of the bottle with him. "We've still got the apartment. We can base ourselves there."

Dean laid twenty Euros under the ashtray after showing it to the waitress, who replied from her barstool with a distracted waft of her hand before resuming her consumption of a soap opera.

———•———

Each hour was bleeding into the next for Gary and Tom. Stretches of prolonged stillness were ruptured by brief disputes amongst their fellow inmates. It was 1pm when Gary rose to his feet at the sight of a police officer opening the door for the hourly toilet break. He joined a line of nine people, two-thirds of the way back. They were escorted around the back of the building in a relay of pairs. Outside, presented with four metallic buckets offering an unenticing selection of bathroom facilities, Gary focused his attention on the unremitting sun that pounded the ground.

On the numerous occasions that it had been Tom's turn to relieve himself in the company of strangers and assorted insects, he'd become awash with a mixture of stage fright and repulsion. Pissing wasn't too bad, but the buckets that were half-full of other malnourished men's faeces tested his gag reflex. He got it over with as quick as he could, breathing no more than twice throughout the ordeal and wiping himself with the paltry toilet paper that had been placed an awkward few steps away, on a low wall. That had been Saturday morning. As he watched Gary depart, he prayed they would be released before a second visit made itself irresistible.

There was a gentle thud beside him and when he looked to his left, the guy in the black hoodie and khaki shorts had reappeared on the bench with that same smile flitting between good-natured and unhinged, emphasised by an extra day's dishevelment. His t-shirt was less white than before and he'd approached unnoticed by circling widely around the room, hugging the walls.

"Troubles?" he asked.

Tom eyed him for a second then looked away, but his visitor persevered and moved his face close.

"I asked: do you have troubles?"

Tom steadied himself: "Fuck off."

The man released his trademark combination of breath and teeth. "You learn that from your friend?"

Tom fixed his eyes on the ground and tried to stay loose.

Laughter again. "It's good to know who your friends are. You find out one way or another, am I right?"

Despite himself, Tom frowned and turned to him, unsure of what to say or do next, until the space between them was filled by Gary, who pushed on both of their shoulders to move them apart so that he could drop himself onto the bench.

"Who the fuck you pushing?" the man yelled, springing to his feet. His question was immediately answered by Gary firing both hands into his chest and knocking him over. Carrying momentum, Gary stepped forward and drove his fist into the man's stomach as he tried to haul himself from the floor, leaving him momentarily incapacitated.

Within an instant of landing his blows, Gary had two men on him, one grabbing his face from behind with both hands and trying to get him into a headlock, the other sweeping round from the side to land rapid-fire body shots. Shaking himself loose from a familiar paralysis in the face of a fight, Tom hurled himself towards the headlocker to execute a rugby tackle that bowled them both across the concrete floor with a hefty wallop, scattering the other inhabitants of a room so cramped that any fight was destined to quickly become one resolved within close quarters.

Freed from the arms around his head and neck, Gary spun and pounded his opponent's body, following up quickly with two sharp kicks to the outside of his knees. They were the last impacts he made as the crowd engulfed him like a whirlpool and his best option became the foetal position, in which he remained even after he heard the doors being flung open and his adversaries being dragged away.

———•———

A lizard made a desperate dash between the bushes lining the pavement outside the airport before stopping in petrified stasis when Dean's head turned sharply in its direction.

"Ever seen a nonchalant lizard?" he asked. "They never seem to go out for a relaxing stroll, do they?"

Morton briefly studied the creature but didn't speak for a while, resisting Dean's attempt at light-hearted distraction. "It's funny, I've been trying to put myself in everyone else's shoes these past few days and the one person I find hardest to pin down is my dad. Always have."

"How did he sound when you spoke to him on the phone?"

"It all sounded like part of a big plan he'd put together. But that's just how he operates. The more chaotic things get, the more he acts like he's in control."

"Sounds familiar."

Morton smiled with an infinitesimal nod. The terminal stood opposite. It was one-thirty. "I know you're talking about me, but you show some of the same traits, you know."

Dean weighed that up. "I've not felt in control for a long time."

"You ever see her?"

"I don't want to see her," Dean shook his head, referring to Caroline. "It wouldn't accomplish anything."

Morton stayed quiet.

"In some ways, I came to terms with it almost immediately; in other ways, it feels like I'm still reeling, two years later."

"It was harsh on you, man."

"Yeah, but in a way that made a brutal kind of sense. We'd always felt so natural together it lulled me into a false sense of security. We didn't fight. Just glided along. And then all of a sudden ..." He took a moment. "She did the right thing. Not the way she did it, that wasn't good. But even as she was telling me—angry and upset as I was—I recognised why she was doing it."

"You're more forgiving than I would be."

"Storing up anger doesn't do any good. I'm not sure I've come to terms with what it says about me, though."

"What d'you mean?"

"I was a spectator through the whole thing. When I talk about it, it's like watching a film for the second time, not believing that I fell for the plot twist the first time around."

"I don't think any of us saw it coming, mate."

"Yeah, but you guys weren't living it. I was there; I should've seen something was up."

"Maybe too close to notice."

"It's over, it's fine," Dean gently dismissed the conversation with a flick of his hand. "I'm just having a problem getting galvanised again, you know? It's like I'm living in muted colours."

Morton regarded him for a few seconds. "Before Camden and I moved over here, you were definitely closing yourself off."

"I know it's not the right way to go about things."

"You don't have to justify yourself. You went through a tough time, and I don't know anyone else who experienced what you did, in the way that you did. Take as much or as little time as you need. Look at what you're doing here: without you, Gary and Tom would be completely stranded. You've been a big help keeping me on an even keel. You're the same friend we've always known, just rearranged."

Morton had a few stones in his hand and tossed them gently into the nearby scrubland. Dean watched him without comment.

"I thought you might have been interested in setting up the business with us," Morton suggested.

"Maybe at a different time. There have been a couple of occasions when I've thought 'what if', but my head wouldn't have been in the right place."

"Talking past tense there. Maybe that means your head's in a different place now." He let the comment hang in the air.

Dean's face conceded little. "Any ideas what you'll do about Salvation?" he asked.

"Too many variables at this point," came the distracted reply, as Morton stood up from his seat on the wall and took two steps towards the dusty car park. His eyes were fixed diagonally left as he moved.

Dean tracked his line of sight and saw two police cars followed by two black sedans driving along a slip road towards the runway.

Morton's feet kept him moving to the soundtrack of an approaching plane—the fourth or fifth arrival in the twenty minutes they'd been sitting—and Dean tried to catch him without breaking into a run. A third police car now navigated the slip road. Morton's walk looked almost involuntary—Dean didn't recognise it.

The automatic doors swooshed open. They entered the terminal building and an aeroplane flashed from right to left across the windows at the far end, having just made its landing. Five steps in, Morton glanced at the arrivals board, where at that precise moment the information about the flight from Gatwick vanished from the screen, which then promptly gave up its transmission and displayed only blue. He glanced over his shoulder at Dean as though this was only the latest in a series of revelations being laid out before them. A police car pulled up outside the glass doors on the runway side, next to which the airport security guards looked as though they were trying out a more combative stance for the first time.

Morton turned as inconspicuously as he could back towards the entrance, beyond which he would gain a freer view of the runway in its entirety.

As Morton passed him without eye contact, Dean's phone jumped in his pocket. *Police Station*, read the screen. Confounded, he slowly exited the doors, watching Morton cross back over to the wall where they'd previously sat and wondering whether the phone call he was about to take was related to the activity unfolding before him.

"Hello? Hello?" the voice on the phone probed. Dean realised he'd answered the call but forgotten to speak.

"Yes?"

"Mr Lockwood?"

"Yes."

Nikopolidis' velvety voice was unmistakable, even under fraught and noisy circumstances.

"Your friends are ready to be released to you."

"That's great news. When?"

"As soon as you get here."

"Wait," Dean said, needing to slow things down so he could keep pace. "That's why you're calling?"

"Of course. Your embassy is a pain in my ass. How quickly can you get to the station?"

"As soon as I can."

He cut the connection with Nikopolidis still talking. Morton had climbed a chain-link fence some thirty yards away and, shielding his eyes from the sun as he twisted, held for a few moments before dropping onto his haunches, hands cupped over the bottom half of his face. Dean traced his friend's footsteps and assumed the same vantage point, from where he saw the police cars and sedans in a semi-circle around the base of the ladders coming down from the front of an EasyJet plane. Morton kept his back to him, studying the screen of his phone. Each sound from their surroundings made itself individually audible to Dean, his senses heightened and his mind incapable of deciding on the appropriate action.

Morton took the decision out of his hands, presenting the phone over his shoulder, its screen lit up and containing a message from Anthony which had been sent two minutes earlier. It read: *Son, they'll arrest me when I land. Stay calm. Be you. It'll be OK.*

Chapter 18

Dean scanned Morton's demeanour as he killed the engine and exited the car outside the police station. Rather than trauma or disorientation, he emitted a relaxed focus on their next task.

There had been no further texts from his father, who presumably no longer had access to his phone nor the free hands to use it. Morton had advised Dean that they would go together to retrieve Gary and Tom from the jail, no more than a few seconds after witnessing the runway scene and before Dean could source the appropriate words.

The more chaotic things get, Dean reflected, and turned his attentions to the police officer standing at the doorway of the station, indicating they should turn right as they entered. This had become familiar territory for Dean in recent days, the setting for his twice-daily conversations with Gary and Tom, fitted into ten-minute windows before Nikopolidis returned, unerringly punctual, to disperse them in their appointed directions and reclaim his office.

Dean clocked that something wasn't right. Nikopolidis was in his customary position behind his desk but looked physically strained and distinctly ill-at-ease. Dean nodded in his direction before turning towards Gary and Tom, who sat delicately on two narrow chairs that were placed with their backs against the roadside window.

"What the fuck has happened here?" Dean roared at Nikopolidis. Morton poked his head round the corner to investigate. Tom's white shirt was tie-dyed with blood and his light grey blazer was folded in three separate pieces on his lap. Gary's clothes were in better condition—ripped jeans being the most prominent damage—but he seemed incapable of uncoiling his vertebrae or finding a comfortable sitting position.

"Don't ever talk to me like that!" commanded Nikopolidis, his right index finger stabbing the air in front of him.

"You told me that my friends were ready to be released," Dean replied without pause. "'Your embassy is a pain in my arse' was what you said. I wonder what they'll think about the condition they're in when they're released."

"Your friends started a fight by assaulting a local man in a room full of local men, all of whom have been locked up for sixty hours."

This was the first time Morton had seen Nikopolidis and he made an instant judgment of a man fumbling to keep his authority intact.

"Detaining dozens of people indefinitely in unfit facilities was your decision."

"They instigated—"

"I'm not going to argue with you about what happened," Dean held up his hand to cut him off. "I don't know because I wasn't there and, clearly, neither were you or your men, otherwise we wouldn't be having this conversation. Now you've mostly been reasonable with me during an unreasonable time. I understand the stress that you're under and how compromised your position is, but what happens after we leave this building depends completely on what happens between this moment right now and the moment we walk out that door." Dean had adopted Nikolopolidis' pointed-finger gesturing to make clear his position.

Nikopolidis breathed in deeply and didn't seem to send the air back out of his lungs. "We've had a doctor check them both. Overall, they are fine, although this one may have cracked a couple of ribs." His gesture didn't make clear which of the two had sustained the injuries, but Gary's tortured expression and shallow breathing dropped big hints.

"I would say his ribs have been cracked on his behalf," Dean corrected.

"There's some paperwork to be completed," Nikopolidis continued, ignoring the interruption. "I'll give you ten minutes with your clients and then we can agree whether the paperwork is to be signed and your clients released, or whether we have further things to discuss."

He maintained eye contact until Dean nodded and gave quiet agreement, at which point his attention turned towards the doorway. "Who is this?"

Hands in pockets, Morton leant against the doorframe as though oblivious to the enquiry.

"If he can't answer simple questions then he can't be in here. This isn't a cafe."

"My business was destroyed in the protests a couple of nights ago. Despite my requests for help, all the police have managed to do is ignore my phone calls and arrest my father. Do you expect my thanks and respect?"

Gary and Tom's mouths gawped at this news.

"Ah. Mr Morton, yes?" Nikopolidis nodded. "While they make their arrangements, perhaps we can talk in private."

———•———

By the time Morton and Dean had transported Gary and Tom back to the apartment, the elation of freedom had capitulated in the face of overwhelming fatigue.

Within minutes of walking through the door, both had changed out of their clothes, paid their first quick—but noteworthy—visits to a plumbed bathroom since Thursday and dragged themselves to separate bedrooms.

The whirring of an insect stirred Gary some time later. His eyes peeled open, and he flicked his hand instinctively around his face, anticipating a mosquito. The whirring stopped, then resumed again from across the darkness. *Phone*, he thought, but stayed motionless on his side, curled up in one of the few positions that didn't send a shot of pain across his ribcage. Four petulant vibrations were all it managed before ceasing. He'd somnambulated into a room he didn't recognise.

Before he could unearth any answers, the vibrations restarted, sounding weirdly more insistent each time. He crawled across to his bag. It wasn't until he searched the fourth compartment that he found the phone, by which time it had given up again. He clicked the button on the front to see who had called: *Jo*.

Not now, he decided, but kept a hold of the phone as he clambered backwards to his previous position on the bed. As he moved to place it on the bedside table, the screen lit up again.

"Hey," he said sleepily.

"You alright?" Jo asked. It was a tone of challenge rather than concern.

"I'm OK," he replied, bringing himself upright.

"Yeah?"

He massaged his forehead with his free hand. "Yeah, I'm fine."

There was nothing he wanted to say, and Jo seemed disinclined to fill the silence.

"When were you going to tell me?" she asked finally.

"Which part?"

She sighed heavily and stifled a sniff. "Do you know how I found out?"

"Does it matter?"

"It matters."

"Lucy," he decided, inwardly cursing his former cellmate.

"She phoned me straight after speaking to Tom. 'Oh my God, can you believe what they've been through?' I felt like such an idiot, having to ask what she was talking about. We both felt like idiots."

"I'm sorry, Jo."

"Why would you do that to me?"

He closed his eyes to suppress the sweep of heat that he felt rumbling around the base of his neck. "Do what to you?"

"A normal person would phone as soon as he got out of jail."

"It wasn't a normal situation."

"Still," she insisted.

"It's been a hard few days, Jo. I wasn't trying to make you look stupid, I just wasn't thinking."

"Weren't thinking about me, you mean." A number of seconds passed before she spoke again. "I'm sorry."

"For what, Jo? Be honest, before you heard from Lucy, were you thinking of me?"

"Of course I was."

"You didn't text or call, not once. Not even to reply when I said I'd landed. And, you know what? That's fine. That's us."

"That's us?"

"We're so remote."

"We're just comfortable with each other."

Gary shook his head in frustrated resignation. It was a call he'd been expecting, perhaps even waiting for. "No, we're not."

———•———

A few hours later, Morton was back at the airport that he now knew with such vivid resentment. Having landed on time, Camden emerged from the baggage area as though he was on wheels, being pushed along from behind.

"Didn't expect anyone to be here with everything else going on. Was gonna call a cab."

Morton refuted the notion with an indistinct syllable and took Camden's bag without invitation. "Not the type of day when sitting around seems appealing," he observed, by way of explanation.

"How are Gary and Tom?"

"Out," Morton said with a restrained smile.

"Fantastic news."

"Yeah. Earlier this afternoon. Seems they had a bit of aggro before getting released."

"They ok?"

"Yeah. Gary might have a couple of cracked ribs but he's holding up, you know how he is. Sounds like their fight was the reason they were let go; that and Dean haranguing the embassy every chance he got."

Camden slunk into the passenger seat and Morton smoothly navigated the snaking roads.

"Was hoping to see two of you coming through those doors," Morton said after a while.

"Things didn't work out that way," Camden said.

"How did you get on?"

"Well, now I've met her family," Camden shrugged.

"How was that?" Morton tiptoed through his questions.

"Not how I'd imagined it."

"Had they seen her?"

Camden slowly shook his head and continued to answer an earlier question. "I met a couple of her friends earlier today."

"Oh? Ones you knew?"

"Ones I'd heard about."

"Could they shed any light?"

"Not in the right places," Camden answered simply. "Been a tough couple of days."

Morton widened his peripheral vision and saw his business partner looking vacantly out of the front and passenger windows, as though being driven to a dental check-up. He'd taken temporary leave of the conversation.

Morton let the silence hang to see what filled it. They were halfway home before Camden spoke again, asking the question that he should have asked within moments of Morton meeting him.

"How are things with the bar?"

Morton gave him a look. "Tough couple of days here, too."

"Yeah?" Camden asked casually.

"Yeah. Hard to know where to begin so I'll start at the end: my dad's been arrested."

"Arrested? What for?"

"Tax evasion, apparently. That government guy on the TV the other day—the day of the riots," he looked at Camden, "he was making accusations. Didn't name names but didn't hold back with his implications. And now he's disappeared."

Camden was quiet for a moment. "I'm confused."

"My Dad flew over after I told him what had happened to us. They arrested him before he got off the plane and transferred him to the mainland. They want him in the same place as the Melas brothers." They exchanged a glance at the mention of the name. "They're all implicated. Feels like they're the real targets of this and my dad's collateral damage, to be honest. Apparently, my dad was working with them on some deal over here. He hadn't spoken to me about it but that's not unusual. Some journalist came around and asked me what I thought about the rumours. Way he spoke about it, they sounded more like facts than rumours."

"Fuck."

"That's not all. All their assets in Greece have been seized. Including Salvation and the canava."

"They can do that?"

"Looks like it. 'All assets appropriated while the investigation is ongoing.'"

"What are we going to do?"

"I don't know. We'll figure it out, step at a time."

"Spoken to your mum?"

"And sister, yeah. They're worried. Been a bit of a battle convincing them not to fly over here."

"I'll bet. Jesus."

"I spoke to the chief of police while Dean was getting the guys discharged. Said you'd spoken to him."

"A couple of days ago," Camden said. "Nikopolidis."

"That's him."

"I went to see him the morning after the trouble, trying to find Crissa."

"He said," Morton nodded. "He seemed interested in helping you find her, once he's emptied his jail of all the people they've got crammed in there."

"Good," Camden said before lapsing back into silence.

"What are you thinking, mate?"

"A million things. Feels like our lives have been tipped upside down."

"What's your next move?"

"I have to find Crissa. It's the only thing I can do."

"Yeah."

"I found out some things about her while I was on the mainland. Things about her past. Her university days and just after. Sounded liked she had some tough times that we haven't talked much about."

"Her friends told you this?"

"Yeah. Nothing drastic, but it feels like there's more there. I just wanted to get back to make sure you guys are alright."

"The rest of them are OK. They'll head back tomorrow. That leaves you and me, and it feels like we have to split our efforts."

"I need to go to the mainland, Morton."

"I know it. And I need to try to get Salvation back on its feet and support my dad in whatever way I can. Just keep in touch. Calm heads will prevail."

Morton left the scene untouched by further words. He felt Camden drift further from the car and into the night.

———·———

When Morton moved to the kitchen to get a final round of drinks before they all headed to bed that evening, Gary followed him gingerly, cradling his torso through the discomfort of movement.

"You OK, mate?" Morton asked, spotting that he had company.

"Yes and no."

"You've had a unique few days."

"And you." He paused to allow Morton a chance to nod agreement. "What's the story with your dad?"

"His lawyer says he'll let me know when anything happens but that I shouldn't expect anything speedy. He sounds like he's used to getting what he wants, which is no surprise: my dad and his business partners aren't the type of guys who shop at a discount."

"I can't believe all this."

"Struggling with it myself." Morton tried to bring levity when he asked: "So, what's jail like?"

"Sore," Gary smiled through a grimace as he rolled his

shoulders and stretched his back. "It wasn't really jail like we would expect. More like an overcrowded hospital ward but without any amenities. You know: whitewashed walls, strip lights, that sort of thing."

Morton could only shake his head.

"I broke up with Jo," Gary added, lips drawn tight.

"When? Before you came out here?"

"No, while you were picking Camden up from the airport. Couple of hours ago."

Morton held his hands shoulder-width apart, as though inviting an embrace. "You OK?"

"Do I seem OK?"

Morton sized him up. "You kind of do."

"I've spoken to my sister. She and her fella will go round to the house and get my stuff, store it at their place. Just clothes and my own things. I don't need any of the rest of it. I don't want it to be … unpleasant."

Morton asked: "Why now?"

Gary leaned back on the kitchen counter. "I should've thrown my hat in with you and Camden from the very start. I wanted to. Just didn't know how to reconcile myself with doing it. I should've heeded my instincts sooner."

Morton put a hand on his shoulder. "In that case, better late than never: welcome to whatever's left."

A smile grew across Gary's face. It felt unrestrained and unfamiliar.

———•———

Gary and Tom shook hands at the airport late the following morning.

"Keep in touch, alright?" Tom urged.

"Look after yourself," Gary replied. They shared a look.

"Let us know how things are going," Dean said as they started to move towards check-in.

"Will do," Morton said.

"Keep him out of jail if you can," Dean added, pointing at Gary, who smiled back in response.

Camden managed handshakes and waves but little else.

As Dean felt Tom's entire body clench in the seat next to him in the seconds before the wheels of the plane left the runway, he tried to focus on things that would occupy his mind. He sifted through some of the details that Camden had divulged about his visit to the mainland and wondered how he'd managed to return home with so few answers. He ruminated on the change of direction that Gary had just taken in his life, both in his dismissal of his relationship with Jo and the sudden distance in his friendship with Tom. And he reflected on how, when Morton had suggested that he join them in rebuilding Salvation, he hadn't given it a moment's thought before rejecting the notion. As Santorini slipped out of view of his window seat, Dean recognised his reasoning: the friendships around him were changing, their motivations existing as much in the shadows as in the light. He was beginning to feel like, until further notice, they were no longer the valuable currency they had once been.

Twelve hours later, Camden's flight descended into the capital towards the landmarks, people, and stories he'd moved between the previous two days. His only luggage was his backpack, which he slipped over his shoulders before disembarking and making for the airport exit.

Time to go looking.

It was Monday, the 5th of May.

Part Two

Departures

Chapter 19

A bench became free as a couple—perhaps them in twenty years—stood up and made their way towards the park exit, lunch hour presumably over. Selena transitioned from a stroll into a comical gait, her stride length halving and its cadence tripling as she raced to secure the seat. She giggled up at Dean from her victorious position.

"Discreet," he smiled. "Don't think anyone noticed."

"I'm a master of the subtle arts."

The mid-June sun broke through the sparse clouds as Dean positioned himself close enough that their legs and shoulders would regularly brush against each other. Selena tried to take a dainty bite from her ciabatta, but its stubborn texture meant she had to twist and rip at it to complete the motion, leaving her to manipulate a huge mouthful into more manageable form. Dean suppressed a grin.

"I see you!" she pointed, covering her mouth to keep its contents in place while laughing.

"I like a girl who gorges on her food."

Selena said nothing further until she had completed her chewing. "You just called me gorgeous." By the time he'd turned to face her, she was looking mischievously away, shoe suspending itself from her gently dangling right foot, legs crossed.

Despite his best efforts, Dean was still a little cagey. "You are gorgeous."

"You're not so bad yourself," she replied. "And you can rub yourself against me anytime you want. No need to feel that you have to get strategic about it."

He smiled and looked across Park Square, on the southwest corner of which sat their offices, in the Civic Quarter of Leeds.

"The jerk chicken must be spicier than normal. You're all flushed," Selena said, moving her head so that she was in his line of vision, her mint green eyes looking up into his.

Four dates in, it wasn't yet clear in Dean's mind what they had. Their boss had hosted a barbecue to mark the year's first weekend of glorious weather a fortnight earlier and Dean had been in two minds whether to attend. He decided to show face, at least until the first few people started to disappear. The office employed a couple of dozen or so and the barbecue boasted full attendance plus partners and children.

As a weather front of smoke from the charring meat spread across the sizeable patio, a few of the younger employees went for a walk towards the koi pond.

"Wow, there are so many of them," said Selena, her unmalleable marmalade hair sitting atop her Y-shaped frame and jangling knees.

"I know," Dave concurred, sidling next to her. Dave was

a barrel and seemed to have an aversion to fastening the top two buttons of any shirt he owned, showcasing a plume of chest hair of which he seemed quite fond. Regardless of his quirks, he was popular in the office.

"I've always thought that having fish would be relaxing," he continued. He'd nurtured a prodigious beard for a few months before being counselled over its unsuitability for a law firm such as McCulloch and Mitchell. Now it qualified as grooming, all neat edges and equal length. It made it even harder to tell whether he was twenty-five or thirty-five. "Although I'd always imagined them being in a tank and having a dozen or so. Nothing on this scale."

"They do nothing for me," said Rav, who sported an excellent side-parted quiff and looked like he could equal Dave's beard growth by late afternoon if the notion took him. He was impeccably dressed as always—as though he shopped by outfit rather than individual garment—and along with Dean and Selena was one of the rising stars of the company.

"Really?" asked Dean. "How come?"

"Never really got the thing about pets," he replied with a shrug. "Don't understand the fascination."

"Depends on the pet," Dave opined, nodding at the pond. "They all serve a different purpose. I can see how these guys would relax you."

"We always had pets growing up," Selena added. "Dogs and rabbits. Taught us a lot about responsibility when we were kids and they become part of the family. We were distraught when they died, though."

"That's the thing, see," Rav stated. "Those things you say are great about them completely turn me off. All I hear is hassle and loss."

"Do you rest your case, Rav?" Dean asked.

"I rest my case," Rav smiled. That had been a stock phrase of his when he joined the firm three years previous, as though it was a legal requirement for him to end any discussion with the words. More driven than Dean and more ruthless than Selena, Rav nonetheless had yet to develop the softer side of his game and had already used up a few goodwill tokens in his two years with the firm. Despite that, Dean liked him and would break his general rule of rarely blending his work and social life to grab lunch together and arrange the occasional game of squash, at which Rav was such a superior player that it made it enjoyable for Dean just to be thrashed by him.

"Food's up!" came the shout from the patio, prompting the group to follow their noses.

"Look at that one," Selena had said, holding Dean in place and pointing to a tiger-coloured fish weaving dynamically through the features of the pool in incessant figures of eight.

"Looks like a simple life," Dean said, expecting his pithy line to be the signal for them to join the feasting.

Instead, Selena placed her fingers on his elbow. "Stop spectating."

Dean felt his throat tighten. "You've lost me, Selena."

She folded her arms across the peach chiffon blouse that sat on her waist above dark denim. "We should talk. How about we get out of here in an hour or so and get a drink somewhere in town?"

"Selena. That's not a good idea," he said after a pause.

"Why not?" she asked, unmoved.

A pause again. "It's not something I'm looking for right now. I'm sorry." And with that, he walked back towards the patio. Within ninety minutes, he was at home alone watching the first of three back-to-back movies.

The next day he woke late and slowly, the uneasy feeling of a recent misjudgment hovering over him. He walked for a Sunday paper, read it over two coffees and a large breakfast and returned home feeling much the same. Before he knew it the clock was showing 2pm.

Selena picked up after four rings and sounded as unsurprised to receive the call as she had been when she was rebuffed the previous day. They shared a few drinks, and she occasionally teased him during the four pleasant hours they spent together before pecking him on the cheek as she entered the taxi at 10pm. It had been their last chaste moment.

The park bench reverberated as his phone squirmed in his pocket. *Unknown Number*. "Hello?"

"Mr Lockwood?"

"Hi—hello," he stammered slightly, flat-footed at the sound of the familiar, heavily-accented voice. He raised an apologetic finger at Selena, leaving her to resume battle with her ciabatta.

"This is Dean Lockwood, yes?"

"Yes, it is." Dean kept his words spare as he moved away from the bench and underneath a tree that offered the type of shade nobody was interested in at that time of year.

"This is Georgios Nikopolidis."

"I know, I recognise the voice," Dean replied, safely out of earshot. "I just hadn't expected the call."

There was a slight silence before Nikopolidis spoke again. "I'm phoning because I need your help. I need to contact your friend, Christian Camden. I have some information that may help him find his girlfriend."

Chapter 20

When Dean got back to the office, he took a couple of minutes to check his emails and paperwork so that, when he then shifted himself to one of the adjacent rooms, it looked work-related. When he'd returned to Selena after ending the phone call from Nikopolidis he'd just about managed to disguise his agitation, hands firmly placed on his thighs to prevent the urge to fidget. Selena hadn't commented one way or the other.

The only room available was bigger than he wanted, making it possible that he'd be disturbed if a group of half a dozen people needed to have an impromptu meeting. No matter: he couldn't leave this percolating in his mind. He placed his notebook in front of him and fanned papers across the table in an attempt to dissuade anyone from casual interruptions, and then found the name he was looking for in his phone.

"You're through to Christian Camden," he was told. "Please leave a message."

"Camden, it's Dean. Hope everything's OK with you, been a few weeks. Listen, mate, I need to talk to you. I've had a phone call from the head of police in Santorini. He thinks he may have some information about Crissa. Phone me back. Whatever I'm doing, I'll make sure I take the call."

He pondered momentarily before dialling a different number.

"Morton, it's Dean."

"Hey, man, good to hear from you. How you doing?"

"Pretty good, mate, pretty good. Look, something's just come up that I want to talk to you about so forgive me for jumping straight into it."

"Go ahead."

"Remember that policeman we spoke to when we were trying to get Gary and Tom out?"

"I remember."

"Well, I've just had a phone call from him." He let the statement hang.

"Really?"

"Yeah. It was pretty unexpected."

"I can imagine."

"He says he has some information that might help Camden find Crissa."

"Right." There had been a pause.

"I've tried to call Camden but I'm just getting his voicemail. Is he with you guys?"

This time there was a short interval before Morton replied. "Mate, we haven't seen Camden since you boys flew home."

"What?"

"Yeah. He flew to the mainland later that same day. Last thing he said to me was that he was sorry but that he had to go and find Crissa. I told him I understood and that things would be waiting here when he gets back. Since then, nothing."

"I had no idea."

"To begin with it seemed logical. I'd do the same in his position. We know Camden and how he can go off the grid: I decided to give him space. Then a few weeks later a letter from him arrived at our apartment saying he was likely to be away for longer than expected and not to worry. Had four thousand Euros in it. To cover rent and expenses, he said. Don't know what he was thinking sending that amount of money through this postal service. I called him, got his voicemail same as you. That was a fortnight ago."

"There were times during our visit when he wasn't acting like himself. What's he up to?"

"I don't know. Listen, I'll talk to this police guy and see where that takes us."

"Thanks." Dean tapped his pen on his notepad. "So how are things with you?"

"Mixed, mate. My dad's out but he can't access his money here or get into any of his properties. He's staying with some friends in the capital, trying to apply whatever pressure he can to change the situation. His business partners are doing the same: they're in the news every couple of days being pilloried. Guilty until proven innocent. They've got some of the best lawyers in the country working on it but no dice so far."

"What about Salvation?"

"Nothing doing there either. Owned by my dad and his partners so I can't get within ten yards of the place. It's killing me: the island's buzzing with tourists and I can only watch it pass on by. Same for the canava."

"Your apartment's still ok, right?"

"Yeah, we rent that and the landlord's cool with us. Gary's moved in and he's ready to help once we can get back into Salvation. His ribs have healed up pretty well, turned out they were bruised rather than broken. In the meantime, it's good to have some company. Think we're both keeping each other sane."

"Tell him I'm asking after him."

"Will do. You heard from Tom?"

"No, nothing."

Dean waited for Morton to speak. "You OK, mate?" he asked when nothing was forthcoming.

"Yep," came the immediate reply, as though he'd snapped back into action. "Just thinking. You sound different, by the way."

"Really, in what way?"

"Not sure. I can tell this is weighing on your mind a bit but there's something else in there. You found yourself a love interest, Deano?"

Dean chuckled. "You scare me, Morton."

"Ha ha. I know the signs. Have fun, look after yourself. I'll be in touch."

Chapter 21

Boats glanced across the water in the caldera, leaving wisps of white wake behind. A cruise liner was approaching, where it would join another which had beaten it to the punch. The north-western side of the island was rugged cliff face interspersed with a clutch of buildings seemingly sitting on top of each other in a way that reminded him of clambering crabs. The north-eastern side was a sparser affair, with collections of houses rather than towns. Although less than ten miles apart, life moved slower there. To the south were the volcanic beaches and their appending tourist clusters, bodies already in situ for another day of hard-earned inactivity.

It was the third Tuesday in June. Tourist season in full swing.

Sweat was emerging under Nikopolidis' dense hair. He mopped it away, folding his handkerchief carefully and returning it to the pocket of his suit trousers. In the seven weeks since the protests had unexpectedly ignited the island, he'd captured only snippets of sleep and fleeting moments of relaxation with his children. They were the reason he'd moved here, to escape the peril and antisocial hours of city policing that he'd endured in his attempts to further his career after graduation. He had met his wife a year before enrolling and saw his chosen profession as honourable, if undervalued. Money wasn't his motivation. His mother had raised him and his elder sister single-handedly and one of the many lessons she'd inscribed within him was that a worthwhile job was one where you worked hard, honestly and for a worthy cause so that you could provide your family with a full, enjoyable life. To her, family, faith, and community were the only truly important things in the world. He wished she could have seen the man he'd become. His sister had told him many times about how proud she would have been of him but, despite being forty-five years old now, he still needed his mother's validation to really believe it.

He reflected on the fact that he'd been described by friends, colleagues, enemies, and his wife as stoic. He hoped that characteristic would at some point pay dividends. Its merits were proving elusive at the present time.

The experience of the past few weeks had been sobering. Never in his years on the force had he received so much attention, and none of it was welcome. He'd been given specific orders to hold suspected protesters for twenty-four hours in order to prevent a repeat, and that would have proven challenging enough. The follow-up order that came the next day—stating that they should be detained indefinitely pending an investigation into the disappearance of the Finance Minister—stretched the boundaries of what he felt was morally acceptable, let alone within the capability of the meagre facilities at the police station. When his superior officer and additional resources arrived three days later, he was upbraided for not better managing a situation with the British Embassy and was left feeling as though every decision he'd made had been in defiance of instructions and conventional wisdom.

And now this. He could really do with a smoke, if only he hadn't given up fourteen years earlier when his wife confirmed she was pregnant with the first of their four children. Now he was spinning multiple plates and felt like they were all too far apart for him to prevent at least some broken crockery. While not officially announced, he could feel the institutional machine circling him as it sought a scapegoat. Part of his conscience prodded him about the local girl who hadn't been seen since the protests and about whom nobody was asking anymore. That would rise up his to-do list at some point soon. In the meantime, Michael Andreas' whereabouts and the accompanying media scrutiny had been hanging over him like a noxious, heavy cloud. The investigation had yielded few results and his accountability for that failure was being made clear to him. It was affecting every part of his life and Gianna Andreas had become ever-present. At the time her husband had made his final public appearance across various media, she'd been visiting their son and some friends in London. Based on Nikopolidis' dealings with her, every indication was that theirs was a strained marriage in all respects. He'd spoken to her over the phone as the search gathered pace: "You don't get to Michael's position without making enemies," she had told him. "They'll have a field day with this."

He watched another plane make its approach into the airport on the east of the island until it was concealed behind the hills on its way to the runway and reflected on how much he and his family could use a holiday.

That felt far off at the moment, however. Nikopolidis could see increased movement from the workers some thirty feet below him, along with some animated chatter and exclamations. He began his descent towards them, wondering which outcome he would most prefer from the discovery that had just been made.

———•———

The two men approaching Nikopolidis had little in common besides their uniform. One was in his late forties, tall, broad-shouldered, and wide around the waist. His uniform may have fitted perfectly five years ago. The other was in his late twenties, well under six feet and weighed less than ten stone wet through. Despite the fact that he'd been on his hands and knees in dusty ground for the past two hours, his uniform was spotless and his hair unruffled. The mannerisms of the taller one suggested he was excited about what they'd just discovered; the shorter one looked pensive. Nikopolidis read them immediately.

A family of five British tourists had been visiting the ruins of Pyrgos' Venetian castle earlier in the day. As they were prone to doing, the three boys—aged between nine and twelve—set off exploring independently of their parents. Calls to them had gone unheeded so their father broke into a jog to corral them. He found the eldest first, sheepishly emerging from behind wire fencing that was intended to allow visitors to view the ruins while preventing them from trespassing. When asked the location of his brothers he reluctantly pointed further up the steps. The father had taken no more than half a dozen strides when he heard an exclamation from the direction he was headed. Breaking into a sprint, he almost clattered into his middle son as he turned a corner. Within five minutes he was carrying his youngest out of one of the many holes that punctuated the castle remains, nursing no more physical injuries than a sprained ankle, but shaken by his discovery of a body that had been buried in a shallow hole and covered with wooden boards.

"Tell me," Nikopolidis demanded, intentionally directing his words at the younger officer.

"It's him, sir."

A haze was settling over the towns below. Nikopolidis felt it as well as saw it.

Chapter 22

Camden leaned his head against the window of the couchette, watching the townscapes that dotted the scenic River Sava skipping by. Over the past day and a half, he'd skirted magnificent coastlines, tunnelled through mountains, and seen green plains open out hundreds of feet below him. He wished he'd seen none of it.

Two young American women in their early twenties shared the carriage with him. They'd spoken to each other incessantly for the first twenty minutes of the journey—seemingly both intoxicated and underwhelmed in equal measure by the discoveries of their travels up to that point—before falling asleep with such synchronicity that it suggested they had been practising for years, barely stirring in the hour since. The initial discomfort they displayed when they realised they'd be sharing with a solitary man seemed to vanish as soon as tiredness tapped them on the shoulder. They carried backpacks half their size and—judging by how they manoeuvred them—twice their body weight. They both wore their hair in practical styles that resembled matching pineapples. They had no idea he spoke English, having uttered not a word to him since entering the train compartment.

Thoughts swirled. It had been a week since the protests had prised he and Crissa apart. He closed his eyes for a moment and woke in Ljubljana.

———•———

When he had left Santorini a few days prior, the mainland had greeted him with indifference. A taxi had brought him to a hostel in Athens that he had looked up online. A short walk had taken him to Stoicheía, and he stood opposite it for a time with a cigarette in his hand. It was only the second time he'd smoked and the first time since university, when he once went for a three-hour walk and battled through a packet of twenty Marlboro before deciding it wasn't for him. The restaurant in which he had met Evelina and Julia the previous day had packed up for the night, so he concealed himself down the side alley between the restaurant and its neighbour. Over the road, Stoicheía looked as though it could alter its dimensions according to the number of its inhabitants: there were no more than twenty people in the place, yet it looked cramped. He recognised no faces.

He returned around lunchtime the following day, at which point staff outnumbered customers two to zero. The guy behind the counter had a beard that looked like it had grown out of laziness rather than design and wore a fitted black shirt lightened through sun exposure and a clutch of string bracelets around his forearm. He seemed keener on tattoos than smiles and had a white towel slung over his shoulder.

"Coffee, please," Camden requested, assuming a seat at the counter.

"Espresso, Americano, cappuccino, latte, frappé? Greek coffee?" The last option had sounded like a dare.

"Double espresso, please."

"Hot milk on the side?"

"Yeah, go for it."

He turned and started clanking instruments in seemingly random fashion.

"Is Malachi here?" Camden tried.

The man disturbed his own rhythm for a tell-tale instant before responding without turning: "Malachi? No."

Camden said nothing more until the coffee was placed in front of him. "Do you know where he is?"

"No." The man was doing his best to look opaque.

"But you know Malachi. We both know Malachi. Everyone does, right?" Camden asked the question of the other member of staff as she emerged from the kitchen at the back, bringing her into the conversation.

She replied with a look of casual agreement, until she caught the scowl of her workmate and immediately froze.

"Don't worry," Camden tried to reassure them, "I'm just looking for someone and Malachi can help me."

They remained stationary, as though posing for an austere nineteenth-century photograph.

"The number I have for him isn't connecting," he continued, trying to break down barriers. "I know he changes them every few weeks. The person I'm looking for, she gave me this number." He held out the piece of paper onto which he had written Malachi's number from Crissa's address book. It had been the latest of a series of scribbled out numbers on the inside back page and hadn't been attributed to a specific name, but Camden had joined the dots and the reaction he was observing confirmed he'd assumed correctly. The guy backed into the kitchen and was gone for a minute or so. The woman stood for a few seconds before deciding she couldn't bear it and disappearing from view.

"Who are you?" the man asked when they returned.

"My name is Christian."

"How do you know Malachi?"

"Through a friend."

"What friend?"

"He would want to know that I'm looking for him."

"Who is your friend?" the man repeated. Camden placed him in his early thirties. He looked like he could handle himself but would prefer to leave those days behind.

Camden sipped his coffee and clenched his jaw muscles as its bitterness knifed its way through him. He added milk.

"The name of this cafe is interesting. How would I pronounce it?"

"Ste-hee-ah," the woman answered instinctively, dragging the start of the second syllable along with her.

"Ste-hee-ah," Camden tried with limited success. "I'm still grappling with the language," he said with a smile, "but I do know what it means."

Hostility was no longer in the man's eyes, although he placed his hand firmly around the waist of his co-worker, a gesture that seemed to suppress any additional assistance until further notice.

"It means Elements," Camden said, adopting a conversational tone, "which you know of course, given that you're from around here. But do you know the reason for its name?"

No response.

"It's clever."

Stillness.

"OK, so you know the reason. Good, that helps."

Nothing.

"The person I'm looking for is actually my girlfriend. The reason I know why this place got its name is because my girlfriend named it." He made sure his eyes landed on them both as he finished his sentence.

They both grew taller. "Crissa?" asked the woman as the man dropped his hand from her hip.

"Yes, Crissa," Camden answered with a pained smile. "Do you know her?"

"We know Crissa." The man's tone had softened entirely.

"Have you seen her?"

"Not for some months now." This time the answer came from the woman, as though they were taking it in turns to make up for their earlier reticence. "Is she OK?"

"The reason I'm looking for Malachi is because Crissa and I had agreed to arrange a meeting through him."

A pall gathered above them. "Malachi rarely stays still, and he tends to find people easier than they find him. Nobody's heard from him since the big protests on Thursday."

"Since The Night," Camden capitalised the words with his eyebrows. "Was he involved in the protests?"

"In arranging them, yes," the man shrugged, "as always. He comes here very rarely these days—this is no longer the hub of the movement—so what I am telling you is only based on what others have told us: he didn't arrive to meet the rest of the group on Thursday, and nobody could reach him on that number you just showed me."

"Is that normal?"

"No, not normal." A decisive shake of the head.

Camden sized up his options. "How would I go about finding him?"

"I don't think that would be possible."

"Not even if Crissa needed me to find him?"

They looked dubiously at him.

"Can you get a message to him?"

"We can try. But if Malachi doesn't want to be found, he won't be."

———•———

A high-pitched yelp pierced the doorframe before he even had the chance to knock. He rapped three times anyway, which only intensified the objections from inside.

"You," Evelina observed coldly as she opened the door.

"Can I talk to you?" Camden asked in a hushed tone.

"Again?" Hands on hips.

"Just the two of us this time."

Evelina looked at him, her hairline and eyebrows looking like they were trying to meet each other halfway. "OK," she said, seemingly in lieu of anything more constructive, and slipped back inside her apartment while keeping the door slightly ajar with her foot. There was a squeaking sound and a scramble of paws. A moment later a tiny dog burst out of the gap of the doorjamb, convinced of its ability to drag its owner along, admirably refusing to accept the limitations of its dimensions. It yapped at him without pause for ten seconds, feet spread as though battle could commence at any time. It looked like it would start more fights than it would win, its legs like suitcase wheels under its squat body and its face carrying a look of mischief that suggested it only adopted its demeanour for light entertainment.

Evelina made a squelching sound from behind her lips and the dog immediately devoted its attention to intently sniffing every inch of the ground it was being led across. "No sign?" she asked in a way that suggested she was confident of the answer.

"No sign," Camden confirmed.

"What are you expecting?"

"Expecting to find? Or expecting of you?"

"Either. There were a lot of questions that you chose not to ask the other day."

They paused under a tree for the dog to cock a leg and confirm it was male. Camden shook his head. "You don't know what you're talking about. And you're a hypocrite."

"Why is that?"

"You could've helped more than you did."

"But not as much as you think," she interrupted. "Crissa and I have influenced each other's lives more than either of us would like to admit. It's the reason we're not in contact anymore. I know her past—which in some ways helps me understand her present and future—but it doesn't mean I can track her down."

"But you could reach out to people who would help me find her."

"Maybe, maybe not. Either way, I'm not going to. I changed direction some time ago and I'm not doubling back. Besides, if Crissa doesn't want to be found, she won't be."

"Second time I've been told that today," he sneered, causing her to stop.

"Who else have you spoken to?"

"I dropped by Stoicheía."

"That wasn't smart."

"Like you, they seemed to take comfort in their inability to help."

She scoffed. "Don't take it personally. They wouldn't have known how to find Crissa anyway."

"I wasn't trying to find Crissa."

Her brow huddled itself together.

"Malachi," he said in reply to her unasked question.

"How much do you know?" she demanded, the dog squinting its head towards Camden as if the information was also of importance to the canine community.

———•———

The first fault lines with Crissa had appeared two months after Camden's move to Santorini. He woke in darkness, the July heat covering his body with a film of sweat under the sheets. It was a common occurrence, usually augmented by the fact that he and Crissa were wrapped around each other. On this occasion, though, his arms—and the bed— were empty.

Shifting his weight onto his elbows, he levered himself up and tried to adjust his eyes to the darkness. He couldn't see Crissa but could sense her. He grabbed his boxers from beside the bed, pulled them on and stood at the railing that ran along the edge of the elevated bedroom. After a few seconds, his eyes rested on the window at the far end of the living room, which was being deftly lit by the moon and contained a shape on the other side of the curtains. He made his way carefully down the ladder and across to her, knees pulled up under her chin as she sat along the windowsill, shoulders visibly tightening as she sensed his approach.

"Hey," he said, joining her.

Crissa let her head slide onto her left shoulder, bringing her knees even closer. Briefly she brought her eyes up to register him, redness visible on her face even through the darkness. Camden tried to avoid asking the obvious question for as long as he could. Crissa remained immobile.

"What's going on?" he said finally.

It took her a while to answer. "Sometimes I find it hard to live with myself."

"What makes you say that?" He became aware that he had now woken fully.

"You only see the best of me. You didn't see me before."

Nothing more was offered in the twenty seconds he gave her. "Same goes for me," he replied. "You can't know the difference you've made to my life because you didn't see what it was like before we met."

She exhaled impatiently, as though he'd missed the point. "Some decisions you can't take back."

He backed off and divided his time between looking blankly at the moonlit sky and Crissa. After a couple of minutes, she loosened her grip around her knees and let them rest against the window, feet splaying further away from her body in a manner that made her look only slightly more relaxed. "Sorry," she said, eyes again flitting to meet his for an instant.

"You don't need to say sorry to me."

"What we have is so intense. Sometimes I have to remind myself that we're still getting to know each other. This is the first time you've seen me like this."

"Don't worry about it. I just want to help."

Crissa made as if she was going to dispute his suggestion but instead her mouth snapped shut and let out a "Hmmm". It could have meant anything.

"Let's go back to bed."

She nodded agreement and was already under the covers and turned slightly away from him by the time he returned from the bathroom. He moved in close and held her gently. She kissed the hand that he placed around her right arm, which he took as a sign that the hug was appreciated but not welcome for long. He turned back onto his side, trying to unpick what he had just witnessed, and was losing himself to sleep again when he felt the bed start to rock lightly with the suppressed sobs beside him.

———•———

Camden observed the lines of people in front of him. Waiting their turns, they variously portrayed a mixture of weariness, excitement, and unfounded guilt. He felt like a replica of himself, as though the vital, sensory parts had been scooped out.

This was where his train-hopping odyssey ended. He was home. It wasn't home.

His line inched forward, another person repatriated every forty seconds or so. He fetched his passport from his black backpack—still his only luggage—and caught a glimpse of himself days ago, just before the start of his journey. Evelina had given him nothing more and Malachi was resolutely uncontactable. And so he had found himself glancing at the clock outside a tobacco store, willing it to be wrong as it ticked off the hours with cruel indifference while he watched the restaurant across the road, wishing in vain that Crissa would turn up as they had arranged, before finally giving up when the tables were stripped of their covers and stacked away, moments ahead of midnight.

Chapter 23

The heat had not yet seeped from the day when Morton and Gary pulled up outside Emporio Suites and Spa.

"How well do you know these guys?" Gary asked.

"Two of them reasonably well: Irini and Sofia. Irini's a good friend of Crissa. Her closest friend here, as far as I know. Good-looking girl, striking. You'll probably start trying to learn Greek once you've met her, now that you're back on the market."

"Steady."

"Sofia's a bit more ... detached? Something like that. Feels like she's always just a couple of steps short of understanding what's going on or what to say next. Nice enough girl but no conversationalist. Then there's a guy that I've seen out with them before who looks like he gets up at five in the morning to polish his pecs and pluck his eyebrows. Fancies himself with the ladies to an outrageous degree. Can't remember his name but if he was a cake, he'd eat himself. I don't really know any of the others."

"Do we have an approach here?"

"Not unless you've come up with one and been keeping it to yourself."

It had been a little over an hour since Morton had ended the unexpected call from Dean.

"Hi," Morton said casually as he approached the front desk.

"Hello," replied a long-necked girl he didn't recognise, her hair sculpted to the contours of her face like a mould. "Do you have an appointment?"

"No, I'm looking for two friends of mine," he ventured, curious to gauge the reaction when he unveiled the name. "One of them works here: Crissa?"

The inquiry was dealt with transactionally. "She doesn't work here anymore."

"Oh?"

"Not for about a month."

"Do you know Crissa well?"

"Me? No," The two words came conjoined into one.

"Are there people here who know her better than you?"

"Sure. Irini and Sofia are good friends of hers. They're with clients."

Morton nodded. "Is the manager in today?"

"Marianna? Sure."

Morton let his smile and expression do the talking.

"Would you like me to get her for you?"

"That would be great."

"OK, I'll ask if she's free."

"Thanks."

As the girl sallied through the door behind her, Morton widened his eyes as he looked towards Gary, who stood slightly behind him and had so far kept out of the way.

"Always a pleasure to watch you tiptoe the line between patient and patronising."

"How did I do?" Morton asked, brightening.

"You just about made it. Probably for the best that the conversation ended when it did."

"Excellent."

Rapid shoe-clicks preceded the entry of Marianna into the room. "Hello, can I help you?" she asked with pleasant efficiency.

"My name is Morton, this is Gary."

She exchanged handshakes and by that point looked keen to see things progress.

"We're friends of Crissa. Her boyfriend is a good friend of ours; in fact, he's my business partner. Camden. You may know him as Christian?"

"I've met Christian. A nice boy." It struck them as a strange expression, given that Marianna would be no more than five years their senior. She showed them to an arrangement of chairs that looked like they were being ambushed by a mountain of cushions.

"When Crissa went to the mainland before the big protests last month, Camden went looking for her. We haven't seen him since."

"We haven't seen or heard from Crissa since those protests," she explained. "She has two good friends here in Irini and Sofia, as I'm sure you know. Irini said Crissa had to go back to the mainland for an emergency and may have to take some time off. At first, we were worried for her; then we were disappointed that she was missing work without even telling us; now we just accept that she isn't coming back."

"You're not worried about her anymore?" Gary asked.

"If it wasn't for Irini being in touch with her when she first left, maybe I would have been more concerned," she shrugged, "but we have a lot of people who work here for a brief period of time. They come and go, often without much warning. I didn't think Crissa was one of those: she was here for almost three years. The customers loved her, the staff liked her." Morton registered the different adjective. "But when I think back to when she first arrived here, it was as if she had materialised from nowhere yet was already a local. Maybe it fits that she's gone again in such a way."

They nodded without conviction.

"As outgoing and strong a character as she could be, it was always on Crissa's terms. After three years of conversations, I can't grasp onto anything that taught me who she really is."

Gary noticed that the past tense had run throughout Marianna's sentences. There was nothing she could give them.

"Could we talk to Irini and Sofia?"

"Of course," Marianna replied, as though she'd been waiting to be asked. "They'll be free in twenty minutes or so. Would you like a drink while you wait?"

"Two waters, please," Morton requested.

"Let me know if you hear from Crissa. And I hope your friend is OK," she said gently as she returned with their drinks. "The girls will be with you soon."

It seemed longer than twenty minutes before they joined them at the sofas, both in dark navy uniforms with thick gold trims and the spa's motif embossed on the left chest.

Morton stood and exchanged kisses with the girls—warmly with Irini, who pulled him close as they embraced; more hesitantly with Sofia, who remained a full step away as she reached towards him and patted his back—before introducing Gary.

"Let's go somewhere we can talk," Irini suggested.

They walked outside without a word, Irini leading the way with Sofia a few paces behind. Gary came to understand Morton's description of Irini: her height and grace made every action look like part of an elegant routine. As she walked, she brought her hands up to the back of her head and set free her blonde hair, which rolled down as far as her shoulder blades. Sofia studied the ground she stepped across, her hands not part of her walking motion.

"Have you heard anything?" Irini finally asked when she'd taken them to the far end of a yard that extended towards the southwest tip of the island.

Straight into it, Morton thought. "No, we've heard nothing," he answered.

Irini shook her head in small, swift movements. "Me neither."

"Your boss said that you'd spoken to Crissa soon after she disappeared," Morton probed.

The head shakes slowed, becoming more definite and less agitated. "I told her that to try to help Crissa keep her job. Marianna is a good manager but she's strict. If Crissa had gone any more than a couple of shifts without phoning in, she would've been fired. As it is, I think that time has passed."

"When was the last time you saw her?" Morton asked, this time directing his question at Sofia, who looked unprepared for it and took a moment to answer.

"The night before the protests. Before she left for the mainland." Her hands were held out in front of her like a squirrel's and her eyes blinked incessantly.

"Same," Irini confirmed when Morton turned his gaze to her. "I spoke to her sister, Nina. I met her once. She's heard from her. Nothing much, just that she's OK. I don't think her parents know anything unusual is going on."

"Do you know her family well?" Morton asked.

"I don't. Crissa and I took a trip to the mainland one off-season, but we didn't meet her parents, only her sister. They may not have even known she was visiting. She wasn't close to them as far as I understand it." She looked from one to the other, but they offered no further questions, so she asked one of her own. "What about Christian?"

"He started looking for her the day after the protests. That's when he spoke to the two of you. On the Saturday he flew to the mainland; spoke to Crissa's family and friends; came back on Sunday without any answers and was gone again by the Monday. 'I can't come back until I've found her,'" Morton quoted.

Chewing her lip, Irini spun on her heels and strode further away from the spa, across a rocky stretch of sparse grass beyond the fence that perimetered the car park. She was no more than three steps from a fifty-foot drop and had her hands dangling in her pockets as though blissfully unaware. The others closed in as she started speaking without looking at them.

"I've got some contact details of people she knows back home. Start with Nina. She's twenty going on forty-five. You get the impression she's understood everything she needs to know about the world since her tenth birthday. She'll know more than she'll be willing to tell you. Try not to get frustrated by that; she'll only be looking out for her sister."

Chapter 24

In the days immediately after the May protests, Crissa
was sequestered to the mainland via an assortment of
islands. Evaldas wasn't with her in person, but she was
certainly moving in line with his commands. The two men
who ghosted her away on the initial leg of her journey had
not provided their names. Instead, as they were approaching
the shoreline of the first island, they told her to pick the
names of two native men that came to her mind: thereafter,
they were called Dimitrios and Antonis. Or at least they
were until a boat drew up alongside them midway between
the second and third islands, at which point she clambered
onto the new vessel and two different men assumed the
same roles and monikers.

There followed a succession of empty apartments down
quiet streets. They were spartan but modern, and conversation
had no place there. One of the men would occasionally take
his turn to catch some rest; Crissa doubted she'd managed to
rest for more than thirty minutes in any single stretch until

they reached the mainland and stationed themselves in the final apartment at dusk on the Sunday. At that point she fell into a dreamless sleep that submerged her like black treacle, before being disturbed by a shake of the shoulder and the face of one of her transporters leaning over her.

"Time to go," he told her.

Crissa blinked her way back into the world. The room was sunlit, and she lay atop the covers. "What time is it?"

"Nine," she was informed, not unkindly. He pointed at three plastic bags in the corner of the room. "Some clothes and a backpack. To keep you going."

She eyed him cautiously, feeling awkward as she repositioned the man-size t-shirt she'd worn since her journey had begun, the neck of which had been pulled down as she slept.

"Ten minutes, then we separate," he said as he rose.

"Wait, where are we going?"

His gaze was level.

"Where do I go?" she asked again.

"I hear you are resourceful."

———•———

In addition to the clothes, the plastic bags had also contained within them five hundred Euros, from which her first investment was a sizeable breakfast. Keen to be unmemorable, she spread her meals across two eateries and committed the necessary effort required to fight the urges of her three-day hunger.

Then she melded together her dormant instincts and discipline, which led her somewhere she never thought she would revisit. She recognised the voice that quietened the barking dog. It had been three years since she'd heard that voice and she wondered if its owner had changed in any way.

She hadn't.

"Come in," Evelina ordered, sounding wholly against the idea, and immediately turned from the door.

Surprise momentarily rooted Crissa to the spot as she recovered from the perfunctory manner with which her arrival had been dealt. By the time she'd taken her first steps into the apartment, Evelina had already positioned herself on one of the two-seater sofas in the living room. Crissa's path to the other sofa was made treacherous by the unhelpful oppositional dancing that the dog performed between her feet.

Contrasting emotions sloshed around the room. Things stayed that way for half a minute before Evelina finally spoke. "I didn't think I'd see you again."

They were exactly the words Crissa had expected to hear, delivered precisely the way she'd anticipated. "By that do you mean you hoped you wouldn't see me again?"

"In many ways." Evelina's tone grew colder.

"How are you?"

"I presume you need help."

"What makes you say that?"

"I see no other reason why you'd be here."

Crissa took a moment. "Yes, I do need help. I—"

"I don't want to know details." Evelina's hand shot out like a karate chop. "A place to stay?"

Crissa nodded. "Probably best to start a chain."

Evelina said nothing but the cogs were turning.

"Do you know of anyone who'd help me start it? It needs to be the lowest of low profiles."

"Don't forget who you're talking to. I lived through those times, too: you know there are a lot of people who would help you in a heartbeat."

An appreciative smile made the briefest appearance on Crissa's lips before deciding to make itself scarce. "Are you still in touch with many of them?"

"No," came the retort and Evelina rose from the couch. She spent the next few minutes in the kitchen, returning with a glass of water and coffee for both of them. They spent another couple of minutes without talking, before a second scalding sip of the coffee prompted Crissa to re-engage.

"You don't look any different," she said.

The comment was welcomed. "Neither do you."

"I feel different," Crissa eventually added.

"Things wouldn't be right if you didn't." It was a slow-moving conversation.

"I don't know where to take this. What to say."

Evelina didn't offer suggestions.

"Should I say sorry? Would that help? I don't even know if it should be me saying sorry. I don't know if I even have anything to be sorry about."

"We know each other well enough. We both have things we're sorry about."

"What's his name?" The dog had been sniffing around Crissa's feet for the past couple of minutes and had finally decided to plant itself right on top of them.

Evelina didn't answer.

"Maybe this wasn't a good idea," Crissa declared, beginning to stand up, much to the dog's displeasure.

"I'll help you," Evelina blurted out, and Crissa retook her seat. The dog wandered to the far corner of the room, clearly unimpressed with such fickleness. "This just isn't easy. There are so many things I want to talk and ask you about, but I don't know if I want to hear the answers."

That made sense to Crissa.

"I can't go back to where we were five years ago." Evelina's voice had turned to a whisper. Her frown looked like it could fold her face in half.

"Once this has all played itself out, I'd love for us to sit down and have a normal conversation. Remind ourselves of who we once were. How we once were."

There was a minimal nod from Evelina, as though her skull had agreed on behalf of the rest of her. "Give me five minutes."

It was more like fifteen, but when Evelina re-emerged from her bedroom with her phone clutched to her chest, she did so with the first three links of the chain in place. None of her contacts knew the identity of who they would be housing; they would only become aware when they saw her for the first time.

A quarter of an hour later, Crissa was gone from her life again. After watching her being driven slowly away in the passenger seat of her contact's unremarkable sedan, Evelina leant against the front door of the apartment and slid halfway down. She held herself there, shaking as tears streaked her cheeks and her chest heaved with unruly breaths. The insular world she'd nurtured had been violated by echoes of their ruptured relationship.

The night that she'd told Crissa she was in love with her was a salient memory. Within an instant they were coupled, swarming each other with hands and tongues. It had felt to Evelina like a culmination, the natural stepping-off point after all the pitch-blackness through which they'd supported each other. Finally, she was lowering her defences. Only good things would follow, for both of them: Evelina would become a woman revealed, Crissa a woman repaired.

Not so. Crissa loved her, but in the cruellest way. Evelina woke the following morning to an empty bed, Crissa having retreated to the living-room couch, from where she offered apologies if her actions had been misleading. She hoped it wouldn't come at a cost to their friendship. Evelina remembered every instant. She replied with all the right words, but her desolation took its toll over time. She felt powerless against it. Their bond seemed to dissolve, and she filled its void with spite. Suddenly, Crissa was no longer around for her to aim her resentment towards. And then, today, from the second she saw Crissa in her doorway, Evelina saw that her feelings were as insoluble as ever. It was a truth that she cherished and hated in equal measure. The past was hurtful but carried vitality with its punches.

Evelina knew her friend was in trouble: she'd seen those eyes before. And yet she'd remained quiet about the visit she'd received from Camden the previous day, just as she would keep Crissa's visit from him when he returned twenty-four hours later, and as she would once more when Morton and Gary came knocking the following month.

Chapter 25

Crissa took the measure of the mid-morning activity breaking out around her. The junior school opposite emptied its children onto a playground that, despite its colourful best efforts, amounted to little more than an arrangement of concrete spaces and shapes. Where grass grew, it did so without optimism. The park in which she sat was seeing increasing footfall as the day progressed. Parents transported and then released their children into the playground with varying degrees of anxiety. Some gave plenty of space to explore and learn through experience, even if that meant the occasional bump or fall; others would almost shadow their child as they navigated their way, perpetually ready to pounce if anything looked like it could go wrong. Despite her hopes to the contrary, Crissa imagined she would be one of the worriers.

Elderly couples and friends had been meandering through the park since Crissa had first arrived, an hour or so earlier. They would typically appear through one of the entrances, walk a path that seemed predetermined for them and then exit by the same gates. Some walked alone and Crissa found herself wondering whom they had lost, when, how. They may look vulnerable now, but she was interested in the things she could never really know. What were they like at her age? Did their losses feel like dead-weights or freedom?

Where was he?

Things were rarely easy with Malachi. A conversation could become a drama with a single misplaced inflection. So many times, Crissa could remember ditching exchanges between them in the knowledge that the only way to regain equilibrium was to give him time to calm down. In the early days of their friendship, she had tried to coax him back to rationality, but soon regarded that as an indulgent error of judgment made by too many people around him. His capacity for self-reflection never convinced her. When his behaviour returned to normality, it seemed more like he had either forgotten about it or presumed that enough time had passed to render any of his outbursts inconsequential. It was no coincidence that her refusal to pander to his mood swings was quickly followed by an increasing infatuation on his part. His all-encompassing admiration was a salve for her after the hurtful rejection she'd experienced in the preceding months, and she was thankful that he wasn't pushy in the bedroom: he accommodated her occasional jumpiness and relished every time she softened up for him. She enjoyed the tender physicality of their sex despite the vacuum she felt.

They weren't destined to be lovers for long, however, and Malachi accepted the truth of the situation while never fully moving on. Their attentions instead focused on the nascent movement in which they were invested so fully, and this became the main way that Malachi strove to prove his worth to her. They recruited; coordinated activities to build the profile of the movement and its cause; published newsletters; spoke outside landmark buildings or in the streets. Things grew.

There were also signs of splintering. Malachi worried that Crissa's intention for the movement to home in on governmental malpractice would bring malevolent attention from the authorities. Crissa viewed Malachi's ideas and activities more as mischievous stunts than pursuits of substance. Crissa wanted to mobilise, Malachi to agitate. A midpoint ended up being the compromise.

They needed financial clout, though, and Malachi had the goods in that regard. He'd grown up in a wealthy household by virtue of his father's successful import-export business and was endowed with financial independence from young adulthood, perhaps a way of his father trying to make amends for his deficiencies in raising Malachi alone after the sudden death of his wife. They eventually butted heads once too often and simultaneously seemed to disown each other, but Crissa knew that Malachi's father had funded some of their group's early activities and kept the pipeline open enough for his son to live comfortably while he drifted between whichever jobs gave him the best balance of freedom, social contacts, and time to devote to the movement. Their political beliefs, at least, were hereditary.

Crissa and Malachi continued to have infrequent sex— mostly at her bidding, against which he seemed unable to defend himself—for a good couple of years before she moved to the islands. She knew she was mistreating him, but it took her a while to break the cycle of mutually harmful behaviour. Throughout that time and even now, she knew that he would still do anything for her—he'd proven as much very recently. All of which made it more troublesome that she couldn't contact him now, this being the fourth time in two days that she had left him a message at one of their former drops to meet at an agreed time and place, and the fourth time she had remained alone.

The previous Thursday, Malachi had woken in a sunlit uncurtained room and immediately hitched onto his elbows in expectation of hostile faces nearby. In his dream, hands had been reaching for him, but they rapidly receded as consciousness gained a foothold. He slumped back onto the bed, let his arms flop over his head and gathered his thoughts. He showered, clothed, and fed himself so unthinkingly that he paused just steps from the front door of the apartment. This wasn't like him. An uncluttered mind was always useful; today, it was borderline essential.

Malachi rarely questioned himself. The mistakes he'd peppered throughout his life were mostly ones he was comfortable with because they came from a position of clarity, based on his beliefs at a given time. *Everyone grows up at different rates*, he had conveniently resolved long ago. *We all do much the same things as each other in our lives if you look objectively enough, just in a different order.* His choices were his own and he wore their responsibility lightly. Had any of his failings been such an issue, he would never have won over so many people for the cause he had championed from Day One.

His relationship with that cause had complicated in recent times. Crissa's defection three years previously had wounded him personally and, in his own mind at least, his standing had taken a hit. To reassert his authority, he would need to demonstrate his worth to those who looked up to him and he had thrown himself into the activities of the movement with such commitment that he sometimes wondered whether he had blunted his own edges.

That was his interpretation of things. The opinions of other members were more equivocal. Many of them had always seen Crissa as their natural pioneer and feared they would be rudderless in her absence, but that had proven not to be the case, after a period of adjustment. The grip she had held so skilfully around the scruff of the group's neck had been exactly what was needed in its early days but could have cut off circulation if maintained for too long. Rather, she had pointed them in the right direction and then trusted them to steer themselves onwards, although they wished she had stood before them to explain her reasons for leaving. Malachi still served a purpose to them—his vision sometimes needed reining in but was an undeniable asset, as were his access to funds and unyielding energy—but they had long considered him as merely *one* of their leaders, not the sole guiding light. Because he wouldn't have accepted such a notion constructively, he was tactfully manoeuvred into the position of figurehead with limited power.

Yet even limited power was power. The impact of that evening's protests would be spread across the mainland

and islands in no small part because of the momentum he had generated over seven dedicated years. He maintained contacts throughout all the major cities, the majority of the significant towns and numerous islands, mostly on his terms. He traded on how easily he could connect with the right people while maintaining exclusivity of who could reach him. He mused over whether he had become the guerrilla equivalent of a boardroom CEO, able to position people but no longer the one who would personally effect action. It was a fair summary of the recent interaction that Evaldas would be preparing to act upon, and it fitted with his plans for the evening, which would focus more on coordination and set-piecing than the angry thrust of the frontline. Certainly, his longstanding feeling of imperviousness seemed to have dissipated, but perhaps that was what was required from here on. Tonight was an escalation, not a resolution.

He'd eaten with a group of friends before returning home to change into all black, other than a white and red sports anorak that would make him less conspicuous on his way to the meeting place. Those anoraks cost five Euros a pop and he had a stack of them on a use-once-and-destroy basis. The apartment he currently called home was a good thirty-minute walk from his destination. Because he liked to make his appearance soon after the first people arrived, he made a move in anticipation of getting there just before dusk. From his first steps outside the apartment, he could feel a denseness hanging in the air above the streets. Shouts emanated from a few blocks away. They sounded like young men playing a role, psyching themselves up. Some passers-by scurried towards refuge, heads down. Small congregations of people dotted the corners and doorways, as though awaiting instructions and as yet unsure of whether or not to follow them when they were given. He could hear footsteps from hundreds of yards away. All senses were heightened.

The first sign of things being awry came when he was midway between the apartment and the rendezvous point: he heard a smash that he couldn't locate and instinctively snaked from the wide street he'd been striding down into an alleyway that dissected the block to his right. It wasn't well lit, but he could see two tall, slim young men standing on either side of its exit onto the main thoroughfare he had been heading towards. They glanced back at him briefly before removing their hands from the pockets of the jackets that they wore zipped to the neck and darted leftwards out of the alley.

Malachi's pace quickened and as it did so he registered a number of dull impacts in the vicinity he was nearing. He stopped at the threshold of the alley and looked to his left, to where the men had dashed with such conviction. They had made their way towards a square that lay around seventy yards away and were emptying the contents of their jackets towards a small but well-ordered unit of riot police, who gave the impression they had expected things like projectiles and charging protesters to be restricted to the capital's centre. To his right Malachi estimated there were around fifty young men and women, with few looking like they had graduated from their teens and some already aware that they had bitten off more than they could chew. He cursed them for their impulsiveness and instantly chuckled to himself at his hypocrisy: they were him a decade ago, and exactly the type of people he would try to recruit now. There was, however, a need for discipline and that wasn't on display here. It was more than an hour before they were supposed to engage with the police and their haste threatened to turn the atmosphere hostile long before the cameras were rolling.

The two youths returned to the group once they had made their deliveries and eight more broke from the ranks, four making straight for the police line, and the other four brushing past Malachi as they swept down the alley. Two had been girls. Sizing up the situation, Malachi decided to retreat and take a more circuitous route when his eye caught a flash of light from above him. He looked up to see another small group standing on the roof of the buildings he was positioned under, holding freshly-lit Molotov cocktails. Craning his head around the corner again, he saw that the police had moved to the front of the square, effectively marking that territory as their red line. The four who had broken from the group were hurling handfuls of bricks and bottles as the first flame was launched from above, landing in the second row of the police and immediately igniting the trouser leg of one. It was quickly extinguished but palpably changed the mood. The group who had shot through the alleyway appeared from the left—far closer to the police than Malachi considered wise—just as the second, third and fourth Molotovs landed. Two landed amongst the police but made little impression. The third hit one of the girls—whom the rooftop group had clearly not expected to materialise at that time—flush on the side of the face and knocked her to the ground. Her jacket instantly caught fire.

Before he knew it, Malachi was in full sprint towards the girl, whose male accomplices seemed not to comprehend her predicament, instead focusing on landing the rocks they carried with maximum effect. Their proximity and the introduction of fire to the situation caused the police to move forwards a few steps, which in turn prompted the remainder of the group to charge at the sound of the screams of the fallen girl. Malachi arrived at her side as her friend had almost succeeded in dousing the flames and saw that she had a gouging wound and what looked like an instant heat scar lashed across her face. He called to the others for assistance, but the sight of their injured companion only enraged them further and they threw themselves headlong towards the first wave of police. Without thought, Malachi lurched towards the young men to get them away from imminent danger and recruit them to help the girl. As he grabbed the shoulder of the first one he came to, a shadow swooped down from the corner of his left eye and clubbed him fiercely just behind the crown of his skull. The sound that left his throat was low and animalistic and he shook his head briefly to try to reset his artificial horizon. He turned—slightly slower than he expected to—and saw the rest of the group less than twenty feet away and the girl being guided to safety. The onrushing group were backlit by what he presumed were cars recently set aflame. The pain in his head seemed to travel backwards from between his eyes towards the centre of his skull. He squinted and held his breath as he staggered diagonally away from both the police and the oncoming crowd. He could sense rather than see that he was clear of everyone, which at first was a comfort and subsequently a worry: things were starting to get fuzzy. He tried in vain to locate the alleyway that had hidden him less than a minute before. Noises, images, and smells encircled him, refusing to offer any help. Although he was no longer capable of seeing it, he was no more than twenty steps away from the entrance to the alley when his foot caught one of the many bricks littering the area. Lacking the wherewithal to recover his balance or even break his fall, Malachi instead got his feet further tangled and, twisting, met the ground with the side of his head and knew nothing more. Three feet away, the corpse of a family's car blazed furiously, its intense heat causing such damage to Malachi's face that, when the doctors tried to treat him in his comatose and badly burned state in intensive care over the coming weeks, they were unable to identify him, as he had purposely carried no personal possessions at the time he was taken away by two attentive paramedics.

Chapter 26

A momentary hesitation preceded Crissa's knock on the door and a longer one bridged the gap between the knock and the peephole darkening. From there, the locks were thrown off hurriedly and the door flung open.

"Crissa!" cried a girl with light brown hair carelessly brushed back from her face and pleating lazily as it made its way down the back of her neck. Her eyes were made up like she had been experimenting with several potential styles and had yet to make a decision. She wore a crew t-shirt and cargo shorts in a way that suggested she generally wore crew t-shirts and cargo shorts.

"Ioanna," Crissa smiled and accepted the hug that was unloaded onto her.

"This is amazing! It's so good to see you," Ioanna continued, not loosening her hold until it registered that Crissa wouldn't converse further until she did. "How long have you been back?"

"A few days," Crissa answered as she was shown inside. They walked through the hallway into a rectangular living room with doors exiting at each corner. Two sofas were taken up by the extended limbs of two occupants, one of either sex, one on either sofa, both in their early twenties. Crissa recognised them: the girl waved from under her curls while the boy grunted diffidently.

Ioanna started swatting her hands at her cohabitants to create seating space, but Crissa dismissed the need: "Maybe we can have a chat, just you and I," she suggested.

"Of course," Ioanna replied, and they doubled back towards her room.

Crissa positioned herself on one of three bean bags arranged in the space in front of the large bay window, which was fully sealed by blackout blinds.

"So, what have you been up to?"

"Still on the islands."

"Luka seems happy to see you," Ioanna added with a grin.

"Yeah, he almost pulled a muscle leaping off the sofa to shake my hand."

"I don't think it's a handshake he would be hoping for."

"Those times have gone," Crissa said with a finality that lent itself to an uneasy conversational pause.

"Were you here for the protests?"

"No," Crissa replied.

Ioanna shook her head and rolled her eyes. "Out of control."

"You were there?"

"On the fringes. Nothing more. My nature, I suppose."

"Things calming down yet?"

"Day by day. Less and less people on the streets each night. Just a combination of the hardcore and those looking for an excuse to cause trouble."

Crissa sized up whether to ask about Malachi but ate the question. Ioanna's expansive eyes were perceptive and inviting. It wasn't a combination she wanted to encourage.

"What have you got for me?" Ioanna enquired.

"A favour to ask." Crissa felt each part of her body gather tension as her fingers spidered towards the bag that lay beside her ankles. "I've got something that's encrypted. I need it deciphered and copied."

"What is it?"

"A data stick. I don't know what's on it, but I need to know."

"Can I see it?"

"I trust you, Ioanna. We've been through things. But this is different."

"Where did you get it?"

Crissa bent down and retrieved it from her bag, where it had been zipped up and its whereabouts checked every fifteen minutes since she had acquired it. "It's the data disk that Michael Andreas waved in front of the screen on the night of the protests," she replied, not quite answering the question.

Ioanna tensed. "How did you get that?"

"Can you decode it?"

"Who knows about this?"

"I understand the questions," Crissa explained patiently, "but I can't answer them. If you don't feel comfortable with this, I get it."

"No," Ioanna instantly waved her away, "I can't let you take this somewhere else. You need someone you can trust; you said it yourself. Let's get going."

———•———

Once the contents of the disk were readable, Ioanna left her to it, returning only once with a glass of water and assurances that she would remain undisturbed for as long as she needed. Whereas she had previously had only one copy of this mine of information, Crissa now held six.

It contained thousands of files—bank transactions, voice recordings, tax returns, business accounts—with a single document acting as a summary of all the people whose details were held within. She'd picked two names at the top of the alphabetised list, consciously averting her eyes from any of the entries and associated folders under the letter M and sussed out how it worked. Next to each name in the master file were multiple addresses, aliases, affiliated businesses, and investment firms, all painstakingly indexed. Once she found the name she wanted, she would be a single click away from a folder full of documents detailing the tax-eluding misdemeanours of that person.

After two trial runs, Crissa snatched her glass and drained it of its contents. Time to check. She scrolled quickly through the first half of the alphabet, slowing when she reached the L's and hitting Page Down to move through the early stages of the M's.

The name Mouriki appeared at the top of the screen, and she pulled her fingers away. A breath. The Up Arrow took her back through the alphabet. A dozen names passed before she released her breath. The name Morton did not appear. Her eyes clasped shut and the realisation came that she was shaking from her elbows down. She jutted out her lower teeth and rested her fingernails on them as she gathered herself. Now her fingers moved quicker again. She raced back up through the Ms and fixed her eyes on the bottom of the screen. Menakis came into view and her eyes drifted up beyond the point of the screen where the Melas brothers should have appeared. She frowned.

There was no relief at this discovery, however. While her eyes had scanned the page, she had picked up an additional, surprising, and unwelcome name: Mavropsaridis. She recognised the address and company that sat alongside, and the forename was all too familiar, having been passed onto his son.

Malachi's father was on the Andreas Archive.

Chapter 27

Morton couldn't remember ever being so grateful to see his father. The first visit they made after their short flight over to the mainland was to visit him at his friend's apartment. In the absence of any form of good news or relief, Anthony seemed to have found a state of defiant relaxation.

The couple playing host were mid-fifties and into their second decade of retirement. It seemed improper to ask about the means through which they had achieved this, given the circumstances, although Morton suspected it would make for enviably good career advice. The husband was sociable and accommodating while his wife created multi-directional blurs as she zigzagged through the high-ceilinged apartment leaving drinks and plates of food in front of their guests. They blended into the surroundings so discreetly that it was barely noticeable when they left the room.

Only once was the subject of his father's predicament broached, and the enquiry was dealt with testily.

"Is there anything I should know about your business deals, Dad? Anything about the Melas brothers worth sharing?"

"News coverage swaying your opinion?"

"Of course not," Morton answered tersely. "But tell me, had I continued to not ask about the complex you were planning to build together near Oia, would you have continued to not tell me?"

"I would've told you." The answer was immediate. "A lot of hurdles need to be cleared for that to become anything more than an idea in our heads."

They segued into safer, more subdued topics—Clare and Adele, the plans for Salvation, the prevailing mood of the country—and it assumed the form of a normal father-son conversation under normal circumstances. There was distance, but there was warmth.

———•———

A hushed phone call had arranged their next meeting, taking them to a busy square with islands of grass dotted around and benches offering shelter from the sun. Nina had instructed them to wait next to the fountain until she arrived. When she did, she was within five paces of them before they heard her approaching from behind.

"She's safe, is the first thing I should tell you."

"Nina? Hi, I'm Morton—"

"Yeah," she replied in a way that ended his sentence. "Walk with me."

They were already four steps behind by the time they started moving.

Nina's gait was unhurried, yet her pace spoke of purpose. She was medium height and, in the few seconds she had stood in front of Morton, he'd registered several physical characteristics she shared with Crissa: their hair was almost identical, as was the shape of her eyes and the way they led onto her slender nose. He anticipated seeing several other familiar habits throughout the course of their walking conversation, but also suspected that they were different in as many ways as they were similar.

The first time she spoke was as she allowed them to catch up with her at the top of three flights of wide, marble steps that led to an even larger open space. "This is Syntagma Square," she told them, before pointing at the neoclassical building they'd commented on from their waiting spot. "And that is parliament."

"Oh wow," Gary responded reflexively, hoping his feedback had done justice to his architectural admiration.

Nina seemed unimpressed. "Mmmm. The National Gardens are only a few minutes away. I love this park. The reason I asked you to meet me here is to show you how comfortably ugliness and beauty sit side by side in my country."

Neither of them knew how to respond.

"Plus, I needed fresh air," Nina said with a grin, cutting the atmosphere.

They entered the park and Morton allowed a further hundred yards of silence. "You said Crissa's OK?"

"Yes," Nina replied simply, "she's safe."

"Have you seen her?"

"No. I've spoken to her a few times."

"On the phone?"

"Or by text."

"Alright, that's good," Morton said with an air of relief. "Do you know where she is?"

Nina's headshake contained sadness and acceptance. "Crissa and I move in different ways. We have complete trust in each other, but we are not alike as people."

It was a slightly offbeat answer and Morton pondered his next question as they skirted around a small lake towards a bridge painted red. Before he had the chance to ask it, Nina was speaking again: "You're very handsome." She was looking directly at Morton as she spoke.

"That's very kind."

"I doubt I'm the first to tell you that."

"Do you know anything about Camden?" Morton asked, slight irritation eking out.

She nodded, laying aside her aesthetic observations for the time being. "Christian? That depends on what you mean. I've met him. He was here recently. He visited us at home soon after the protests, which I presume was when he was first looking for Crissa. But I think the question you're asking me is: 'do I know where he is?' I'm afraid I don't know that." Worry made a brief appearance behind her eyes.

"Crissa hasn't mentioned his whereabouts to you?"

"No. I'd presumed they were back together again."

"How often do you speak to her?" Gary asked.

"She's on the move at the moment but she checks in every few days."

"What did you mean when you said you presumed they were back together again?" Morton enquired.

Nina stopped to give the question thought. "Crissa and I have always had a close connection. We could go a month or more without talking and it would be fine. Any time I've spoken to her since she has been with Christian, she's seemed happy. That hasn't always been the case in the past, at all. It seemed like she was finding her place."

Gary nodded; Morton remained still.

"Something obviously happened a few weeks ago. At first, she was really agitated and asked me not to tell Christian where she was. I guess she must have expected him to come looking for her and figured it would be more convincing if he was genuinely in the dark. But that calmness has returned to her voice the last few times. I put the pieces together and took it that they'd found each other again."

They had reached a path lined by columns, with convex railings entwined with leafy branches to form an archway through which they walked. Halfway along was a bench, which Nina decided should be put to use.

"Why do you think she didn't want Christian to know where she was?" Morton asked from under a frown.

"I don't know," she replied with a shrug. "Crissa's complex. When things have been really tough in her life, she's always started contacting me more, and that's happened again recently. She lets me know she's safe, but she compartmentalises her life. There will be a reason that she wanted to be alone for a while, just like there will be a reason she's told me enough to stop me worrying but not enough that I have all the answers you're looking for."

As he processed Nina's words, Morton concluded that he was speaking to someone who realised that, like them, she was a peripheral character in a game that was moving around them.

———•———

They followed breadcrumbs.

Nina gave them two recommendations, and the first was to visit Evelina. It was made with both conviction and hesitancy, and left Morton and Gary wondering whether it would prove fruitful or fraught. By the time they knocked on her door, it felt like oxygen was becoming increasingly hard to come by. They had many questions to ask her.

She sneered as she wrenched the door open. "More of you. What do you want?"

"We're looking for a friend of ours—" Morton started, charm turned up full.

"Spare me," she cut in. "I know: your friend was here recently. She hasn't turned up yet?"

"No. We're hoping you can help."

"I can't help you. I don't speak to Crissa anymore."

"I know," Morton said, "but we have questions about things that happened a few years ago."

"I can't help you," she repeated through clenched teeth, making to close the door on them. Morton put his foot in the way.

"Why would you turn your back on your friend when she's in trouble?"

Evelina's face turned to stone. "Crissa and I haven't spoken for a lot of years for a lot of reasons. My life's been better ever since and I'm not dredging up my past mistakes for anyone. She'll be fine, she always is. Now leave me alone. And if you've got Julia on your list of people to harass, cross her off. She's not around anymore. The last visit from your friend saw to that."

A stamp on Morton's foot caused him to reflexively draw it back for long enough to enable her to slam the door and ring an echo through the hall.

———•———

Nina's second recommendation took them to the University of Athens. Hidden in its bowels was an office housing four people. Three of them were comfortably into their sixties—two women, one man—and briefly looked up at the interlopers before returning their attention deskward. The person they'd come to see was a bundle of bones wearing spectacles whose frames took up almost three-quarters of their surface area. She had a slender face that tapered off at the chin like a Munch painting and seemed so enchanted to see them that it suggested visitors were rare.

"How can I help you?" she asked them in flawless, eager English.

"Thanks for your time, Rosa. My name is Morton, this is Gary. We're looking for two friends of ours: one is a British guy, about our age," Morton pyramided his hands towards his chest in a way that said 'like us'. "The other is a Greek girl who we believe you know from a few years ago. Younger than us, far better looking," he smiled ingratiatingly. "Her name is Crissa Papanikolau."

An audible intake of breath spoke of excitement to hear the name. "Crissa? How is she? I haven't seen her in so long."

"She's doing well. We know her because she is in a relationship with the friend we're looking for. They're very fond of each other."

Rosa's head tilted to one side in contentment. "She deserves a good man."

"But the reason we're here," Gary picked up, "is because both Crissa and our friend—Christian—are proving hard to find. This isn't the first time they've gone away unannounced: we both live with Christian, and he and Crissa have taken trips for a few days at a time before, but it's important we find them. Christian's mother has been taken ill back in England and we need to let him know."

"Oh, that's terrible." A hand shot to Rosa's elfin lips.

"Nothing too serious," Morton immediately reassured her. Nina's advice had been to accentuate positivity throughout their chat with Rosa and they were working from a fictitious, loosely rehearsed script. "She fell down the stairs at home. She's fine, but she and Christian are very close, and I know it would mean a lot to them both if he saw her."

"I understand," she replied sincerely.

"We all live on Santorini these days," Morton told her. "In the time we've known her, Crissa's spoken of several friends here on the mainland, so we thought we'd try them. You were one of the names." His accompanying smile suggested Rosa should take that as a compliment, and it seemed to do the trick.

"Oh, Crissa," she said wistfully. "I miss her. Such memories. We were so young! It feels so fresh and yet so long ago."

She pulled open a drawer and rummaged for an eternity before handing them a photo of four girls with their arms resting round each other's shoulders, looking up at a camera with gleaming smiles and optimistic eyes. It looked like it had been taken from a few feet away—halfway up some steps or on a low balcony—after a few drinks but with the majority of the night still in front of them.

"This is a great picture. When was it taken?"

Rosa flipped the photo around in his hand so that the back was facing him. It read "2007" and then a scrawl that he couldn't understand.

"Neither of you have changed at all," he lied.

"I don't know about that." She showed them another, this time in a larger group. The four girls from the first photograph were again in shot for what was clearly a more formal occasion. "The year after," Rosa said, anticipating the question. "Near the start of our second year of university. It was a fundraising dinner; I forget what for." She turned the picture back towards her and studied it, as though searching for clues.

"Who are the other girls?" Gary asked invitingly, admiring the first photo, which lay on the table in front of them.

"Adrianna has the straight hair; Evelina the curly hair."

Morton and Gary both made a conscious effort to avoid each other's eyes.

"Are you still in touch with either of them?" Gary asked.

"Adrianna actually lives in Germany now. She's been over there for a few years. We keep in touch online. Evelina was always more Crissa's friend than mine."

Morton took her tightening lips as a cue to adjust the flow of the conversation. "I bet you had some great times."

"Wonderful times," Rosa agreed, blinking. "Did you go to university?"

"We did," Gary answered, flicking his hands between himself and Morton. "And Christian. We've stayed close, a good number of us have."

"Everything's in front of you. Everyone was so open-minded, like they were happy still to be learning to look at the world in different ways."

They let the thought hang.

"Crissa didn't graduate in the end, though. You know that, right?"

"Yeah, she told us."

"I never really understood what happened there. Crissa and I rarely spoke about our secrets or our troubles—we didn't confide in each other necessarily—but we would talk about our hopes for the future. Our dreams. She had so many plans," she continued falteringly.

Morton smiled encouragingly. "What did she dream of?"

"Mostly of helping people. She wasn't sure exactly how, but she had so many options open to her. She was so smart and organised. Had a real presence. And she was a romantic at heart, so she hoped she would find someone and raise a family. Not that different to a lot of people, I guess, but it just seemed more attainable for her. And then"—a shrug and a waft of the hands—"she was gone."

"Was it sudden?"

"It seems sudden now, looking back. There were probably signs at the time."

"Do you know what triggered it?" Morton asked, trying to keep the tone airy.

"No. Even now, I couldn't put my finger on anything. It just felt like she started moving in different circles and then withdrew completely."

"Well, she still speaks fondly of you," Gary told her.

"What does she do now?"

"She's a masseuse at a spa on Santorini. It's very nice. Quite exclusive. I've only known Crissa for a year or so, but from what she has told me she's happy that she moved there."

"I'm so glad she's happy."

"Would you know anyone here in Athens that she would be likely to be staying with?"

"Have you tried her family?"

"We're on our way there next," Morton fibbed. "We don't want to alarm them so we're trying to talk to anyone else who might be able to help first." He'd intended his comment to inject a sense of urgency into Rosa's hazy memory recall, but it was hard to tell if it had made any impact.

"I'm sorry; I wish I could help more. I'm not really in touch with any of the people from my early days at university. I'm afraid I've never been a very curious person."

Morton was unsure whether he agreed with that assessment as he stood up to leave. He wore his smile uncomfortably as he thanked her and left behind his details. A couple of corners away from Rosa's office, they turned into a corridor where a man in his late sixties stood in front of them, his balance wavering slightly and giving him a frail disposition that complimented the rasping voice he used to beckon them into a nearby room. They followed him hesitantly into a dark, dated classroom with two-thirds of its space occupied by chairs and desks and the remainder left mostly clear. The man stood with the lights off, the sunshine prevented from entering by fully drawn roller blinds.

"I've worked here a long time," he said, unbidden, "and I know the girl you were asking about."

Only at this point did it register with them that they were looking at one of Rosa's colleagues, whose departure from the office they hadn't noticed.

"Is she missing?" The way he asked the question cut through the fabrications they'd presented to Rosa and impelled them to answer truthfully.

"Yes."

"And your friend?"

"Yes."

"Do you think they're together?"

"No, I don't think so. Our friend left to search for her." It was Morton doing the answering.

"When was this?"

"A few weeks ago."

The man eyed them like they were giving him a low-ball offer for a used car.

"What do you know about Crissa?" Morton asked.

The man allowed himself a hollow smile. "A wild girl," was his assessment.

"What does that mean?"

"I'm retired now. I work because I enjoy being around people. I used to share an office with some of the personal assistants to the more senior staff here at the university. You hear a lot of things in such an environment. You learn people's habits. Even if you don't gossip, it is impossible not to pick things up. I'm a watcher. While other people are talking, I'm taking in things around me. I've always been the same." He paused, perhaps feeling that his efforts merited appreciation.

"The Rector here at that time was a consumptive man. Driven in many ways, not all of them good. He enjoyed women and disposed of them easily. For most of them, this was no problem. Even for his wife, this was no problem," he exclaimed. "All part of their arrangement. Your friend changed that. She affected him. He was different around her."

"Wait—Crissa was seeing the head guy here at the university?"

"Privately, yes. I saw them three times, and that was three times more than anyone else."

"You're losing me here," Morton said.

"The first time," the man said, holding up his index finger to count, "was outside a restaurant in the city. It was clearly the start of something. They got into a car together.

"The other times were extremely late, when they thought they were alone in the building. The last time I saw them, it was a huge row," he said, circling his arms like windscreen wipers to illustrate scale, "very loud. He was trying to quieten her down, calm her. No chance: she was incensed." He delivered the final word emphatically, suggesting that his sympathies lay with Crissa. "She was distraught, I don't know about what."

His eyes pierced the gloom in a way that discouraged questions.

Up came the second finger. "The second time was an intimate moment."

"I don't understand what this has to do with us," Morton said.

"Her name is Crissa?"

"Yeah."

"Yes," he nodded, "I'm very good with names and faces."

"And we just used her name when we were speaking to Rosa, so that's hardly impressive detective work," Morton cut across him.

The man waved away his protests. "They seemed destructive in many ways, but I've never seen two people burning so brightly for each other as Crissa and Andreas. It consumed them."

Morton snapped to attention. "What did you just say?"

"Ah, you see—you should listen instead of being impatient," he scolded, relishing the opportunity to do so. "The Rector of the university at the time that Crissa was here was Michael Andreas."

"The government guy who's gone missing?"

"The very one. And now both he and the girl have vanished. If you had seen what I had seen, you would not call that coincidence."

———•———

"What about Camden?" Anthony had asked Morton towards the end of their visit earlier in the day. "Any sign of him?"

"No. Been over a month since he left. He was in touch early on. Nothing recent." He explained the contact that Nikopolidis had instigated with Dean and, in broad brushstrokes, their visit to the spa. Anthony seemed phlegmatic. "I don't think we'll see him again until he finds Crissa," Morton concluded.

Anthony's lips twisted slightly in a way that looked like an unfavourable appraisal of Camden's actions.

"We're all different, Dad."

"One of the things about love," came the reply, "is that it can be disproportionate."

Chapter 28

It was around the time of night when things tended to go one of two ways, and recently the preferred route had been less conducive to scholarly pursuits than to funny stories recounted through the fuzz of the next morning. Tonight was starting to assume a similar form. Crissa was happy to roll with it.

It was October 2008. She had heard tales that her second year of university would need more commitment to her studies than the first, but that had not yet proven true. Academically she wasn't feeling challenged, but the social payoff more than made up for that. Tonight, they were a group of four—Crissa, Rosa, Adrianna, and Evelina— and had decided to start the evening off with a meal at an affordable restaurant on the other side of town from the university. They'd made the usual comments about having just a single bottle of wine between them before acting in contravention to that pledge at each opportunity. By the time they left the restaurant towards the first bar, they'd made their way through a bottle each and counting. Crissa, who could hold her drink well, cast an eye around the group as they hit fresh air for the first time in two hours and immediately questioned whether they'd compromised the rest of their evening: there was a lot of wobbling and swaying going on for 9.30pm.

"Maybe we should pace ourselves so we make it through the night," she proposed. It wasn't taken up as an option. Instead, the girls began the half-mile walk and seemed to regain composure as they progressed. After a while they came to a group of upscale restaurants that had always caught Crissa's fancy. An ardent people watcher, she found herself checking out the diners—she had long had a habit of lightly attaching to them assumed personalities and circumstances—until her attention was diverted by a solitary figure eating at a table towards the rear of the restaurant. He seemed at ease without company, slowly working his way through a mouthful and taking in the surroundings.

She'd met him once before and had been struck by the sincere way he gave everyone his full attention when they spoke. There had been rumours when he was appointed Rector that his past contained more than its fair share of volatile moments, but that didn't chime with Crissa's experience. She had found him magnetic.

She told her companions that she'd seen a friend in the restaurant and that she'd catch them up once she'd said hello. With perfect clarity, she decided to change the direction of her night and her life.

Entering the restaurant, Crissa permitted herself a smile of gratitude that their earlier dinner plans had led to her choice of outfit that evening being more elegant and refined than may usually have been the case. It was a fitted white dress which showcased the sweeps of her figure while challenging the imagination to at least do a little work.

Andreas had looked her way as she had first walked through the door, finding it unusual for an attractive girl on the cusp of her twenties to turn up at a restaurant so late and alone. After that initial inquisitiveness, his attention returned to his meal and didn't shift again until Crissa had slalomed between the tables and positioned herself— weight shifted gently through her right foot—in front of him, hands joined lightly in front of her stomach, around her clutch bag.

Taking in the view presented to him, Andreas carefully dabbed the sides of his mouth with his napkin and reclined in his chair. "That's a beautiful dress," he observed.

Crissa's head dipped in a way that suggested the compliment was welcome but not unexpected. "Thank you."

"Not that you've given it a chance to be anything else."

She simply smiled. It was the first experience he had of the confident challenges she would set him on many occasions in the future.

"Do I know you?" he asked, glancing furtively around, conscious that some of the looks that had followed Crissa's path through the restaurant had yet to detach themselves from her.

"We met once."

"I thought I recognised you," he said as he took his wine glass from the table.

"The fundraiser at the start of semester."

"Crissa, isn't it?" He held the wine glass towards her as he spoke.

"That's an impressive memory," Crissa replied after an unsteady moment.

He appeared ready to shoot back with another comment before instead grinning to himself, nodding, and taking a brief drink. "Are you waiting for someone?"

"No."

"Oh. Dining alone?"

"I've already eaten."

"I'm not going to ask you why you've walked into one of the best restaurants in the city when you don't have an appetite."

"Then I won't tell."

He took another drink and gestured with his palm at the seat opposite. "Please."

She watched him pour her a glass of wine as she sat.

"No food at all?"

"No, thank you."

"Do you mind if I continue to eat?"

"Not in the least."

"Maybe you can join me for some dessert."

She raised the glass to her lips and lifted her eyebrows in an unreadable response.

"So, you're a student at the university?"

"I am."

"Are you enjoying it?"

"Aspects of it."

"Oh? Which aspects?"

"The social aspects."

"You know I should frown upon that sort of attitude to your studies," he said good-naturedly.

"Don't misjudge it: I'm serious about my studies, but I don't find them stimulating."

Andreas' back straightened slightly. "Well, we need to do something about that. In what ways are they not stimulating?"

"Do you find working at the university stimulating?"

"What do you study, Crissa?" he enquired. "I'd put money on it being something that allows you to question people's thinking."

"Political Sciences," she smiled. "Year Two."

He nodded and formed an approving upside-down crescent with his lips, clearly enjoying their exchanges. "Do you consider yourself political?"

"I think we're all political, whether by choice or circumstance. That's going to be ever more the case in the coming years."

"What makes you say that?"

"Is that an expensive suit?" she nodded at the jacket he'd folded carefully alongside him on the banquette.

He gestured to the waiter, who whisked away his plate within seconds. "There's a pattern to how you converse," he told her, leaning forward on his elbows as he placed them where the plate had laid.

"What is it?" she responded, mirroring his posture.

"You don't answer two questions in a row."

"Does that tell you something about me?"

"It suggests you like to be in control of conversations."

Her wine glass and eyebrows went to work again.

"Am I correct?"

"I'll leave you to your own judgments."

"And I don't think you lose many arguments."

The wine was good.

"It says something about you that you made that observation," she contended.

"Really? What does it say about me?"

"That you trust your instincts."

He allowed himself a fleeting moment of self-pride before she swept it out from under him.

"And that the relative success you've experienced in your life has led you to believe that you're right far more often than you're wrong."

"I'm wrong a lot of the time."

"Do you admit to it?"

He couldn't help himself laughing. "Not often, no."

They took their drinks in tandem.

"I do like to be in control," she said in a low, steady voice as her glass settled back onto the table.

"I'm getting that impression."

The waiter re-emerged with dessert menus: Andreas took his when it was offered to him; Crissa demurred.

"No?" he asked her.

"Not tonight."

"A shame. And now I feel guilty having one while you don't."

"I'll leave you to it, then," she said, draining her glass and standing up.

"You don't need to leave."

"I think it's best. Enough fun for one evening. It's Wednesday: isn't this supposed to be the least fun night of the week?"

"I like Wednesdays."

"Why?"

"It's the best food I have all week. I eat here every Wednesday during term time. I'm away from my wife and children from Monday to Thursday. I tend to work late, eat a great meal, and then retire to my apartment alone, grateful for the late start on Thursday."

It occurred to him that she didn't blink often. She leaned in towards him and kissed his cheek. "It was a pleasure to meet you again. Sorry for imposing."

"Not at all," he replied as she spun and glided towards the door.

———•———

A week later, as the lights of the city spilled through the undrawn curtains of his apartment bedroom and caressed her form with shadows as she lay on her back beneath him; as he had pulled her close to him upon stepping into the empty living room and raised her arms above her head, resting her hips against the wall while he kissed her neck and she let his hands run free across the black and gold dress she'd poured herself into; as, laying on the bed, he removed the final piece of her clothing and slowly made his way back up from her ankles, kissing every part of her body and savouring the smoothness and smell of her skin before being swept away when he tasted her for the first time; as he stared at the ceiling, trying to balance the ecstasy that her mouth brought to him with the urgent desire to control himself for greater treasures ahead, before she held him in her hands and guided him into her as she lowered herself down; as later she arched her back, pulling herself up from all fours and craning her neck so that she was kissing him as he climaxed for her for the first time; throughout all those moments—and the dozens of other trysts they committed themselves to so fully over the coming months—he knew he was embarking on something that was far more than physical, but which was indeed very physical.

It had been an inevitable sequence of events from the moment he had arrived at the same restaurant the following Wednesday to find her sitting alone at the table adjacent to where they had spoken the previous week, replying to his enquiry of what she was doing there by asking him: "Why else would you tell me exactly where and when to meet you?"

Chapter 29

After terminating the broadcast of his speech amidst the escalating protests, Andreas was enveloped by silence. He allowed Alex's second attempt at contact to go unanswered. Deeming it his best shot to clear his head and fend off the inevitable calls from his wife and boss, he switched off both mobiles and disconnected the landline. He closed his eyes and concentrated on his breathing, accompanied by the soundtrack of the serene lapping of the sea below. It helped, to a point.

This was hardly the first time his headstrong nature had proven to be a double-edged sword. His first memory of it was in a schoolyard, aged six, when he summoned up every sinew of rage in his body to swing a tree branch bigger than him and connect with enough impact to send a boy three years his senior crumpling to the ground, clutching his head. A moment after contact, Michael knew that retrieving his prized football from the older boy's grip was unworthy of either the damage he had just caused or the repercussions that would follow. His parents had been appalled, although his mother had privately worried for some time that, although much improved from his days as a small child, her son's temper controlled him rather than the other way around.

His childhood was a succession of tender moments punctured by outbursts. They became trademarks. Time lessened but didn't eradicate them, and while they made for amusing tales at social gatherings, they also had the ability to make him cringe. His desperate drive to escape his modest upbringing was paradoxical. The youngest of three brothers, he felt ashamed that he found the lives of his parents and ambitions of his siblings so small, yet he knew who he was. Family get-togethers and learning a trade would provide insufficient sustenance for his future; there was no point pretending otherwise. And yet his desperation could also prove his undoing. Ironically, as the family's only careerist, he was also the only one who would display such indiscipline.

For example, he experienced exhilaration when he pinned his boss to the wall by the throat in his first full-time job at an electronics company after one too many dismissals of what Andreas felt were the solutions for the company's problems. As two security guards ejected him from the building, it dawned on him that he would have to get creative and humble when explaining the lack of a glowing reference from his gap year as he reset his aim on a sparkling university career.

Once that misdemeanour proved not to be an insurmountable issue, the tale became one he retold with vigour and a twinkle in his eye until, upon being appointed

Rector of the University of Athens, his alma mater and the country's oldest university, in 2004, his face appeared on the front page of Estia. Across four pages, an unflattering profile was painted of an academic whose newfound power sat uneasily with a national publication largely intolerant of his leftist leanings. His gap-year transgressions were only one example selected by the newspaper to illustrate his indiscipline. The time he faceplanted a fellow student into her bowl of pasta was another. A photo evidencing the crooked nose of a late-night opponent who claimed he was an innocent, defenceless victim—despite the fact that he started an unsolicited fight with Andreas outside a nightclub in 1993—also featured.

He had tried meditation, even lightly studied Buddhist philosophy. The teachings resonated but didn't reshape him. Impulsiveness still stalked his moods. It was to his immense frustration that his weaknesses—lust, ostentation, a desire for admiration—rendered him no better in his mind than those he felt both above and apart from: frivolous, powerful people who strengthened their positions by denying equal access to their subordinates. He was, by his own admission, stronger on philosophy than deeds.

Gianna knew of his indiscretions. She recognised him for who he was when they first got together in their late twenties, accepting and resenting him on steady rotation. To their friends, they were compatible at a macro level, less so upon closer scrutiny. They shared dreams and aspirations rather than common interests or mutual affection. And yet they endured because they worked at it and constantly reminded themselves—and each other—of the benefits that their union brought to them.

Twenty-two years on, they had two sons, one attending university in London, the other in Massachusetts. Gianna would see Michael two or three days a week. They put time aside for a Date Night every fortnight. It felt like a healthy stab at routine rather than a regular renewal of their romance. They moved in identical or separate circles as it suited them. It was contractual.

———·———

Andreas clearly remembered the day in the early autumn of 2008 when the Prime Minister first approached him about a role in government. They had met twice before at public dinners, when Andreas was university rector and the Prime Minister an up-and-comer in the opposition. The call had come in during a meeting with his senior staff; his secretary informed him who was on the line and promptly emptied his office on his behalf.

"Michael," said the voice.

"How are you, sir?"

An audible smile made its way down the line. "You told me you would only call me sir once I am Prime Minister."

"I'm getting into practice, sir. I figure those days aren't so far away."

"That is kind but premature. It is also, in some ways, related to the purpose of my call."

It had been an unexpected offer and the fact that it had caught Andreas off-guard was the primary reason for him declining it: a role in the struggling opposition party was not immediately alluring, yet it spoke to his desire for a greater purpose which he believed himself well disposed to serve.

Six months passed with him stewing over his decision, receiving no further contact until another unarranged call made its way to his office, this time at 7pm, as he was preparing to leave for the night.

"Working late?"

"I wasn't expecting any calls, let alone this one, sir."

"This one?"

"A call from you, sir."

"Stop with the 'sir'. That's one of my two conditions to this conversation continuing."

"Understood."

"The second condition is that you open the door when it knocks in thirty seconds."

He arrived unescorted and unnoticed by anyone other than the somnolent security guards at the entrance to the campus.

"Why do you think I'm here, Michael?" he asked once they had both taken their seats.

Andreas paused before answering. "I think it's wiser for me to hope than guess."

"Very well. Why do you hope I am here?"

"To ask me the same question you asked me six months ago."

He nodded in affirmation. "What has changed in that time?"

"I've had six months to reflect on my error of judgment."

"Anything else?"

Andreas was puzzled. "Such as?"

"I want bold people in my government, Michael: that's why I am here. You've impressed me every time we've met: the way you carry yourself, your accomplishments. But

I believe that it was caution that caused you to reject my offer six months ago, and that is why I asked if there was anything else."

"There's nothing else."

"But I'm right about your caution."

"You are. It was against character, which is why I've regretted it since."

"What I am presenting to you tonight is a second chance to make that decision."

"My answer is yes."

"I am glad to hear that, Michael. Promise us both one thing."

Andreas nodded.

"Be true to yourself from now on. This offer is made because you are a clear and strong-minded thinker. That is what is needed. Trust your instincts and be resolute. That is the Michael Andreas I want."

They stood, both bringing their left hands on top of the handshake, as though that made it more sincere and binding.

———•———

Five years on, he knew the Prime Minister would be trying to reach him. His instincts had been trusted and his resolution unwavering, but an unsanctioned broadcast was at best unwise, and its provocative nature was unlikely to have won him favour.

Andreas had graduated to whisky after his address to his outraged nation. He threw it back and pondered the remnants in the glass. It was Japanese and had been named the world's best a couple of years previous. That discovery had staggered him at the time but less so after a few sips. Planting himself on the sofa that looked out onto the water, he placed the glass on the table and closed his eyes with a sigh. It felt like he had drifted off for a minute or two when his eyes sprang open with a sudden realisation that caused the hairs on his arms to rise.

He was no longer alone.

———•———

Evaldas' mission was as well planned as something can be with only four days' notice and no prior knowledge of the building in which it would occur, yet as he took in its layout from a crouch position with a slow sweeping movement that took his head beyond the threshold of the bathroom and into the corridor, things rapidly coalesced.

Seconds earlier, his shoeless feet had soundlessly met the bathroom floor after he'd flattened out his body to slide himself through a gap prized open under the window. Maintaining the crouch and keeping his feet spread wide, he swept his torso back into the bathroom, looked over his shoulder and held up three fingers at the hidden faces that monitored his progress from the window. All three were to follow him in.

Michael Andreas' subconscious jolted him from his slumber at the realisation that he was no longer the sole occupant of the villa, but his transition from disorientation to self-preservation happened much too slowly. Before he'd even cantilevered himself up from the sofa, Evaldas' body was being projected towards him with such precision that within an instant the bicep of one arm was wrapped around his throat and the other around his torso, holding his arms tight in against him and rendering his top half immobile. He was on his back, Evaldas underneath him yet still able to use his bulk to pull Andreas groundward. His legs flailed as he struggled for freedom—it struck him that it was freedom rather than air that he was searching for, as the grip around his neck was purposeful but not suffocating—yet he couldn't gain enough ballast to effectively fight back. The kicks became more desperate, and he made contact with something solid. Any vain hopes that it had inflicted enough damage to effect his release vanished with a metal clang—he'd succeeded only in toppling over the stool next to his laptop. Suddenly his legs were no longer moving, instead being held in place by another body while a third wrapped something in tight loops around his ankles and then calves, then knees, then thighs. Andreas had an awareness of all these things happening, yet they didn't demand as much attention as the knife that glinted in front of his eyes when the second and third bodies appeared. It carried with it the stark truth that compliance was his only option, and he felt the heat of his pores letting loose with sweat and the embarrassment of tears filling his eyes. There remained a foolish pride that he had controlled his faculties up to this point. The knife was held by Evaldas, who first presented its flat edge before rotating it to exhibit the serrated blade. He tilted Andreas' head back slightly to expose the throat, touching the skin there so deftly that Andreas switched his entire concentration to resisting the urge to swallow. With his mind so frantic, it felt like a near impossible task.

Evaldas levelled his breathing and strove for strength in stillness. His two fellow restrainers went to work, binding

Andreas' arms completely to his body. The fourth member of the crew had completed a recce of the premises—inside and out—and reported back with astonishment that there were no security cameras, only an alarm system that had not been activated.

"This will be a flick of the wrist away from your throat the whole time," Evaldas advised Andreas in low tones. "You've seen what we do: don't test us."

Wet blinks agreed with the recommendation.

Within two minutes they had vacated the villa, the bathroom window resecured, the side door used as their exit. Their boat was a tight fit for five so Andreas was laid along the bottom of it, the four figures positioned along the length of his body, offering no escape. It was all he could do to prevent passing out, and he wasn't sure he fully succeeded.

They headed southwest—away from the main island—before circling back east half a mile out to sea and mirroring the southern coast from a safe distance before travelling up its east side. It was one of the others who now held the knife to Andreas' throat. Evaldas raised his head into the gentle breeze created by the speed of the boat so that the air ran across his eyes and lips, the only parts of his body that were uncovered.

This was far from the first criminal act of stealth he had committed, but it was the most brazen and high-stakes. It troubled him how natural the whole thing had felt.

Chapter 30

Seventeen hours before Salvation opened briefly for its sole evening of business, Camden taxied back to Crissa's apartment in a smitten haze. He'd taken his leave of Morton and their recently-arrived visitors, fending off their protestations with a single-minded determination born out of equal parts devotion and lust. It was important to him to make clear to his friends the extent of his bliss with Crissa, and incessantly talking about it had filled his brain with an overpowering desire to make love to her before losing her to the mainland for a few days. The lights were still on when the cab pulled up outside. As he hit the night air, he was glad he'd been having water along with the shots they'd been imbibing over the last hour or so.

She was sitting at the kitchen table, having seemingly expected him to enter at that very moment.

"Hey," he answered, a few seconds passing before he became aware that things were not about to turn instantly amorous. "You OK?"

"I need to talk to you. There's been a change of plan."

"Hmmm?" He wasn't wearing his most intelligent expression.

"I'm staying here. I'm not going to the mainland for the protests."

"Oh." Camden's chest emptied itself with relief. Up until that point, Crissa's words had carried an air of alarm. "OK, great. Are you going to come to our opening night?"

"Sit down with me." She nodded at the seat, and he robotically placed himself opposite her. "There are going to be protests here."

"Here?"

There was no need for a response, verbal or otherwise.

"Why here?"

"It's the right moment." As though the answer was self-evident.

"You've never mentioned them bringing any protest activity over here."

"I don't head things up anymore, Christian. But I still have credibility and I'm needed now. There have never been protests on the islands. They need coordination from people who've been through it in the past. You know I've done it before."

Camden leaned back in his chair, searching for internal calm. It proved elusive. "The most frustrating thing is that I won't be able to influence you at all."

Again, no reply needed.

"Do you want me to list the reasons? Your safety; our future; your job; our opening night." He counted them off on his fingers.

Her eyes bore into him. "Do you understand why I do this?"

There was a beat before he answered. "Yeah, we've spoken about it." He cursed himself for sounding like a churlish juvenile as he answered, chin buried in his chest.

"But do you understand it?"

"I understand parts. That's all I can understand. You don't give me enough to fill in all the blanks."

She watched him process things.

"I can't go back and live through your past with you, much though I wish I could," he continued.

"You wouldn't want to."

"If it helped me take away some of your pain I would."

She shrugged her shoulders coarsely. "Pain shapes us."

"Is that supposed to be profound?"

Crissa briefly rolled her eyes to the side and chuckled under her breath.

"What was that for?" he asked angrily. "Don't dismiss me for caring about you."

"You don't understand, Christian."

"Which suits you perfectly," he shot back.

"You've not been through what I've been through. You don't get to turn up years later and talk like you would have made it all OK."

"I can't do anything else."

"I know. So just accept that. You don't have any other option."

They said nothing for a time.

"Pain is why I have to be here when the protests are happening."

This was where Camden had lost the full flow of Crissa's logic, and he wished he'd pulled her up on it at the time.

"Tell me you won't be directly involved," he pleaded.

"I won't be, but even if I was, it would be nothing to worry about. The protests will be peaceful, not like in the pictures you see from the cities. People there are downtrodden and angry. That kind of discontent has never really reached the islands. There's a disconnect between the reality here and the reality on the mainland and it needs to be addressed. Most foreigners who visit Greece head for the islands. What they see is idyllic and untroubled. They see pictures on a TV screen of the streets of Athens and it seems remote; they don't draw a parallel between those images and the experience they have while they're sunbathing and dining with a sea view. Tonight will be the first time that they'll witness the trauma of the mainland transported to the islands. We will protest. It'll be alarming to a lot of people here, but it will be peaceful, and it will be honest. It'll strike a chord. It's the right time to do it. Tourists are arriving. Time to publicise."

Silence pervaded the room, disturbed only by the obsequious ticking of the wall clock.

"How can I help you?" Camden finally asked.

"By not telling your friends."

"Why?"

"They don't know my background and I can't have them learning it. The way things are right now, I'm one of thousands of people demonstrating against the government. I'm one of the crowd. I need to stay that way."

"I'm not used to lying to them."

"I know. It's the only help I need from you, but it's important."

"How will I know you're alright?"

"I'll be fine."

"I can't just act like everything's normal while everyone around me is revelling in our first night and I'm wondering whether or not you're safe. Can I—"

"I won't have my phone," she said, anticipating the question.

"Why?"

"Think about it. I don't even have it now. It's already gone."

Camden's face hardened. "So, the wheels are already in motion. This was all decided before I even walked through the door."

"This was always about telling you what I'm going to do. Neither of us ever need to ask permission about anything."

"This was never going to be about asking permission and you know that."

"OK, how about this?" Crissa held both hands in front of her as though at the beginning of a hesitant prayer. "We have two scenarios. The first one—the one that *will happen*," she bulged her eyes to emphasise the point in what she hoped was a light-hearted way, "is that you drive back to my apartment once everything is done at Salvation, once you're closed up and have banked that monstrous amount of cash you're going to take on your opening night."

Camden awaited further permutations.

"Second scenario is that you see or hear something that you're not happy with. If that happens, I'll have a contact waiting somewhere ready to meet you."

"A contact?" The phrase sat poorly with him.

"Tristan. I've known him a while and he's back on the

island. He'll be in Cafe Rock just off the town square all night, ready to bring you to wherever I am."

"OK. One condition. You do that for me, and I'll do what you're asking."

"What's the condition?"

"That you tell me the worst part of your past. Right now. As long as you hide things like that from me, I can't accept my role in your life."

"OK," Crissa agreed. "The worst part."

"And tomorrow: first sign of things going wrong," he replied, "and I'm finding Tristan."

———•———

Inside Salvation, Camden felt himself detach from the scene around him.

The television played a cavalcade of unwelcome images: advancing riot police; unruly crowds; cars ablaze; faces contorted with terror at the shift from antagonism to violence; thick jets of water knocking people from their feet and propelling them across the streets.

He couldn't suppress it any longer. He had to see her.

Camden raced to his right as soon as he hit the streets, barging his way through a cascading mass of bodies infused with fear, invigoration, horror, and excitement. The catcalls that trailed in his wake went unheard as he took the steps up from the cliffside paths towards the main town square three at a time. He reached the top of the climb quickly and adjusted his stride to hit full speed as he bulleted towards Cafe Rock. It was all but empty, the evening's customers presumably having recently become otherwise engaged.

No sooner had Camden entered the doorway than a thin-hipped man with slicked jet-black hair was released from the shadows at the far end of the bar and walked towards him in a decisive manner that still managed to look like a saunter. "Come with me," he said as he passed.

Camden turned around. "Tristan?"

Tristan didn't confirm or deny, instead retrieving a helmet from the luggage box of a scooter parked outside and tossing it in his direction. "A good time to avoid a ticket," he said, pulling on his own helmet, climbing into the seat and gripping the handlebars. He didn't look back but showed no sign of leaving until he had a travelling companion.

Within seconds they were pulling away from the Town Square towards a narrow alleyway that had not been constructed with two-wheeled transport in mind. Camden briefly wondered about the rationale for the route Tristan had chosen until, upon glancing right in the split-second before the alleyway walls closed in around them, he saw twenty or so police officers, fully equipped and walled by Perspex, marching in formation towards the steps he had just taken at such pace.

Chapter 31

Darkness was making itself comfortable as Crissa nudged open the door of her home. Maintaining silence as much as she could, she squeezed it closed behind her and carried her bicycle until she arrived on level ground near the square at the heart of Emporio. Once there, she clambered onto the seat and her legs took over from her autopiloting brain, which flitted between worries and memories. The wheels turned sedately through the town before picking up pace as she passed the last house and took the road which would take her first west, then north.

Her gloved hands gripped and released the handlebars. She rode through air that slid warmly across her face as though trying to soothe her anxiety. She bore the look of an exercise enthusiast—a mid-grey zip-up hoodie over a purple t-shirt and dark grey leggings. Her trainers also sported a purple streak. She had avoided all-black attire.

Camden was a constant buzz around her mind. She knew she was being unfair to him and that he was making things easier for her than she had a right to expect. How much of her future life should she risk for the sake of her past? Her feelings were true and bone-deep: she hoped he knew that. What thoughts would be tumbling around inside him now? How well would he be reconciling the images that would be weaving before and behind his eyes, balancing the opening-night joy he was supposed to be feeling against the fear he had to suppress about her welfare?

Crissa had been thrilled by the process of discovering things about him, quite unlike anything else she'd known. Within him he held a belief—or simply a need for a belief— that a better life was there for the constructing. Even when she had told him the previous night about her affair with Michael Andreas—and all the torment that she carried from those days—he focused purely on how she'd never have to endure anything like that again. It was instinctual for him to foresee a future for them both that was unfettered by the past. She had been careful not to derail it. She knew that it meant he'd do anything for her.

Instant attractions had been sprinkled throughout her youth—driven first by a desire for love; then lust in assorted guises, transmitted to her through confidence, resolve and, ultimately, power—but with Camden she'd experienced the closest thing to wholeness she'd known. It was beyond what she'd imagined for herself, revelatory if occasionally constrictive. She would work through it. The years leading up to Camden were dead time, best written off and erased, if only that were possible.

Travelling clockwise around the lower part of the island, she would soon complete an almost-circle of its tallest part, atop which sat Profitis Ilias Monastery, before slicing through Kamari—still under half-capacity at this early point of the tourist season—and hoisting herself up a steep, winding single-track road to Ancient Thera, Santorini's second highest point. There she would wait alone for a short while.

Pedals churning beneath her, she didn't pay attention to the car that passed her the opposite way, slowing as it did so before resuming its previous speed.

———•———

The sea beneath Crissa gave off an obsidian glimmer as she first caught the sound of an overmatched engine. 10:30pm, her watch told her. She had been here alone for a little over thirty minutes. She stood in an excavation site—one of several on the island—with astonishing views of the surrounding seas and towns below. But it had been chosen for its quietude, not its aesthetic merits. Crissa became fleetingly aware that she had instinctively positioned herself in a part of the site where not only would she see any incomers before they saw her; she would also be advantaged by the raw light of the moon haloing her face while illuminating theirs as they blinked into it. She crouched behind a small wall, in front of which was a ten foot by ten-foot square of dusty ground without any ancient architecture waiting to be disturbed.

The engine—which had clearly found the climb quite a challenge—clicked off, its sounds replaced by what she interpreted as four feet stealthily crossing the ground. Crissa dipped and moved her head into the sightline she had sought out. The footsteps were not for making themselves easily identifiable, however, and she returned her head behind the wall, remaining still for a couple of seconds while she considered a next move that was rendered unnecessary by a single word.

"Tristan," was the word, said plainly from a distance of no more than twenty feet.

Crissa stood straight in recognition of both the word and the voice, which emanated from a point in her past that seemed both distant but inescapable. Tristan stood poised and calm, hands by his side as he took in the woman before him. Crissa returned the action before her eyes jumped leftwards to Camden, whom circumstances seemed to be taunting. "Hey," she said to him.

"What's happening?"

Instead of answering, Crissa turned her attention back to Tristan, who nodded, spun in place and made his way back to his scooter. Camden watched him go and Crissa's arms were there for him when he turned back around.

"Why are you here?" she asked him.

"We're standing on the most remote part of the island—same question goes for you."

"Waiting for someone."

"Who?"

"A few people. They should be on their way."

"It's gone crazy in Fira."

Crissa's eyes narrowed.

"The streets were full of people. It wasn't like you said it would be," he said, leaning back to see her as he held her in his arms. "It wasn't all peaceful. Some people were looking for aggravation there. When I met Tristan, there were riot police starting to move across the town square towards the front streets."

"Riot police?"

"Yeah, they were—"

"Ssssh," Crissa said abruptly.

They both heard wheels on gravel.

"What's going on, Crissa?"

"Come with me," she instructed, resuming her position behind the wall, "and don't move."

Camden looked at her as though seeing her for the first time.

"Wasn't Tristan worried about announcing himself like that? It wasn't exactly discreet."

"He would have realised when he arrived that I was the only one here. And his name isn't Tristan."

She shivered. It wasn't cold.

Chapter 32

When he'd arrived on the island three days earlier, Evaldas had worn a foldaway backpack containing three plain t-shirts, three sets of underwear, a zip-up hoodie, spare pair of shorts, basic items of hygiene and a pair of running gloves. A backwards-facing cap covered a head that had been shaven since his hair had first made its retreat in his early twenties, more than a decade ago. He wore aviators and a grey lightweight V-neck with khaki cargo shorts. Broad shouldered and carrying his height in full, each athletic step possessed grace and menace. Everything was utilitarian.

His expectation that he would be the first to arrive proved correct. The rest would assemble in stages over the coming hours.

His instructions could be divided into an unambiguous first act and a second act rife with risk. As was his wont, he focused on the part he could control. More than the variables that he would need to negotiate in the coming days, the thing that caused him most pause was his suspicion that the instructions had been passed onto him as a result of emotional attachment. That was outside of his wheelhouse, but he owed a favour, and it was the type of favour that demanded substantial repayment.

Everything had checked out: the addresses contained the people they were supposed to contain; the verbally-drawn maps were representative of the key landmarks; and the rhythms of the days of those he watched had been described to him with such accuracy that he doubted he was the first person to be sent to the island on reconnaissance. The key difference was that his mission was far more than mere reconnaissance.

The patterns of Crissa's life were easy enough to shadow. She worked at a desirable spa hotel and her breaks seemed to consist of enjoyable chats with two colleagues, with whom she also spent some time outside of work. She seemed especially close to one of them—a statuesque blonde who was either unmoved by or oblivious to her physical attributes—and they both in turn seemed protective over the third member of the group, who appeared capable of finding stress and difficulty in the most rudimentary daily interactions.

The boyfriend was even more straightforward: he was either with Crissa or working in the bar that he was due to open with his business partner, at least until the Wednesday, when a flurry of activity saw him drive to the airport to collect a group of friends who'd flown in from the UK to celebrate the bar's inaugural night. Together they'd had celebratory drinks at assorted establishments throughout Fira. None of this was a surprise to Evaldas because it had all been laid out for him before he had boarded his boat.

Taking note of where Crissa and the boyfriend had parked, Evaldas made sure he was on his way back there the moment Crissa withdrew from the evening's festivities. Thirty steps short of her car, Crissa altered her stride and direction, and at that point he knew she'd been part of the movement. It didn't leave you quickly.

"It's OK, Crissa," said one of two nearby men who had, until that point, seemingly been deep in conversation, "he's been sent by a friend of yours."

Crissa stopped despite knowing better and stared at the men, who nodded and resumed their dialogue as though nothing untoward had just occurred. By this time, Evaldas was by her side. "Will you walk with me?" he asked.

"No," she said defiantly.

"I won't force you." His voice was inexpressive and surprisingly feminine. "I'm only here because Malachi asked me."

"Malachi?" Crissa took a half-step, as though to stride away from him, before aborting it and remaining in place. The two men were no longer in sight.

Evaldas' demeanour gave nothing away. "Is there a better place to talk?"

It was evident to him that Crissa was searching for a suitable venue—away from the town in which her boyfriend was carousing; distanced from the place she called home; out of earshot of casual listeners; without risk to her personal safety—so he tried to resolve the quandary for her. "Two choices: we can mingle with the tourists and go to one of the towns in the south, or you can park up at your place and we can talk in Emporio."

"What do you know about me?" she asked him.

"Before Sunday I had no idea you existed. After I'd spoken to Malachi, I realised you were important to him. They're not attachments he accumulates carelessly. And now I'm striving to find out nothing else about you. It will help us both in the fullness of time."

"Why should I trust you?"

"Can I borrow your lighter?"

"Why?" she insisted, opting not to ask how he knew she still carried a lighter, even though it had been more than three years since she had last lit a cigarette.

His eyebrows raised in a miniscule display of impatience, in response to which she handed it over. A reporter's notebook was brandished, and he scribbled quickly with a biro before ripping out the page and holding it out so she could read it. Her facial muscles constricted and then disengaged completely. Evaldas lit the paper, let it burn and then dropped it on the floor, making sure that the only section to remain uncharred was the one in which he had avoided writing.

———•———

Five figures moved towards Crissa and Camden, laid out like dots on a dice, the central figure blindfolded and gagged, seemingly directed by a hand placed halfway up his back.

A glance from Camden asked if these were the people Crissa was expecting, and she nodded without taking her eyes off them. Drawing her zip slowly up and bringing her hood tightly over her head, she rose to her feet and the figures adjusted their path slightly to bring themselves to her. Camden nervously took his place by her side. None of them spoke, but Crissa and the one at the far right exchanged a nod, similar to the one she had traded with Tristan. The scene struck Camden as being almost comic in its high drama, until a reflection from the moon caught his eye and it became apparent that—rather than a simple hand being held at the back of the man in the centre of the group—it was a serrated knife, which was now in the process of being moved towards his throat. Camden's mouth was suddenly dry, and he was caught unaware when Crissa sat back down at the base of the wall behind which they had crouched. It seemed an incongruous time to take the load off.

The front two members of the group fanned out to either side and the blindfolded man was brought to within a few feet of Crissa. Evaldas stepped forward and handed something small to her which she instantly pocketed. She then rocked back onto her feet and remained motionless for several seconds, appraising the man standing before her and seeming to strategise on the spot. A mischievous smile appeared on her face as she glanced at Evaldas and walked towards the man holding the blade. The man in the blindfold allowed his head to move the tiniest amount as a different smell announced its presence nearby. Two pathetic grunts made their way from his terrorised throat through the gag that wrapped tightly around the lower half of his head.

Crissa laid her hand gently on top of the blade-holder's and maintained complicit eye contact until the knife was released into her possession. Keeping it softly pressed to Andreas' throat, she moved it around in her hand so that the tip grazed the tightly stretched skin.

"Thank you for the hard drive," she said breathily in her native tongue, leaning slightly towards him as she did so. Andreas grew three inches taller with fear at the sound of her voice.

Crissa directed her eyes to Camden.

"Is that him?" he mouthed silently, stitching together parts of the conversation from the previous night and becoming cognizant of the meaning of the scene taking shape in front of him.

Crissa nodded in response and raised her eyebrows, as though asking a question of him.

The man from whom she had taken the knife loosened the gag so that it hung limply from Andreas' mouth and unbound the blindfold. As he did so, Crissa bowed her head slightly so that its crown was facing Andreas as he blinked furiously at the first light he had seen in two hours. No sooner had he gained some semblance of bearings than Crissa raised her face towards him, then pulled back the lightweight hood with her free hand, keeping the other steadfastly in place at his throat. She seemed to enjoy watching his realisation coming in stages.

All these things happened in front of Camden like a sadistic parlour game, with the leading role being played by the woman around whom he was building his life and who now appeared to him in a different form than ever before.

His horror grew exponentially as Andreas grasped what the eyes he was looking into were promising him and managed the start of the word "No!" before it was savaged by Crissa withdrawing the blade slightly and thrusting it upwards with unrestrained vehemence, driving it deeply into his neck and burying it there as time slowed, after which she dragged it to the left, shearing straight through the windpipe and then removed it suddenly, releasing her grip as she did so and letting the blade hit the ground.

From the moment the tip of the knife pierced the skin, nobody had made a coherent sound, and it was Evaldas who reacted first to rip off his hoodie and wrap it around the throat of Andreas as he fell forward, no longer sentient, to prevent the propulsions of blood spreading uncontrollably across the dried ground on which they stood.

Camden found himself incapable of speech or movement as he tried to digest what he'd just witnessed. As his world vortexed around him, his mind quickly grasped the reality of Andreas' death and instead diverted to Crissa, whose body seemed to have been reinhabited by her usual self, as though free of a transitory possession, and landed her knees on the ground, shaking and croaking, eyes pulsing out of their sockets as she tried to hold her attention on Camden but found herself unable to stop glancing over at her former lover and the devastation she had wreaked upon him.

The four figures around them moved efficaciously, equally stunned by recent events but intent on taking the necessary steps for them all to escape their predicament with as few traces as possible.

Camden held Crissa tightly to him, waiting vainly for the shaking to stop.

Chapter 33

As 2008 became 2009, his world interrupted, Andreas had taken to spending more nights away from Gianna and the children. Work demands always made for plausible obfuscation. By now he was seeing Crissa twice a week and the gaps in between dragged out excruciatingly.

The future was taking multiple forms, a wicked concoction of potential and constraints. It was the month of his forty-fifth birthday, and he felt both surprised and foolish to view each new week as ripe with possibility. He could palpably feel the absent heartbeats each time he caught first sight of her, all the more so if they occurred before she saw him: there were few things that drove him to greater desire than seeing her moving unselfconsciously, his interpretation of beauty at its most natural. He knew such feelings were teenaged.

By necessity, their meeting places became less conspicuous. The act of him sitting alone in a bar—no doubt appearing to his fellow drinkers as another nondescript middle-aged man contemplating the pressures of his life—only to have a radiant twenty year-old inexplicably come straight up and lead him outside by the hand after speaking no more than a single sentence had swollen his ego enormously, but they both knew it was a one-time deal, too egregious to be repeated.

Today's meeting point was a shopping centre, with him resting in standby mode in a formulaic eatery. Other times he would browse stores or stand outside like a reluctant shopping companion, roused into action only when Crissa walked past him without eye contact, the dance of her hips and the cut of her clothes her only acknowledgement of him as he struggled not to affix his eyes to the body that he found so delectable. From there, it would be a matter of minutes before they were alone somewhere—his car, a lift, wherever they could steal a few seconds. Their time together was basic: they fought to contain their urges until retiring to his apartment, where they immediately released themselves, shorn of clothing and the various distractions from their other lives. Andreas savoured every touch and sensation her body gifted upon him, yet there were times when he caught himself wondering if he cherished even more the conversations they would have between bouts, their sharing of small revelations. It had been almost six months since she had stood uninvited at his restaurant table.

An oppressive sorrow hung over him as Crissa drifted into view at the far end of the food hall, a lightweight camel trench coat falling open to her hips, displaying a stylish chocolate rollneck. He'd long ago taught himself how to assimilate every feature of people with a single swift look and had elevated that skill to art form during his time with Crissa. A flash from inside her mouth as her lips parted slightly upon spotting him signalled that she had yet to remove her tongue stud, despite her misgivings amid their recent circumstances.

Attention glued to his mineral water as she took her last strides past him, he took a drink until the ice cubes lapped against his lips, swilled the last remnants in a lazy circle and emptied the glass. Rising, he laid bills on the table and made his way towards the escalator.

The far doors of the shopping centre opened onto a car park, with his vehicle in a quiet, but not deserted, corner. He was fifty yards away when he unlocked his car without removing the key from his pocket and saw a smudge of light browns as they swooshed inside the vehicle.

Like many days in that flurry of months, it lived vividly in his memory for years to come.

It was fear of loss that made his decision for him. Success galvanised him, all the more so when it was visible to others. Once he had exited the most tempestuous phase of his youth, he secured impressive university qualifications and converted them into regular promotions, the foundations of his career built upon his unshakable self-confidence and an ability to convince most people he met that his was the side to be on.

It had seemed too much to give up—the one thing that was irreplaceable if its impetus was checked—and so the decision had unveiled itself to him as he stared through the bedroom ceiling of his family home in the early hours of the previous Sunday, his commute back to the capital encroaching as the darkness faded through the curtains.

His choice of a neutral venue had been multi-faceted:

Firstly, he was of the opinion that this type of thing was always best done in places of solitude, where the unpredictable directions of the conversation and its aftermath could be contained with little collateral damage.

Secondly, it was less cruel if the memories of such moments remained attached to locations that were unlikely to feature much in their futures. Nothing haunts more than the knowledge that you're approaching a place where you experienced seismic distress; that desperate hope that this will be the time that you'll feel nothing but catharsis.

Thirdly, there were no expensive or personal objects within reach.

Finally, there were no witnesses.

They had walked for thirty minutes to this spot—a small clearing containing its own minimalist natural soundtrack—where Andreas' true intentions were dragged into the open.

"Why are we here?" she asked him.

Andreas heard the truth in Crissa's suspicion, retreated a half-step and then spoke. "This can't go on, Crissa."

"You fucking asshole." Her words were instant and vociferous.

"There are too many things in the way."

"Name them."

"My children." It had seemed the most failsafe of reasons, if not the most honest. "There's Gianna."

"Yeah? The woman who doesn't do all the things you tell me that you love me doing? How many more things will you list as reasons until you mention your career?" Every word she delivered was at a volume dictated by rage.

"That's one reason, but only one of many."

Crissa expelled air through her nose and thrust her hands onto her hips, facing him square-on.

"What we've had has been amazing. You're a wonderful girl, and you deserve better than to be with someone who can never devote himself to you." He felt an active loathing of the words that left his mouth, but it had to be quelled. "I'll never forget the experiences we've had."

"You mean the fucking?"

He rolled back onto his heels.

"If this is the end of us, then all the enjoyment or special memories will involve fucking—you trying to recapture a glimmer of your youth, playing out fantasies you never thought you'd be able to enact again; me following you down a rabbit hole of empty promises that already seem pathetic. But there's more to it than that and you know it!" Her voice was straining at maximum capacity now. "You're a fucking coward!"

She started to pound his chest and he languidly brought his hand up to defend himself, in response to which she suddenly switched tactics and started striking his face with clenched fists and forearms.

"Stop it. Enough!" he yelled as he finally wrestled her into neutrality.

"You can't do this!"

"I'm doing it, Crissa."

A calm authority had entered his voice, and she dropped her hands from his at recognition of it.

"You're right. You deserve the truth. I don't have feelings for you. You're beautiful and you've been an enjoyable diversion. But that's all. Now something more important has come along and I have to make a choice. It's an easy choice to make."

"Yeah?"

He nodded nonchalantly. "After everything that's gone on in these past few weeks, I'm only glad that we both got out of this unscathed."

As soon as the words left his mouth, he knew they were irretrievable. Despite knowing that he'd had to switch to coldness to make the break as clean as he could, he wished he'd found another way.

"Just remember that it's not only me you're saying those words to, you fucking parasite."

"I'm sorry," he told her, unable to help himself.

"Sorry means nothing," she told him hatefully. "You made me give up everything and you're running away without suffering a single loss that you care about."

He watched her stride away, head held determinedly high as she did so, a single swipe of her hand across her face the only concession she would allow the turmoil she felt. And so Andreas looked upon the woman he loved the most leaving his future, feeling not for the last time that he was certain he had done the right thing in the short-term but that the regrets would reveal themselves in time.

All of these thoughts coursed through his mind as the tip of the blade was thrust into his throat by the mother of his unborn child.

Chapter 34

"Another wine?"

Crissa shook her head.

"Coffee?"

"No way. I plan on being like Sofia soon," she replied, glancing at the third member of the group, who had wafted into sleep within minutes of arriving at Irini's home. It was the end of their second summer working together and the spa's traditional end-of-season celebration had taken place that night, coming to a close at different times for different segments of the staff: whereas the more tenured members of the payroll had long since taken their leave, Dimitrios and several of the other males continued their pursuit of the perfect night out and had no plans to call it quits until morning. Much to their disappointment, Irini, Crissa, and Sofia made their exit around two, correctly interpreting the signs that if they didn't do so, they'd be subjected to advances that would make their next meetings with their work colleagues awkward in the extreme.

"Can I get you anything?"

"Do you have hot chocolate?"

"Actually, hot chocolate sounds like the perfect way to end the night. And you're in luck," Irini said, reaching into a nearby cupboard and producing a jar. "How strong do you want it? How many spoonfuls?"

"How big are your spoons?"

"I have options to suit all appetites."

"Then I'll trust you to judge my appetite."

"Dimitrios likes you, you know."

"That'll be down to my killer combination of pulse and vagina."

"More than that," Irini laughed. "Most girls he treats like prey; you he treats with respect, like he knows he's not worthy."

"I'm not interested."

"Anyone else you're interested in?"

"No." A smile and a shake of the head.

"Bad experiences?"

"We've all had them, right?" came the reluctant concession.

"Actually, I've never had a bad sexual experience, or at least not one I've regretted. I've fallen a bit quicker and heavier than I should have for people who weren't right for me, but the sex part has always worked out pretty well," Irini said with a smile. "Not the same for you?"

Crissa merely shrugged. They moved to the unoccupied sofa with their drinks.

"Eighteen months we've known each other," Irini ventured, "and we've become good friends, right?"

Crissa nodded expectantly.

"And yet we still only talk about things that are safe and superficial."

"Should I have taken you up on that offer of wine?" Crissa smiled wryly.

"I'm not prying," Irini raised her palms, the gesture met with a doubtful tilt of the head by Crissa. "Or not prying for the sake of it, anyway. I've had tough things happen to me, too. I consider you a genuine friend who I trust. Our pasts are on show whether we like it or not."

"Do you always lure vulnerable friends back to your lair and make them tell you their darkest secrets?"

They shared a smile.

"I lost my older sister when I was fourteen," Irini said, as though it was a run-of-the-mill discussion topic.

"Oh my goodness, Irini. I'm so sorry." Crissa only knew of Irini's elder brother, who lived nearby with his wife and young family. "How old was she?" The words left her mouth with an air of inappropriateness.

"Eighteen. Due to leave for college a couple of months later."

Crissa was taken aback.

Reading her thoughts, Irini instead took the reins. "It was a car accident. You know how the roads can be between Fira and Oia. She was with her boyfriend, a great guy—we all loved him. They seemed made for each other, as far as you can tell those things at such a young age. He wasn't a crazy guy or a reckless driver that we knew of." She tailed off. "But too much misplaced confidence and adrenaline; only takes one misjudged corner on those roads."

Crissa placed her hand on Irini's thigh as they sat facing each other and Irini nodded as if to approve of the gesture.

"My father found them."

Crissa's eyes widened.

"He was a paramedic. First on the scene with his partner and he didn't recognise the car because it was so mangled. Can you imagine what that must feel like?"

Crissa could only shake her head.

"It broke him, really. Trying to hold it together, thinking it would be the best way of keeping our family strong, was the worst thing he could have done. He kept trying to stay upbeat in the early days—inappropriately so, saying things like we should be thankful for what we have rather than resentful of what we'd lost. There was truth in it but none of us needed to hear it and it drove my mum away from him to the extent that they never recovered.

"My mother used to love vinyl. She had so many records and would play them all the time. Clara and I used to love singing and dancing to them with her." A smile launched itself onto Irini's lips as she spoke her sister's name. "Sixties pop and soul, Motown, she adored them all, especially if there was a female vocalist. She stopped playing them as soon as Clara died, like they represented a part of our lives where pure enjoyment was deserved and that those times had passed. One day I went to visit her and found her record player and all her records sitting in a big box next to the bin, ready to be collected with the garbage that day. I didn't tell her, but I took them in my car and played them when I got home. They'd obviously been left in the sun for too long and had started to warp. That sums up how mum's been since Clara died: the melodies and words are still there but out of tune. Incapable of joy."

"She still lives nearby, right?"

"Yeah, she still lives in the house I grew up in, about ten minutes from here. But she doesn't go out much anymore. The outside world holds nothing but worries for her these days. Her life's just become a cocoon."

Crissa sighed and hesitated before asking her next question: "What about your father?"

"Gone within five years. The whole act about being grateful for what we have and focusing on life's gifts was a very thin veneer. Before long it had been scraped away by nightmares about what he'd found at the bottom of that ravine, the bright future of his firstborn child rubbed out and turned into a statistic. Drink is an insidious friend. In most of my last images of him he's yellow and slow to react to everything around him. I wish they were images I could shake."

"I have absolutely no idea what to say to any of that, Irini."

"That's ok, there's nothing to say. It's just made me the person you've known, so I guess that's why I told you the story. Clara was my idol. I always wanted to be just like her, and she was always so kind to me. I still get proud when I see photos of her and see how alike we look." Irini finished with a smile. "I get the feeling that your story is less tragic but just as deeply felt. Am I right?"

"You've got a gift for reading people, Irini. And your sister would be very proud of you—kindness is the first word I'd use to describe you."

"Thank you. That's a lovely thing to hear," Irini said softly, then let the conversation vacuum prompt Crissa into action.

———٠———

Crissa's story was more honest with its emotion than its details.

She spoke of her ambition as a nascent student. "A definite work-hard, play-hard girl. Maybe work-hard, live-fast would be more apt. I wanted everything yesterday. Very headstrong. Not so unusual but I was toward the extreme end of the scale."

She hopped easily onto the topic of her attraction to Michael Andreas without naming him.

"He was charismatic and good-looking, in a distinguished older-guy way. When I became pregnant, it seemed the natural continuation of the most natural experience of my life. Now I look back on it as the point where the naturalness ended. There was a romance about things but also a reality that we couldn't ignore. He was married with children and an increasingly prominent career. I was less than half his age." She stopped there, as though no other reasons beyond age were occurring to her. "We arrived at a decision fairly quickly in the end. It seemed like we'd talked about it a lot, but I don't know if that was really the case. He made a lot of promises, and I accepted them too willingly. The circumstances as they were at the time were … unsuitable." A sad smile made a brief cameo. "I made the mistake of thinking that the future was promised. Within days I'd terminated the pregnancy. I hate the phrase: terminated. So cold and impersonal. I allowed my baby to be killed inside of me." Crissa's lower lip wobbled and re-settled, a heavy blink and a backward tilt of the head stifling any progress that tears may have made down her face.

"I remember him sitting beside me in the private clinic he'd arranged for us to attend. He never let go of my hand once as the doctor spoke to us about what would happen. He was there when I woke up, took me back to his apartment and laid beside me as I slept and recuperated. He did all the things I hoped he would do." Her words faded away and showed no immediate signs of restarting, yet Irini remained patient.

"When we first started out, my entire world felt different. Like each moment had become worthy of being concentrated on. Part of me was desperate to share how I felt but I was so protective of my privacy that nobody knew what I had been doing. They may have had their suspicions, given how often I would disappear, always dressed up, but nobody knew a single detail beyond that."

"Did you ever tell anyone?" Irini asked.

"My sister, Nina, but not until later. She's five years younger than me. More worldly-wise, to be honest, but I wasn't about to tell my fifteen-year-old sister about the decisions I'd made. I didn't want her to feel let down. She's my little sister. Two years down the line, I wasn't exactly living a model life and she tracked me down and we talked about everything. She's the only one who knows."

"About the affair? Or the pregnancy?"

"Both. And she's the only one who knows who the affair was with."

Irini eyed her uncertainly.

"You'd know him. He's in the public eye."

"Really?"

"Michael Andreas."

Crissa watched Irini's face screw up as she tried to locate why that name rang familiar. "The politician?"

The question was allowed to answer itself.

"A few weeks after I aborted the pregnancy, he ended our relationship. It was like a surgical procedure in itself, done in isolated woodland, all the words well-chosen and vague, as though he'd used them a dozen times before. It was the dishonesty of it that cut the most."

"Dishonest in what way?"

"The reasons he gave," Crissa said, nodding in a way that showed lingering bitterness, "I didn't believe them. He told me that I didn't mean anything to him. Spoke like I'd just served a purpose for a while and that the problems I could cause him were bigger than the happiness I could bring. It all just felt fraudulent. And then within two months he'd left his position at the university to join what was then the opposition party."

Irini nodded. "That explains some things."

"Yep. I think he'd been told his ticket was going to be called and he made a choice."

"You deserve better."

"The worst thing," Crissa said, not seeming to hear Irini's words, "was what he said about our baby."

Irini didn't move a muscle.

"He said he was glad we both came out of our relationship unscathed. That's the cruellest thing anyone has ever said to me. How could he say it? How could he ever have thought I was unscathed?" Tears were beginning to fall, droplets jumping onto the carpet. "How could *he* have been unscathed? Whether or not the rest of it was true—whether or not a baby with his mistress would have stopped him from achieving his political ambitions—our baby didn't deserve to have that said about it."

Irini waited to see if Crissa offered herself for a hug, but she remained self-contained.

"Was that the last time you saw him?"

Crissa didn't answer immediately, as though waiting for the right phrase to reveal itself in her mind. "Nothing could be gained from us seeing each other after that."

Irini briefly remained still before lifting the empty mug from Crissa's hand and taking it over to the sink with her own, the pressure valve of their intense conversation released for as long as Crissa wanted. Opposite, Sofia stirred then rested.

Unsaid words kept Crissa company on the sofa. The undignified downward spiral that had followed the breakup was kept to herself. She was conscious that her account of things placed the blame squarely on Andreas, whereas the anger that she truly couldn't let go of was directed at herself, brought about by how easily she felt she had been manipulated into giving up her baby simply because it didn't fit with his career plans. There was no need to share the tales of the times when she appeared unannounced at Andreas' apartment or work, increasingly desperate and unable to fulfil her promise to herself that she would treat the end of their affair with equanimity. And there remained nobody that she had ever told—not even Nina—about the time that she stormed into Andreas' family home just after he'd arrived back from work and confronted him in the presence of his wife, laying bare the predicament in which he'd put her and unsparing in her lurid accounts of the mechanics of how they had arrived there, all the while oblivious to the disbelieving, emptying eyes of his teenaged sons who were sitting at the kitchen table.

Those weren't stories to be shared.

Irini returned to her seat. "I often think about what I'd say to my sister if I ever saw her again."

"What would it be?"

"That I loved her and that I was so proud of her. Nothing original, but I'd mean every word of it. What would you say if you saw Michael Andreas again?"

Crissa thought for a moment, as though considering the prospect for the first time. "It depends whether I saw him from the perspective of what he did to me or what he did to our child. I'm not really sure how I'd react."

Chapter 35

On the night that his future changed for a second time, Camden held Crissa tightly to him, waiting vainly for the shaking to stop.

"Look at me," he urged.

Her eyes were unfocused and unreadable, like freshly shaken snow globes.

"Crissa, look at me," he insisted, cradling her face in his hands. "We'll figure this out."

She nodded vigorously, more through desperate hope than conviction. Her eyes were still unmoored.

He looked around at the faces looking down at him and gave a small nod to reassure them. "OK, here's what's going to happen. I need you to pay attention; there are only a few things for you to remember. OK?"

"Yeah."

It was a breathed syllable rather than an engaged response, so he tried again. "Come here," he told her, wrapping his arms around her and bringing her close to him. A wail let loose from her chest, as though he had squeezed it out, and was immediately followed by a series of convulsions that delivered streams of tears that he felt through her hair. Once the cries had subsided, he released her and held her at arm's length. "I love you."

"I love you, too."

"I need you to listen to me. Can you do that?"

She expelled air from her cheeks as hard as she could, and this time nodded in a more convincing way. "I can do that. I can do it; I'm just struggling to think straight." Her hands shook in front of her as she spoke.

"I know. These guys are going to get you out of here. I don't know where and I don't want to know just yet. We need to get you somewhere safe and obscured."

Crissa nodded.

"Once things have calmed down, I'll find a way to meet you. We'll arrange a time and a place."

"How?" she asked.

"Malachi."

She nodded.

"And if we don't hear from each other, we'll meet at the place where you asked me to take you for your birthday last year, near your old university, OK?"

"OK." She nodded. It looked to Camden like it was hitting home.

"If you've not heard from me by next Thursday, we'll meet there at 8pm, OK?"

"Got it," she replied, this time meeting his eyes.

"And if that doesn't work, then that place I told you about back in Scotland. You remember?"

She nodded maniacally.

"I'll be there."

The figures around them were shifting restlessly.

"You need to go now," Camden told her.

"I love you."

The words almost gave way to more tears so he grabbed her and held her as tightly as he could, kissing her on the lips and then peppering her face and head with as many more as he could manage. "I love you, too, with all that I have," he said as he let go, the figures coming to help her on her way. He tried to force himself not to look back as he walked off but couldn't do it. The noise of the boat sounded dangerously loud when it first started up but soon diminished into nothingness. As the silence of the night throttled him, his legs demanded that he stop. Dropping to his knees he felt helpless as he fought back tears. Looking out to the caldera he could see a fire burning. In the capital—a good seven miles away—blue lights decorated the night sky.

Soon he would be walking back to friendships he'd already surrendered in his mind, to a life he was willing to reshape to whatever form fitted. He steeled himself as he began to lay the foundations in his head. He could build on them as he needed to, and he knew that such a commitment would contain risks that would need careful tending. The lies would have a shelf life, but he had to stretch them out so that they gave him the breathing room that he and Crissa needed. The woman he had watched murder the former lover who had caused her such permanent pain was different from the woman he had known up to that point, but she was still the same woman he had fallen in love with. If life couldn't be reshaped for that, what was it for?

He rested his head gently on hands and tried to establish his breathing; everything after that had to reflect normality, even though normality had just imploded.

He took his first steps back towards his disembodied life. Time folded in on itself.

Chapter 36

Not a sound from inside. Taking two steps to her left, Irini peered through the window, the early afternoon sunlight making it difficult to make out much from within the unlit home, curtains half-drawn.

An hour passed, at which point she had to make tracks. Her shift began soon, and she'd had to pull a few strings to finagle a later start as it was. A note would have to do it. It had plagued her thoughts since Morton and Gary had visited the spa two days earlier.

It was now six weeks since she and Sofia had seen Crissa riding her bicycle, legs pumping furiously, as they passed her on their drive home from work. Confusion blended into the darkness of the car: Crissa was supposed to be with the protesters on the mainland.

"What should we do?" Sofia had asked.

"I'm not stopping," Irini had answered instinctively.

"That was Crissa, though, right?"

Irini forced silence upon the car. The next day, she had scanned the news websites on her phone upon waking and was out the door within seconds.

"What about all this trouble?" Sofia's mother asked disapprovingly as she answered her door, as though Irini and Sofia carried responsibility for the chaos that had erupted while they were working their shift at the spa the previous night. Irini had known Sofia since their first days at school and she couldn't recall anything which her mother had deemed deserving of commendation.

"Terrible," Irini replied in a neutral tone. "Wondered if you felt like a walk?" she asked, directing her words at Sofia.

Sofia nodded and stepped outside, as though following directions rather than her own volition. Irini led them up the hill to the right, away from the house, where the homes quickly petered out and were replaced by fields where the contest between flora and dust was decisively tilted in favour of the latter.

"Seen the news?"

Sofia nodded again.

"Do you know what I'm talking about?"

"Michael Andreas."

"Have you tried to call her?"

"No."

"Try."

"Voicemail," Sofia said moments later.

Irini nodded to show she had experienced similar results.

"It could be unrelated." Sofia had a habit of delivering hopeful words, devoid of conviction.

"That would take a lot of dots to be unjoined."

Sofia took her time comprehending Irini's words. "Do you think Camden knows about Crissa and Andreas?"

"I don't think that's something she'd want him to know about. She doesn't even know you know. She thought you were asleep."

"What do we do?"

"Until we can figure out what's going on, we have to protect Crissa. Whatever it is, she'll have her reasons."

Now, standing outside the empty home of Morton and Gary—where only weeks ago Camden had been building his life with Crissa—Irini remained unclear on those reasons, but knew the time had come for greater disclosure. Michael Andreas had been missing since the night they saw Crissa cycling. Until either he or Crissa showed up, too many things were unexplained.

Come and see me at the spa as soon as you get this, she wrote on the note that she slipped under the front door. *It's urgent. Irini.*

—————

At dinner the previous night, Morton and Gary had arrived at a theory of what was going on and a consensus of how they should act upon it. They hadn't discussed it since.

As Morton strode towards the entrance, Gary trailed a half-step behind and briefly pondered how many people automatically fell into that formation in Morton's company, as though a natural order of things dictated that the limelight was his to inhabit and that support was welcomed rather than required. Soon they were standing at the reception desk of a building that seemed deserted compared to their last visit there. Gary felt the atmospheric conditions around him tangibly change.

The head behind the desk spoke with little enthusiasm or decorum. Although he could have comfortably engaged in dialogue in Greek, Morton opted to stay silent, forcing the head to lift and give him its full attention. It belonged to a man in his mid-forties who sensed an unspecific familiarity in Morton's face and shifted across to Gary's, at which point the recognition was undeniable. The man coughed, "Can I help you?"

"Is Mr Nikopolidis in?" Morton enquired.

Reflexively, his eyes shot to the right where they could see Nikopolidis waving them towards his office, in which he was taking a phone call with the door closed.

They walked towards the office without further interaction and entered discreetly. Nikopolidis directed them towards chairs and held up two fingers and then an open palm to manage the expectations of their waiting time. He rotated the wedding ring on his finger and spoke quickly in a disengaged manner that suggested he was keen for the phone call to reach its conclusion. He looked like he had lost weight. The room was slightly dim despite the roller blind being fully retracted. There was a musty odour laced with a hint of coffee. Morton observed the family pictures and wondered whether the difference between how Nikopolidis acted when on and off duty had lessened over the years.

The call ended and they stood and exchanged handshakes and brief greetings. "Would you like a drink?" he asked them.

"We've just flown back from Athens," Morton told him as he held up a hand by way of declination.

"Ah," he replied, before diverting his attention to Gary. "You're looking well." The words held within them an apology, which Gary straight-batted with a nod and a simple thank you. Nikopolidis seemed willing to endure a brief moment of awkwardness before turning back to Morton. "You've spoken to your friend. Dean Lockwood." It had taken a moment for the name to emerge from the policeman's memory banks. Morton wondered if he only operated in full names.

"He phoned us after speaking to you the other day."

"I'm surprised you didn't come and see me immediately."

"We found it unusual that you contacted our friend in the UK instead of us, given that we're only a short walk away."

"I knew that your friend Christian Camden wasn't with you and that you didn't know where to find him."

Morton straightened in his chair. "And how did you know that?"

"I can't discuss that with you," Nikopolidis said, retaking his seat.

They let the words descend into the floorboards and regrouped.

"What took you to Athens?"

"Mr Nikopolidis, we're trying to be helpful here, but it's not proving easy to figure out the best way to help. When you spoke to Dean, you told him that you had some information that might help find Crissa, Camden's girlfriend."

A shallow nod in response.

"What was the information?"

After a brief pause and a solemn sigh, Nikopolidis seemed to sink deeper into his chair as he spoke: "I'm afraid I can't tell you that."

Morton didn't hide his exasperation.

"Did you find what you were looking for in Athens?"

Morton felt his eyes flicker as something dawned upon him. "You still don't know where Camden is. Nor Crissa." They were statements.

"I think they've both decided not to be found for the time being."

"We went looking for Crissa. We haven't seen Camden for some time."

Nikopolidis squinted at him. "Would it be normal for your business partner and friend to just leave at a time when your business has been badly damaged?"

"Things haven't been normal," Morton pointed out, letting his words land before continuing. "It's not uncharacteristic of him to want his own space."

"Go on," Nikopolidis encouraged, retreating to listening mode, the wedding ring continually being manipulated.

"We didn't find her, but that won't come as a surprise to you."

He concurred without moving or talking.

"But we did find out some things."

Nikopolidis patiently parted his hands, palms up, and then clasped them again in a gesture of invitation.

"Michael Andreas." Morton said.

Nikopolidis stopped fiddling with his wedding ring.

"Any idea of his whereabouts yet?"

"No." The voice had suddenly gathered considerable edge. "He remains missing. Don't toy with me, Mr Morton, my patience is finite."

"We found out some things about him. Did you know he and Crissa were a thing a few years back?"

"A *thing*?" The phrase seemed unfamiliar.

"An item. A couple."

"Mr Andreas is a married man."

"Apparently that wasn't sacrosanct."

"Where did you hear this?"

"Someone who worked at the University of Athens when Crissa was a student there and Andreas was Rector."

"Did you corroborate this information?"

"No, but it felt right and it's the type of thing that a man in his position—both then and now—would want contained, so it's doubtful it's about to get advertised anywhere. The information's there, take it or leave it."

Morton left an inviting pause that went unrequited.

"This colleague said he had 'never seen two people burning so brightly for each other'. Feels coincidental that they've both suddenly become thin air."

———•———

Later that evening, Irini faced them down with a look of dismay and disbelief.

"Why didn't you tell us about Crissa and Andreas?" Morton asked.

"Crissa's a private person." The venom in her voice surprised her.

"It could have helped Camden."

"Everyone has a right to a past."

"Doesn't look like it's buried in the past anymore."

Irini had heard their theory: that Crissa and Andreas had pounced on the opportunity of both being on the same island to rediscover the passion they'd regretted deserting, for unknown reasons, years before.

"I don't buy it," she told them, shaking her head.

"It adds up," Gary suggested.

"Only from the angle you're looking at. I'm basing what I believe on what I've seen and heard from Crissa before and since she got together with Christian."

She spoke with conviction and gently closed her eyelids. Perhaps that would help determine her next step. "I wish you'd spoken to me first."

———

When situations dictated, Nikopolidis had a remarkable ability to subdue the need for words without it looking unnatural. That gift had been fully exploited in order to keep his counsel until Morton and Gary had left his office earlier that day.

It was three days since he had received the phone call from an Athens number. The caller had told him that the Andreas Archive had been decoded by a friend of his and named Crissa as the person for whom that transaction had been conducted. It was a male voice and seemed pleased to be divulging the information, as though personal satisfaction was being derived from the act. The address of the decoder wasn't revealed, but there was mention of a number of locations where Crissa had briefly sought respite.

That was how the link between Crissa and Andreas had first been revealed to Nikopolidis, but its nature had now been reshaped into a form he hadn't anticipated. A useful technique he'd cultivated in his years as a policeman, husband and father was to strip away his interpretations and preconceptions and just let information stand on its own merits in front of him, where he could see it at face-value and figure out if it helped create a mosaic that worked. As he did so with the information from the past few days and preceding month, a question gnawed at him: if Crissa and Andreas had rededicated themselves to their abandoned love, why would she arrange to decrypt a disk containing valuable information that he already had access to?

———·———

The phone call that Nikopolidis made to Gianna upon the discovery of her husband's body was memorable for many reasons, all abhorrent. Before he was able to complete the sentence he'd rehearsed, her shrill exclamation caused his head to jerk away from the phone. He returned it to his ear at the same time that a sharp crack exploded down the line, signalling that the phone had fallen from Gianna's hands as her motor skills endured an interregnum. For the remaining two minutes until he decided it best to abandon the call, the only sounds that could be heard were sobs, becoming ever more disconsolate as they travelled to the phone across the tiled floor on which Gianna lay, crumpled.

By dusk she was on the island, devoid of her earlier fragility and instead full of fury and determination that someone be held accountable through the media and justice system, for all the faults she perceived of both. Unhelpfully, she brought with her such scant insight into the daily workings of her husband's life that she offered little value to the investigation.

Andreas' assistant, Alex, was the most helpful. Quickly he realised that his impenetrable discretion—such essential second nature in recent years—would no longer be in his boss' best interest. Having fought the impulse to fly out as soon as he lost contact with Andreas, Alex had instead stayed put, keeping the ministerial office in working order as best he could in the subsequent days, including feeding disinformation to the Prime Minister and other cabinet colleagues to deflect from the fact that his boss had gone incommunicado at such an inopportune time. It was there that he received the news of Andreas' death. The day that he had spent on Santorini proved useful to Nikopolidis but unpalatable to Gianna, who clearly viewed him as an agitator to Andreas' infidelities. She almost hissed at him as she jabbed her finger in his direction when they were both in the police station. He was gone the next day but left insights behind him.

He had given a hollow laugh when asked if Andreas was a faithful husband. "Michael was a man who enjoyed indulgence and struggled with self-control."

"Did he have extramarital affairs?"

"Many." The word was laid in front of Nikopolidis by mahogany eyes that told him Alex wished he had been capable of doing more to change his answer.

"Were they relationships or one-night events?"

Every answer was preceded by a brief pause, as though waiting for confirmation in his ear that it was acceptable to disclose details. "They were both."

"Did he have a preferred type?"

"Typically, quite glamorous. He was handsome, self-assured, and influential—it came easy to him. He liked them curvaceous, appreciated good legs. I'm telling you all this based purely on his retelling of things. I never met any of them. I didn't want to become implicated in any of that. My interest was on how Michael could do good work for the country.

"He seemed to prefer if they were quiet, for numerous reasons. It may sound uncharitable, but I sometimes felt that the thing he found most irresistible about a woman was if she was attracted to him. But he tried to be selective. Family and career had to be segregated as much as possible."

"Did his wife know?"

Another scoff. "She knew. I'm sure Gianna wasn't entirely faithful either, although not with the same vigour. For as long as I've known them, they've maintained separate existences. Michael seemed physical and flirtatious with every woman other than his wife. I can't imagine living like that but, by the time I appeared on the scene, it was already the established way of things."

"Are you married, Alex?"

"No," he said sharply, with a few heavy blinks.

"When did you first start working for Michael Andreas?"

"The summer of 2009, not long after he joined the opposition."

"Did you know him before then?"

"No. I'm good at what I do and was recommended to him."

"Did you enjoy working for him?"

"I did," he replied defiantly. "I believed in him. He had his faults and contradictions, as do you and I and all the people who take the easy option of judging from a distance."

When Alex left the station to take his taxi to the airport, Nikopolidis felt that he'd caused offence multiple times in the course of their conversation, yet Alex's loyalty had led him to help through gritted teeth as much as he could. A notepad page full of contact details was on the table in front of him, a collage of names of varying natures: governmental, family acquaintances, benign ex-lovers, former colleagues from his time at the university.

There was nothing to do but work the most significant and oppressive case of his career.

———·———

The following day, the Crissa-Andreas connection spun again.

Gianna Andreas stood resolutely in front of Nikopolidis in his office, full of opprobrium. His efforts to locate and, latterly, seek justice for her husband were lambasted, his competence derided. It was at the point where his integrity was questioned that he broke his silence.

"I believe my main failing here has been that I have at times tiptoed around some delicate matters when speaking to you, Mrs Andreas," he ventured.

"I have no idea what you mean," she retorted.

"I'd like to ask you some questions that are quite personal. They may be upsetting."

"Ask them," Gianna instructed tersely. "There's nothing that can make these days harder."

"How would you describe your marriage?"

"Hard work," was the answer. "The spark was long gone from it. You'll recognise the dynamic, I'm sure." She dipped her head towards the photos on his desk. "But the extent of Michael's appetites never softened. At first, I was blind to it. Then it became clear. Initially I was mortified. I found the humiliation hard to overcome. Then, after a couple of years the embarrassment turned to pity. He was trapped by something he found insatiable. I found it pathetic. By that point, we were together for the children." She shrugged. "Mostly. Our lifestyle suited us."

"Did any of the affairs last long?"

"I didn't want to know. Before the children grew up, I had my own escapades, but they were never rewarding, and I switched them off." It struck Nikopolidis as a strange but pointed choice of words.

"Did you meet any of the women?"

An uncomfortable silence occupied the room. "A few."

"I can imagine that was difficult."

"It was." Nothing else was offered, but Nikopolidis decided he would not be the next to talk. Eventually, Gianna resumed. "I understand why you should have asked these questions when Michael went missing but I don't understand why they're relevant now," she pressed, emotions again coming to the fore. "Ask the questions you need to ask, don't dance around me."

As he made his next movements, Nikopolidis was keyed in on Gianna's every tic and sinew as he prepared for her reaction to what she would be shown. He was both hopeful and fearful of what it would tell him: the hope driven by a return to normalcy if he could make progress with the stalled case that was devouring his life; the fear brought about by the oppressive sense that he was several days too late in acting on his intuition.

"Do you recognise this woman?"

When he said Crissa's name and passed her photograph across the table, Gianna knocked over her chair as she sprung to her feet, her face at once drained and enraged.

Chapter 37

At a similar time on the same day, Crissa ordered a second espresso and re-read her words. She'd chosen the cafe with her next destination in mind, and it was a pleasant surprise to find that they served glorious coffee. There was a time when instances like these would be accompanied by a cigarette. No longer.

Her writing filled two pages of the paper she had bought—along with a half-decent pen—with this specific purpose in mind. Beside it lay another letter—this one taking up six pages and folded into quarters—with an envelope wrapped around it. The lengthier composition had been easier to write; the shorter one was more pragmatic, its combination of instructional and personal content never quite finding form. Still, it was unambiguous. She was sure its wishes would be honoured.

Camden was omnipresent in her thoughts, hardly an unusual occurrence but one that had become unbearably acute these past few weeks. She could feel the lack of his hands touching her face, the absence of his words to ease her doubts. Perhaps it was possible that the simple act of being enfolded in his arms would partially cleanse her. Perhaps.

Three weeks earlier she had sent him a package, addressed to Oliver Arnolds. She had smiled to herself as she wrote it, an in-joke about an Icelandic musician whose work he'd introduced her to and whom she was amazed that she liked—it was rare that music suited both of their tastes.

Yet their mutual use of the moniker also had a deeper and more essential purpose.

It was during one of their disrupted sleeps in the dark, early hours of an August morning when the notion surfaced unbidden and shaped itself into thoughts and words between them.

"If anything ever happens with us, I'll make sure there's always a way for you to get in touch with me," he'd told her. She'd looked at him with astonishment that their minds had both arrived at a similar point.

"You've got my parents' number, even though we don't really talk," he continued. She nodded confirmation. "I've also got an uncle. Well, he's not really my uncle but I called him that when I was a kid. I don't see him so much since I moved away but we're in regular contact and I trust him completely. If my parents aren't the right people to reach out to, he's the best alternative."

She clasped her hand around his. The wetness of her eyes shone amidst the darkness.

"If we ever need to stay apart for any length of time, I've got a place I could go. Away from things. I'll come up with a pseudonym." He had smiled and it was both boyish and grim.

It was to this address that the package went, containing two data disks, a red thumb-sized keyring in the shape of a heart and a photo of the restaurant where they'd been due to meet up again in the days following the protests, Andreas' demise, and their necessary separation. She wrote *8th May* on the back with three dots after the date, hoping it would communicate to him how much she regretted not being able to meet as planned. It felt too much of a risk to describe anything further.

On the date they'd been due to reunite, Crissa had been in crippling pain. Not long after she had been hidden away in and around the capital, she found herself cramping and retching, unable to hold down food, accumulate sufficient sleep or get around easily. That was bad enough, but one time she passed out while trying to get from her makeshift bed to the toilet. By her estimation, she came to a couple of minutes after she had fainted. It was a game-changer. If that had happened to her in public, she could have found her efforts to meld into anonymity undone to disastrous effect. Much though she hated the consequences, she decided not to venture out in public until she'd regained control of her health. Any transfers between hideaways were accompanied. Malachi continued to be unreachable, so she couldn't get a message to Camden in advance. Instead, she was shipped to her latest place soon after rush hour— when people are at their most distracted as they shift their personas from professional to private—cooked some tinned food, immediately rejected it, and sank into sleep. She woke a while after midnight smothered by a dizzying, jagged headache, checked her watch and clattered her head off an unfamiliar shelf as she tried to mobilise quickly enough to turn back time. One of the many downsides of staying in unfamiliar places was that there was always furniture lurking, ready to spring a surprise. She tried to gather herself and made it as far as the front door before the fresh air hit and unsteadied her still further. It just wasn't wise, she decided, and returned to the uninviting bed. Malachi remained her best bet as a conduit—by using his network, she and Camden would reach one another again soon.

It had felt much longer than seven weeks. Crissa placed the letters into the stamped envelope she'd handwritten earlier and drank the remainder of her coffee, tipping back her head to get every last drop. Everything that would come next was unknown.

A phone call had brought her to this, Ioanna on the line in tears and panic, splurging details about Luka informing the police of their recent meeting. *I never should have told him what you'd shown me,* Ioanna had moaned. *We'd had too much to drink, I have no filter when I'm drunk, I'm so, so sorry.*

"You helped me, Ioanna," she had told her. "Thank you for always trying to help me."

She held the phone to her ear as she exited the cafe and embarked on the final journey over which she would have full control for the foreseeable future. Her letters were deposited into the mailbox that was soon to be emptied as the ringing down the line was replaced by an enquiring, business-like voice.

"It's Crissa Papanikolaou," she announced.

The sound of a floundering mind was almost audible. "We need to talk urgently," said the voice, its words tentative and taut. "Where are you?"

"Four hundred yards short of Syntagma police station in Athens. I'm guilty of the murder of Michael Andreas and I'm going to hand myself over."

The line clicked softly yet it caused Nikopolidis to jump as he heard it, the phone almost falling from his hand.

Chapter 38

Rain met windscreen with such velocity that the wipers laboured to keep pace. The metallic sky looked like it had been in situ for days. Britain in late June. Welcome home.

Morton's mood matched the conditions. They'd landed three hours earlier into Manchester, the cloud so dense that it had buffeted the plane on its descent and only unveiled the ground to them in the final two hundred feet of their approach. Quite a contrast to their stopover in Munich, where the sunshine had been eye-straining.

Dean had been there to collect them, greeting Morton with a few words and a reassuring pat on the shoulder.

"Any more news?"

Morton shook his head. "This is Nina, Crissa's sister," he stated by means of introduction.

"Nice to meet you, Nina," Dean said, offering his hand. His discretion told him that further questions should wait.

She took it and said, "You too."

"Let's go." Morton lifted the overnight bags he and Nina had packed for their brief visit and jerked his head towards the car. Dean noted the lack of warmth in the gesture and how Nina chose not to acknowledge it.

They were on the road before eleven and now, with the time ticking towards one, they crossed the Scottish border via an A-road that looked like it could pose tangential challenges at any time.

Not many words had been spoken on the way, a tendency not unique to the northward drive.

Meet me on the mainland, Nina had told Morton. *I'll explain when I get there.* Since her phone call two days earlier, there had been a deficit of explanation. He'd already known about Crissa's surrender: it had been headline news across the country for the previous twenty-four hours.

Nina again met him at the fountains in Syntagma Square. He arrived expecting her to unload onto him all the details of Crissa's predicament and how it connected to Camden. Instead, things came in fragments.

"I visited Crissa today. The place where she's being held is not good."

"How does she look?"

"Numb. Like she's already accepted her fate."

Morton couldn't tell whether the rationing of the information was being determined by what Nina was leaving out or by what Crissa had kept to herself.

"I got a letter from her yesterday. She posted it just before she handed herself over to the police."

"What did it say?"

"Asked me to visit her—alone, as soon as I could. That she loved us. Our family, I mean. There was a letter for

Camden folded inside it, with instructions that I put it into its envelope without reading it and hand it to him at an address in the UK."

Nina showed him the address. It was unfamiliar to Morton, and the name of the premises left him agog.

"What the fuck? What's he doing there?"

Nina answered a different question to the one he had asked. "I'm hoping you'll travel with me. He's your friend and he may need support when he finds out what's happened to Crissa. I don't know him well and he won't have heard the news, given where he's staying."

The contents of Morton's brain were being rattled around. It was hard to arrive at the correct questions and responses. "Did she say if she did it?"

"She did it," was the immediate reply.

He hated asking the next question. "Did Camden know about it?"

"That wasn't a question she wanted me to ask. I got the impression that he wasn't involved but knows what she's done."

"Jesus Christ."

A sense of paralysis had hit Morton when the news broke. His first thoughts were of Camden and his own father. When he had finally got through to him, Anthony had seemed decidedly unshaken, his words sounding like unruffled interview answers rather than a conversation between embattled father and worried son.

With Camden he felt rudderless, like he was reaching for strands of the friend he tried to convince himself he knew. *How much of this did Camden know?* If he knew of any part of it, that rendered all of his actions after the protests as artificial on at least some level. Clearly, it was hugely suspicious that he'd vanished so soon afterwards.

Gary had almost burst down the door when he returned after seeing the news on a TV screen in town. Morton was still on the phone to his father at the time, after which Gary asked him all the same questions he'd asked himself and they agreed that clear answers were scarce.

"Does this mean Camden's in danger? I mean, where can he be?"

Two more questions that Morton could only meet with confounded headshakes.

He'd phoned Dean to let him know. The call consisted mostly of disbelief and gaps in conversation.

"Have you spoken to the police?" Dean had asked at one point.

"Not yet."

"You should."

"You're probably right."

"That guy Nikopolidis: maybe he could help."

"Part of me is worried what he'll tell me."

Morton had only managed to reach Tom's voicemail and was still waiting for a call back.

The news reports had latched onto the extramarital affair between Crissa and the murdered politician. The more salacious outlets were already publishing photos of the apartment Andreas had owned at the time, which had been their primary meeting place. Each new detail added weight to the story's legitimacy, yet it still seemed incompatible with any reality Morton could understand. Crissa's role as murderer seemed to him like a revelation that couldn't possibly have substance.

"Did she say why she did it?"

"The past," Nina said simply and inadequately.

Declining to interrogate further on that point, Morton instead focused on the task at hand. "Did she say what's in the letter?"

"No."

"How do we know he'll be at this address?"

"They arranged it."

Morton blinked rapidly and shook his head. "You're not making much sense."

"Everything I'm telling you makes sense," she responded. "It's just hard to take in."

———•———

Dean's tyres scuttered over shale as they entered the car park, the satnav having picked out a destination that seemed to have no possibility of existing until signs started popping up two miles back.

A path led them towards a building that looked like it might contain a reception. They each noted in their own way the ornamentation dotted around the complex: the gates, the stupa, the prayer wheels. A reverence hovered around each item. The building they had picked out looked as though it could have been constructed at any time in the past one hundred and fifty years—the windowsills looked older than the building itself, as though the bricks had formed around them—and the reception was inside, a cluttered room that wouldn't have looked out of place in the administrative section of a primary school. Boxes were stacked against one wall, crates of leaflets against another, mountains of miscellany elsewhere. If there was a filing structure in place, it was enigmatic. A man of indeterminate age—bespectacled, shaven-headed and wearing orange-trimmed maroon robes—turned away from his contemplation of the items dominating the room and asked how he could help.

Morton began to speak but stopped at the unexpected sound of Nina's voice.

"We're looking for a friend of ours. Oliver Arnolds?"

It took Morton and Dean a full second to recover from the use of such an unfamiliar name. The man clearly noticed but Nina remained unaffected. Morton softened his furrowed brow: another piece of information withheld.

"He's been staying here for the last month or so," she continued. "We have some news about someone very close to him that we think he'd want to be told in person."

"Can you sign the visitor's book, please?" the man asked, committing nothing further. They complied.

"I'm sorry if this is unusual. We're not sure how things work here, but we've come a long way. It really is important news."

"Is he expecting you?"

"No," answered Nina as the other two shook their heads. Spreading her index finger and thumb to point at herself and Morton, she continued: "We flew in from Greece this morning; he doesn't even know we're in the country."

It was as though this detail was a tipping point for the man, lending enough weight to their credentials as carriers of important information that Oliver Arnolds was better off knowing.

"He's out for a walk at the moment. You'll be able to find him." He gave them brief directions. "There's an entrance to the forest a couple of hundred yards along there, at the bend. He usually takes a path straight down into the woods. You'll meet him on his way back."

"Thank you," Nina said, her tone full of sincerity.

"Be careful of the traffic when you leave the complex and get onto the main road. A lot of people drive quicker than the road would like."

———•———

The stillness of the place was bracing. The cars that allegedly sped along the roads were clearly taking the day off. There was a house at the bend where the path lay. It looked like it had been transplanted from the suburb of a minor city. No life was identifiable within it. Each step along the gravel path sounded improperly loud.

From a distance of several hundred yards, a figure emerged over the brow of a hill. Dressed and depilated in a similar style to the receptionist, its walk nevertheless unmistakably belonged to Camden. To Morton, who checked his stride as he caught sight of him, he looked nothing like an Oliver.

They reached each other within a minute. "Morton, Dean, Nina." Camden addressed each of them in turn with a pleasant, empty smile. He didn't offer his hand for his friends to shake, nor an embrace for Nina to receive, and instantly realised his judgment on that count had been correct.

Dean nodded at him, unsure of what to say.

"Hello, Christian," said Nina, her earnestness snatching his stomach from him.

"Oliver," said Morton.

Camden acknowledged the comment. "Forgive that. I guess you know by now why Oliver became necessary." He looked at all three. Despite their collective lack of reaction, he knew that he had again judged things right.

"How are you?" he asked, the question applicable to the whole group but directed towards Morton.

Morton's gaze didn't waver as he took a good ten seconds to decide on what should be said. "You look well," he said finally.

"Thanks."

"Different haircut."

"The barber's still in training." It sounded like a much-repeated line.

A gap emerged in place of words.

"Am I right in assuming this visit isn't going to be conversational?"

Nina answered his query by assuming control. "Crissa asked me to deliver a letter to you personally. I asked Morton to come along to provide support. Dean was good enough to drive us." She presented the letter, and he took it and held it in front of him, his eyes moving agitatedly between his two friends.

"When did you land?" he asked.

Neither of them reacted.

"Read the letter, Christian," Nina instructed. "Maybe sit down as you do."

Chapter 39

"This way."

When reading Crissa's letter, Camden's face had been a slideshow of expressions: there was the pain brought about by longing; the relief of feeling a reconnection to what made him feel most worthy; rapid tears and a quick exhalation, as though the words had leapt from the paper to punch him in the gut; and utter conviction by the conclusion of his reading, as though it contained the teachings of sacred scripture.

Now, having been allowed to walk wordlessly ahead of them from the woods into the monastery grounds, he led them through the living quarters into a simple room where clutter seemed an alien concept. He pulled out a small, padded Jiffy bag from the back of his bedside drawers and passed it to Morton, who thrust his hand inside and held two data sticks in his hand when he withdrew it.

"The fuck …," Morton managed to say. "Are these …?" He didn't get to the end of his question.

"Everything you need is on there," Camden told him. "Two copies."

"Have you read them?"

There was a pause, as though Camden was unsure of his own powers of recall. "No."

"But you know what's on there." Morton seemed sure he was right.

"I now know the important parts."

"When did you get the disks?"

"Three weeks ago."

Morton nodded angrily, jawbones clenching and unclenching. "That wasn't worth a phone call? Or some type of contact?"

"That wasn't an option."

"How did you get them?"

Camden gave a look that said the answer was obvious. "Your dad isn't on there."

Morton pushed out his bottom lip as he received this information.

"Nor are the Melas brothers."

"Well, that makes things straightforward, then." He took a couple of steps forward until his nose almost touched Camden's. "Except for the fact that while you've been sitting on that information for three fucking weeks, my dad's been under virtual house arrest trying to clear himself of corruption charges that you had the information to disprove! What the fuck is wrong with you? His life will never be the same. Our lives—the ones that you and I were meant to be building on Santorini—they're ground into nothing now."

Camden hadn't flinched. "I'm sorry." It was a sincere statement, yet plainly unsubstantial.

Their eyes remained fixed on each other for a long time.

"What was in the letter, Camden?"

"I know that Crissa killed Michael Andreas."

"You knew that already," Morton shot back. "Didn't you?"

A few seconds passed as Camden selected the parts of his story he was willing to release into the wild. "I saw everything."

"You were there?"

Camden didn't feel the need to answer.

"You saw her kill him?" Without realising, Morton had taken a small step backwards at this revelation.

"I saw everything, Morton," Camden repeated.

"What happened to Crissa after that?"

"That's a question that's best left unasked and unanswered."

Morton let that sink in. "And then you came back to Fira the following day and acted like nothing had happened."

"Hardly."

"Right, you were spinning the web by then. Going to the police about your missing girlfriend but not pushing them too hard. Travelling to Athens alone to search for her as if your life had fallen apart."

"It had fallen apart. I was trying to piece it back together as best I could, just not in a way I could share with you."

"You lied to me. You lied to all of us. Systematically. Consistently. And then instead of helping my family you turned the other way."

"I had no choice."

"Yes, you did!" Morton pounced and shoved both palms onto Camden's face, ramming him back against the wall and causing him to hit his head with a thud.

"Morton!" Dean exclaimed and put a warning hand on his shoulder.

"You had a fucking choice! You don't get to take the easy way out; you had a fucking choice!"

Flecks of spit were hitting Camden as Morton shouted at him, but he offered no resistance. Instead, he waited it out until Morton released his grip.

"My world changed that night, too," Camden said finally. "I didn't expect it to happen. Wish it were different. But if you'd seen what I'd seen, you'd have known there was no changing it."

He took a seat, his back perfectly straight.

"You're right: I had a choice. But only one. I had to protect the parts of my life that are most important to me. That was my choice, and that was Crissa. I had no idea how to do it. It wasn't a set of circumstances I'd ever imagined myself being in so I improvised as best I could while my life was crumbling under my feet. I hate that I've hurt you and your family—I'm sorry about that. I didn't want to lie to my friends. Didn't want most of what's happened." His eyes worked over all three of his visitors as he concluded. "But there are parts that I really do want. And I'm not willing to give them up."

Morton waited a couple of seconds before speaking. "Well thanks for clarifying which parts of your life you're OK with sacrificing. At least now we know where we stand."

He turned and made it as far as the door before stopping.

"I'm going to do whatever I need to do to clear my dad's name," he told Camden, holding the Jiffy bag in the air. "I'm going to be asked how I got this disk, and I'm going to give a straight answer."

Camden nodded, which seemed only to irritate Morton.

"This false tranquillity you've surrounded yourself with here: it's just another facade you've assembled."

"There's nothing false about it," Camden countered calmly, standing up as he did so.

"And it won't last once I give this to the police."

"Not in its current form," Camden agreed. "Goodbye. And I am sorry, whether it counts for much or not."

"I'll be in the car," Morton informed Nina as he left the room, in a way that suggested Camden hadn't even spoken. Dean was close behind him, a picture of perplexity.

Chapter 40

Reds and golds filled Camden's vision and he tried to focus on them to still his mind. It was a fruitless endeavour.

Beside him sat the lama who'd been so supportive of his training, and who'd provided a living example of how to simplify how he dealt with the world. A sideways glance confirmed that the lama had his eyelids down, although Camden imagined he would still be aware of the look being cast in his direction: he seemed so acutely aware of everything around him. It was rarely clear what thoughts he held at any given time, but Camden hoped they were prayers for absolution on his behalf.

Once his visitors had departed the premises, Camden had waited outside the temple. Soon after the sounds of chanting and gongs ceased, the lama slipped out of one of the doors and, immediately registering that Camden was in a state of distress, took him to one of the anterooms. Having listened to all that Camden had to tell him, he then spoke unhurriedly, with a quiet authority that brought sharp focus and an unexpected urgency.

"If you want to help and do what you describe as the 'right thing', start by looking at the purity of your motivation. Why would you make the choices you're considering? For your good or for the good of others? Admiration and thanks don't make you a better person. Don't use that as a basis."

———•———

"Will you come?" Nina had asked him after Morton and Dean had left them alone in his room.

"Of course," he replied.

"You'll be giving up a lot."

Camden breathed in slowly and considered that for a second. "I'd be giving up more if I didn't come."

Nina's final act before she said goodbye with a stifling hug was to give him an envelope that she had kept to herself, containing names, numbers, and addresses that he was likely to need in the coming months.

There was no questioning what had to be done from here, only his capacity to see it through.

———•———

"Everything I've done and am going to do is because I love her." It was an attempt at clarification, maybe justification.

"Attachment is about wanting happiness for yourself," the Lama replied. "Instead, look for what will make others happy. And be realistic about your own capability to help.

You have to make progress with yourself before helping others."

Camden had recently made a habit of allowing the words of other people to settle in his mind before responding and it felt like now was the most salient example he'd experienced. As he sat quietly, the lama rose to his feet and placed a hand on Camden's shoulder. "You know what you need to do."

And so now he awaited the arrival of the police—whom he'd recently contacted and who would be in the process of negotiating the winding thirty-minute journey toward them—in a room filled with vivid colours, and with the currents of his mind smacking furiously against each other, he turned over in his head the words from Crissa's letter, not needing to read them a second time, so imprinted onto him were they at first pass.

———•———

My darling Christian,

From the most blissful year of my life have come the most tumultuous days.

Know this: I've never known anyone like you in my life and my love for you is all-encompassing. You've changed so many things in a positive way for me. I only wish I'd met you sooner. Maybe then I wouldn't have been carrying so much baggage by the time our paths crossed.

I'm impulsive. You know it. It's probably one of the reasons you love me. I always marvel at how you love the parts of me I resent the most. There was a plan for the evening that changed our lives, but only up to a point. I found out late that Michael Andreas would be on the island, and it only needed a few strings to be pulled for him to be brought to me. I tried my best to bury my past. My regrets, my anger. But when you know where they're buried, the temptation is always there to go digging. I never intended for you to be there, nor to do what I did. Instead, I've accumulated another collection of horrible mistakes and regrets. It's like I've become a hoarder. The instant that normality returned to my mind that night I knew I'd lost everything close to me.

And yet that is not the case. By the time you read this I will be in police custody. There will be no doubt about my guilt, only consequences. There is one other element that may play a part here and it's the most important of the many reasons why I need you. In the past few weeks, I've discovered that we are going to have a child, Christian. It's a magnificent thing in so many ways, something of which I would never even have dared dream until I met you. On the other hand, of course, the timing is somewhat cruel. I know little of what will happen next, but I know that someday I'll return to what will become our family and a different version of our blissful beginnings will play out.

Let me take a sidestep; it's an important one. Please hand the data disks to Morton. His father and his business partners are innocent, the disk will prove that. I should have told you sooner and I'm sorry if it has cost you friendships. Malachi's father will be implicated, and it may severely damage the movement—that was why I held back that information and I was wrong to do so.

Come to me, Camden. In whatever way you can, come to me. And stay. I can't imagine that a future exists without the two of us together.

———·———

There was a scraping sound. He could hear noises of things rubbing together. The chair was moving beneath him, his limbs convulsing of their own accord. Droplets were striking the floor. They were tears of joy at the intimacy brought by her words. They were tears of longing, tears of frustrated rage at the things they would miss out on.

To Greece. To Santorini. To the life he'd imagined for them, spun around, chewed up, spat out and still worth living.

To Crissa, to whom it seemed all his possible futures had always led.

The door opened behind him. Footsteps and official voices.

He nestled the letter in his hand as he stared ahead, unblinking.

About the Author

Robert McNair was born and raised in Gretna, in the south of Scotland. He has spent his adult life in Yorkshire and the United States.

After graduating as a teacher, he worked as a barman and football coach, determined to get all the fun stuff out of the way first. He currently works for a multinational corporation.

Salvation is his second novel.

www. robertmcnair.co.uk